W9-ATF-329

*ELUSIVE*
An ON THE RUN Novel
Published by McGuffin Ink

Copyright © 2012, 2016 by Sara Rosett
Cover Design: Alchemy Book Covers
Editing: ManuscriptProofing.com

ISBN: 978-0-9982535-5-8
Second Paperback Edition: November 2016
First Paperback Edition: November 2012

This is a work of fiction. Names, characters, places and incidents are either the product of the author's imagination or are used fictitiously, and any resemblance to actual persons, living or dead, business establishments, events or locales is entirely coincidental.
Printed in the USA.

Interior Format

# Praise for Sara Rosett

"Some cozies just hit on all cylinders, and Rosett's Ellie Avery titles are among the best."
—*Publishers' Weekly*

"Tightly constructed with many well-fitted, suspenseful turns…"
—*Shine*

"Thoroughly entertaining. The author's smooth, succinct writing style enables the plot to flow effortlessly until its captivating conclusion."
—*RT Book Reviews* (four stars)

"Sparkling…"
—*Publishers Weekly*

"…keeps readers moving down some surprising paths—and on the edge of their chairs—until the very end."
—*Cozy Library*

# ELUSIVE

## BOOK ONE IN
## THE *ON THE RUN* SERIES

# SARA ROSETT

# CHAPTER ONE

*Dallas, Tuesday, Noon*

IT WAS SUPPOSED TO BE an easy job.
  "Cake," Rick had said.

Sammy Dovitz tossed his binoculars onto the passenger seat then shifted restlessly within the confines of the black KIA. It *should* have been an easy job—no dog and no sign of an alarm installed. The large cottonwood in the front yard hid some of the two-story house and made it difficult to see what was going on upstairs, but that situation also worked to his advantage—he'd take mature landscaping over barren new lots any day. High hedges, shrubs, and towering trees made it possible to move around unnoticed.

But for it to be an easy job, the woman had to leave.

Sammy pulled a small hand towel from below the binoculars and wiped his sweaty forehead. He'd been sitting in the car for five and a half hours. It hadn't been too bad at six-thirty in the morning, but now the windshield acted as a magnifying glass for the sun. The dark clouds of the approaching early spring thunderstorm were sliding across the sky, but they were still far enough away that they didn't block the sun. He'd moved the car three times already, to stay in the shade—and he didn't want to remain in one place too long.

He threw the soaked towel onto the passenger seat. Rick hadn't told him the woman worked from home. Sammy hated work-from-home people. His line of work depended on empty houses, not that this was business as usual. This job was some sort of special case. Sammy usually worked alone, but when Rick offered to let him in on this job, the payoff had been too big to pass up.

Sammy's phone vibrated. Rick didn't bother to say hello. "He's left the office. You got it yet?"

"No. The woman's still there. Is he coming here?"

There was a muttered curse, then Rick's scratchy voice, pitched higher than usual and with a layer of nervousness vibrating through his words, came back on the line. "Doesn't look like it. He was still in his suit. He's driving to the Tollway. Sammy, man, you've got to make this happen. Get on it, right now. Did you hear me? Right now."

"Yeah, I got you." Thunder rumbled, and Sammy looked at the approaching mass of clouds. Another half hour and they would be directly overhead. The bottom of the cloudbank was dark, nearly black, and flat as if sliced with a knife, but the top was bumpy with bloated white columns. Not good. A downpour would only complicate things.

"Do it now," Rick said. "My part is done. I'm out of here."

"Half an hour," Sammy said and turned off his phone.

Looking at the house again, he sighed. It was going to be the hard way. Instead of a quick and dirty, in and out, he'd have to do the job with the woman in the house—not impossible, but time consuming and riskier. He wasn't worried about a confrontation with her. He knew he could take care of her, but it would be better if she never knew he was there, which meant slow and careful and quiet.

Sammy pulled a gray shirt over his white T-shirt. He fastened the buttons, making sure the collar covered the chain link tattoo on his neck. He removed his diamond earring, dropped it in the console, and then picked up a small clipboard and black baseball cap. The name of the game was blending in—that was key. You couldn't stand out. Tattoos and diamonds were memorable. Sammy wanted to be practically invisible. Both the shirt and the cap had the logo of a local cable company, a multi-colored starburst. He pulled the baseball cap low over his eyes and strolled across the street to the gate that opened into the backyard of the two-story house. Despite the large tree in the front, he couldn't risk being seen picking the lock on the front door. It would be too chancy in this neighborhood of occasional walkers and joggers. He could leave through the front door, but he wasn't going inside that way.

The gate was unlocked, so he slipped inside the fence after a quick glance up and down the empty street. He moved to the back of the house and eased up to the small window placed high on the wall over the kitchen sink. His hand tightened on the rough brick. She was still there, all right, motionless except for the movement of her fingers as she bent over a laptop, which was a useless piece of trash. He'd hoped to do a little business on the side during this job—something Rick didn't need to know about—but if that was the type of merchandise in the house, he wouldn't even bother. It wasn't worth his time.

Sammy inched his head away from the window. No sudden movements. When he was clear, he went to one of the windows on the opposite side of the house, an extra bedroom filled with boxes. He sighed with satisfaction. Finally, something was breaking his way. Sammy tucked the clipboard into his waistband at the small of his back then slipped his knife out of his pants pocket. After examining the screen and window for an alarm, he used the knife to pry the screen out of its track.

He set it on the ground then slid the knife into the thin space where the upper and lower window casement met. With a flick, the thumb lock released, and he pushed the window up. A cool, air-conditioned breeze from inside the house engulfed him.

X

ZOE STOPPED TYPING AND STARED at the exposed rafter of her kitchen ceiling, listening.

It was too quiet.

The air conditioner whirred and there was the faint plink from the leaky faucet in the hall bath, but there should have been noise from upstairs. A quick glance at the digital clock on the oven confirmed that it was almost twelve-thirty. Jack should have finished his daily run and be in the shower by now. She had heard him come inside, hadn't she? She must have. He moved through his schedule with a precise, unwavering regularity. Despite their best efforts to steer clear of each other, their daily lives crossed at certain points. They couldn't completely avoid each other. Even divorced, non-communicative ex-spouses tended to run into each other when they shared a house.

It wasn't an ideal situation, but because the bottom fell out of the housing market right about the time they divorced, they didn't have a choice. The house was underwater, meaning they owed more on it than they could sell it for, so they were stuck—with the house and with each other.

To keep their sanity and prevent a shouting match that would have the neighbors calling 911, Jack and Zoe kept to their carefully defined regions. Jack used the front door and the stairs to reach his half of the house, the upstairs. Zoe used the back door, which opened into the kitchen. The first floor was hers. The stairs were a sort of No Man's Land, a 38th Parallel. The first floor had more living space, but Zoe really only cared about the kitchen. She'd gladly ceded the master bedroom because she couldn't live without a kitchen. The guest bedroom downstairs was fine with her. She didn't understand how Jack made due with a hotplate and a mini-fridge, but apparently he lived on cereal and sandwiches.

Zoe swiveled on her barstool, legs dangling, as she considered checking the driveway for his car. Then she heard the distinctive creak of the floorboard in the hall, followed seconds later by the far-off squeak of the upstairs bedroom door. Zoe gritted her teeth and turned back to the keyboard. She couldn't remember how many times she'd asked him to spray some WD-40 on those hinges, but did he ever get around to it? No. He could make time in his schedule for anything related to his small business, but minor household repairs never showed up on his to-do list.

When the knock sounded on the back door five minutes later, Zoe looked up from the spreadsheet to check the time and cringed. Helen wouldn't be happy.

"It's open," she shouted, as she leaned over to flick on the overhead lights, since the light in the kitchen had taken on a golden cast as if the sun were setting.

"I knew it," Helen said as she opened the door and plunked down two brown bags dotted with grease stains.

"You stood me up again. And for your laptop, no less. Why did I even bother to go to Chez Madeline? I should skip that step and go straight to a drive-thru instead. It would save me at least fifteen minutes." She tossed her long golden brown bangs out of her eyes and put her hands on her hips. "Did you even remember we had a lunch date?"

The aromas of grilled hamburger and French fries filled the kitchen. "Sorry. I forgot to call you to cancel," Zoe said squirming, but she knew that Helen wasn't seriously mad at her. Helen was never seriously mad about anything. "I'm a terrible friend. I got two short notice assignments this morning. They were urgent. Since I finished the copy-edit on the Italy book, things have been a little slow." Zoe reached around the laptop for a French fry so hot she could barely touch it. "I don't know why you put up with me."

Helen dropped her combative stance and rolled her eyes as she climbed on the barstool beside Zoe. She began to unload food from the bags, careful not to get grease on the cuffs of her silk Michael Kors blouse. "It's probably because you taught me how to fold a dollar bill into a ring in seventh grade and passed all my notes to Ned Billings in history."

"I did dissect your frog for you in biology, too, so you wouldn't fail. Don't forget that."

"Please—we're about to eat!" Helen shuddered, causing the topaz pendent on the thick gold chain at her neck to wink.

"I'm just saying…I do know all your secrets."

"That's definitely part of it," Helen said as she unwrapped her burger and inhaled deeply. "And I know you need the money."

Zoe licked her fingers, gave them a brisk wipe on her shorts, typed a final entry, then attached the document to an e-mail, and sent it off. She pushed the laptop back and picked up her burger. "That I do."

"When will you get the next travel book?" Helen asked.

Copy editing books for a small but popular independent travel company, Smart Travel, was the main reason Zoe's checking account stayed just barely in the black—most of the time. "Should be in a week or so," Zoe said. "England and Ireland this time."

"That will be a nice change from gladiators and gondolas."

"Are you saying you don't like to hear interesting trivia that I pick up when I'm copy-editing?"

"Oh, no. I think it's fascinating to learn about the construction of the Colosseum and how archeologists excavated

Pompeii. I'm invincible at Trivial Pursuit now."

"Right. I forgot history was your least favorite subject, next to biology, of course."

Helen shrugged. "I can't help it if all those dates mash together. Anyway, you like it and that's all that matters." Helen changed the subject. "Want to go to the club with me tonight? It's Yoga night."

Zoe shook her head. "Can't. I have a spreadsheet to finish and then I'm walking my neighbor's dog." Normally, she had several dog walking appointments around North Dallas, but the last few weeks had been slow and she only had her neighbor's dog on her schedule today.

Helen put her burger down and took a long sip of her soda as she glanced at Zoe out of the corner of her eye. Casually, she said, "Gary's quitting."

Zoe frowned. "Who?"

"Gary. Gary Wilson. In the clerk's office. You know, he's got the third cube on the left."

Zoe closed her eyes briefly, but it wasn't because she was enjoying her food. She knew what was coming. "I don't want to work at the County Clerk's Office," she said quickly.

"Why not?" Helen pounced. "It's a good job. Benefits. Steady pay. You wouldn't have to take all these different jobs to scrape along, and you might be able to save enough money to actually visit some of the places you'd like to see instead of reading and dreaming about them," Helen said as she pointed a French fry at a mason jar half filled with coins that sat on the window sill. A curling and faded sticky note with the words, "Passport Fund," was stuck to the outside. "You could finish this," she added, looking up at the exposed wood and pipes that ran overhead.

Water damage from a leaky pipe had forced Zoe to rip out the drywall a few months ago and she didn't have the money to hire a contractor to put up new drywall after she paid the plumber.

Zoe plunged her fry into ketchup. "I'll travel someday and I've decided I like it this way."

"You do not. You just say that to make it seem better."

"No, I do like it," Zoe replied firmly. "Those exposed pipes and wires might drive you crazy, but you don't live here. I do. They give the place character, a uniqueness. I know exposed beams would never go over in your corner of suburbia, but here in Vinewood, it's okay.

"They're not exposed beams," Helen said, exasperation lacing her tone. "They're two by fours."

Zoe shrugged. "So? Who says you have to have drywall on your ceiling?" Helen took a deep breath and Zoe wrinkled her nose. "I'm frustrating you, aren't I?"

"Yes!" Helen swiveled on the barstool and touched Zoe's arm. "I worry about you—living here in this old house. You know it will need more repairs. How will you pay for them? And your car, it's already got what—a hundred thousand miles on it?"

"Two, actually," Zoe said, placidly.

Helen threw up her hands at Zoe's tone. "What will you do if your car breaks down? How will you get to your dog walking clients to make twenty bucks?"

"Fifty bucks—for an hour's work. Even you have to admit, that isn't bad," Zoe said as she finished off her burger. "That's more than you make an hour, isn't it?"

"But you don't make fifty dollars every hour. You make fifty here, ten there, and it's not steady work. You don't know if you'll have anything tomorrow."

"Yes, I do know that I'll have something tomorrow. Tomorrow is April first, and Jack's rent is due."

"Oh, there's great security in that…renting office space to your ex is not the smartest business move. Don't you think he'll look around for someplace to move his office as soon as the lease is up?"

"No, I don't. I know you're not Jack's biggest fan, but he's… steady, solid. He's not going anywhere. I can count on him."

Helen narrowed her eyes. "I've never understood what happened between you two….but it begins to make sense now."

"Why we divorced?"

"No, why you got married in the first place! I mean, I understand why he fell for you—you're vivacious and beautiful and fun, but Jack is so…well, dull. Sure, he's good looking—that dark hair and those blue eyes." She raised her eyebrows and nodded. "I totally got *that*, and he can be witty in a sort of dry way. But after you get over his looks, he's kind of stuffy. But you've hardly ever had anyone you could count on. Who knew," she mused, "stodgy as sexy. Well, there are plenty of guys who are down right dull at the county offices. You can have your pick of them."

Zoe cleared her throat. Helen had hit a little too close to home. Zoe didn't want to dwell on why she'd jumped into a hasty wedding. Once the fireworks had fizzled, she and Jack had found themselves at opposite ends of the spectrum in almost every area of life. She was a live-in- the-moment kind of girl. Jack lived by his calendar. She loved surprises. Jack loved routine. They were just too different.

"Look, Helen. I know you're trying to help, but I'm not like you. You've gone all domestic and settled down with Tucker. You've got a great job. That's terrific for you, but I don't want to live like that. I don't want to dress up and go to the office every day. I like wearing this to work." She gestured to her droopy, oversized waffle weave sweater. It had been navy blue, but now she'd washed it so many times it had a faint gray cast to it. Rumpled North Face khaki shorts, boat shoes, and jingly miniature coin earrings completed her look. Helen stared at her for a moment, a hurt look spreading across her face. Zoe said hurriedly, "I'm not saying there's anything wrong with your life, just that I don't want it."

"But how can you not want it? How can you live from paycheck to paycheck, or, actually, job to job, not knowing if you're going to have enough money?" Helen leaned forward. "Think of all the fun we could have, if we worked in the same building. My cubicle would be down the hall from you. We could eat lunch together everyday and see each other a lot more than we do now."

Zoe's stomach clenched. "And be trapped in an office all day, filing papers and typing on a computer, a cog in the massive machine of government." She shook her head so adamantly that a few strands of her dark red hair came loose from her low ponytail and brushed her cheeks. "No way."

"You make it sound like a death sentence. You type and file papers here all day."

"But I only do the work I want. I turn down jobs, if I don't want to do them. I'm in control."

Helen narrowed her eyes. "When was the last time you turned down a job?"

Zoe busied herself gathering up the trash. "A few weeks ago. I told Kendra I couldn't housesit."

"Because she has a cat! Come on, Zoe, tell the truth. You didn't take the job because you're allergic."

Zoe turned away, dumped the trash, and then hid behind the refrigerator door. "It wasn't the cat. It was the fact that Kendra is the devil incarnate. Looks like we're going to get some rain." The overhead lights in the kitchen seemed to glow brighter as the light outside shifted. The thick layer of dark clouds slid across the sky, bathing the landscape in sepia tones. "Want something else to drink? I've got water and ice tea."

"Water's fine." Helen had her arms crossed, and a stubborn frown crinkled her forehead. "Don't try to change the subject."

Zoe filled two glasses with water from the sink. "The point is," she said as she crossed back to the island, "that I can set my own hours. I value my freedom, and whatever happens, happens. I can't control things. If the Jetta dies, I'll find something else or get it fixed. And, I'll always have some income, thanks to Aunt Amanda."

"At least you've got one sane relative," Helen said.

Zoe's Aunt Amanda believed real estate was the ultimate investment. When she'd moved to Florida to live in her Sarasota condo, she'd asked Zoe to act as the property manager for her commercial properties, two stand-alone offices built side-by-side, like a duplex, in a business park. After five years, her aunt decided to live in Florida year-round and she'd deeded the commercial properties to Zoe, saying she had plenty to live on from her other real estate investments. Zoe had tried to talk her out of it, but Aunt Amanda had refused to listen and told Zoe to consider the properties an early inheritance.

"Amazing that I'm even halfway normal, isn't it, considering Mom carted me from one audition to another from the time I turned three months old until I was eleven."

"Well, at least you got to live on a tropical island for three summers in a row. I was jealous."

Zoe sipped her water, then said, "Yeah, the island was great, but the downside is that now the three most mortifying years of my life are available on DVD for $14.99."

"What is your mom up to these days? You haven't mentioned her lately."

"She's at a spa outside of Sedona for the next two weeks for a 'Freeing Serenity Treatment,'" Zoe said.

"What's that?"

"Not sure, but it involves total separation from the stress of everyday existence and silence. No television, no music, no phones, no computer."

"Your mom is going a week without TV? Without E!

News? How will she survive? And why would she do that to herself? Won't she go through withdrawal?"

Zoe shrugged. Her mom lived in continual hope of a new reality show contract and followed celebrity news like some people followed politics. "I think it has something to do with a certain producer's wife being at the spa during the same time mom is there."

Helen said, "It all makes sense now. And I bet she expects you to be in it, too."

"Which I never will. If only I'd known what *emancipated minor* meant ten years ago." Zoe said it flippantly, but she was only half-joking.

The floorboards at the top of the stairs groaned. Helen looked at Zoe. "Is that Jack?" Zoe nodded and Helen asked, "What's he doing here?"

"He lives here, Helen. He always stops here after his run to shower and change before he goes back to the office," Zoe said, listening for his tread on the stairs.

"I don't think it's good for you, living this way," Helen said with a glance at the ceiling. "Still together."

"What is this? Pick on Zoe day? Well, I can play the same game. When will you have a baby?"

Helen held up her hands. "Okay, I get it." Her tone softened. "I worry about you, that's all."

"I know you're concerned, but it's not like Jack and I are living together. We live in the same house. It's really no different than living in an apartment building or duplex. We hardly see each other."

"But you're still…connected to him," she said, her tone gentle. "You've got his drawings on the refrigerator, for God's sake," Helen said, swinging a hand to the fridge. Jack had a tendency to draw when he was bored. Not crosshatches and squares that Zoe made while she waited on the phone, which turned into splotches of ink that only resembled a blob of

Play-Doh. Jack's impromptu sketches were more art than doodles. Zoe looked at the fridge where she'd used poetry magnets to attach Jack's sketches. There was the Dallas skyline drawn in the margin of the phone bill, a sketch of a book splayed open in the corner of a sticky note, and her favorite, ivy leaves climbing into the text of a magazine article like the words were bricks in a wall. "They're just little sketches," Zoe said. "It doesn't mean anything."

Helen didn't reply, only dropped her chin and looked at Zoe with a sorrowful look.

"You've still got that *Pirates of the Caribbean* poster with Johnny Depp—the one you got when you were fifteen. I know it's on the inside closet door in your guestroom. You haven't thrown it away."

Helen shifted on her barstool. "That's for my nieces. They stay in there when they come to visit. Besides, a movie poster is different from personal mementos. And if I had any personal mementos from Johnny Depp, they wouldn't be tucked away in a closet, let me tell you," Helen said with a grin and they both laughed, breaking the slight tension between them. They might argue, but they were good enough friends that they *could* argue.

Another noise from upstairs caught their attention. "Will he come in here?" Helen asked.

"No. He never does." She paused, listening for his rapid descent and the solid thump of the front door as it closed—Jack always came down the stairs fast, but it was absolutely quiet.

Helen raised her eyebrows at Zoe. "Is he gone?"

Zoe walked over to the kitchen doorway. Unlike the popular open floor plan of Helen's newly constructed house, Zoe's house was designed in an earlier era when each room was self-contained. Nothing flowed, and there were few open spaces, which suited Zoe and Jack just fine. The choppy design was exactly what they wanted, but it meant that Zoe couldn't see the stairs or the hallway that ran along the stairs to the front door. She leaned around the doorframe then peered up the stairs, listening, but the only sound was a crack of thunder.

"Jack?" she called. She returned to the kitchen, flexed a large envelope, and pulled out a stack of pictures. "He missed these," she said with a little frown. She and Jack communicated mostly by message. They left notes or bills on the hall table, which was where she'd placed the envelope, figuring he'd pick it up on his way back to the office. She debated invading the upstairs for a moment to leave it in his room, but dismissed the idea. She wouldn't want him poking around in her room.

"Oh, pictures," Helen said, wiping her hands on a napkin. "Let me see. You hardly ever see actual pictures anymore. Everything's digital now."

"These aren't mine, and they aren't high quality. They're on printer paper. Connor mailed them," Zoe said, referring to Jack's business partner. "I have no idea why he'd mail anything snail mail in the first place or why he'd send it here."

"Maybe he forgot the office address?"

"But remembered Jack's home address? No, I don't think so. I don't know Connor's address off the top of my head."

"Where were these taken?" Helen asked, squinting. "They're cute. I love the cobblestones and the sidewalk café, but they're so grainy they're almost Impressionistic."

"I couldn't figure it out either. Connor's afraid of anything made after 1995, so he probably took them with his phone, which has a terrible camera. I heard him complaining the other day about how he couldn't use his regular camera because he couldn't find a place to develop film, if you can believe it."

Zoe flipped through the pictures again, which were all street scenes, except one. She paused at a close-up of a Madonna, the paint faded and crackled. The figures were flat, almost one-dimensional, barely standing out from the blue background with its sprinkling of stars. She fingered the corner of the photo, thinking it was an odd sort of thing for Connor to photograph. He wasn't especially religious or interested in art, either.

"Weird," Helen said, handing the pictures back. She stood and slipped her Coach bag on her shoulder. "Well, I have to get back, too. Maybe I can beat the rain. Looks like it's going to be a huge storm. Think about the job," she instructed as she left.

"Fine. I'll think about it," she said to placate Helen. As she shut the door behind Helen, she felt a twinge of misgiving. A job at the county would be a smart move—secure and safe, but she couldn't do it. It might be wise, but she'd be miserable. She knew she would, and it's not smart to make yourself miserable, she reasoned. A prick of doubt wiggled inside. She squashed it down and went back to work.

Half an hour later, the storm unleashed torrents of rain, and she spent fifteen minutes in the hall bathroom after the tornado siren sounded. She emerged from the hall bath and noticed that besides missing the envelope, Jack had also forgotten to lock the front door. "That's odd," she said to herself. He was such a stickler for locking doors and windows. Strange that he would forget.

*Dallas, Tuesday, 1:15 p.m.*

JACK ANDREWS PUSHED THE WINDSHIELD wipers to HIGH. Rain pounded his windshield in thick torrents of water that drowned out the local news on the radio. He'd hoped to catch the latest market report, but he could do that when he got to the office. GRS, an abbreviation for Green Recyclable Services, was located in a business park made up of single story stand-alone businesses designed to look more like homes than offices. The developer hadn't skimped on trees, sprinkling islands of oaks and cottonwood trees along with plenty of hedges for privacy. Most of the tenants were dentists, accountants, or small medical offices.

He wheeled the car into the slot directly in front of the door to GRS, still slightly amazed at the heavy rain. These Texas thunderstorms that swept across the plains were unlike anything he'd seen growing up in middle Georgia where rain usually meant steady storms that skimmed overhead, gently soaking the land. Here, thunderstorms were vicious, bearing down quickly with winds that drove rain slicing through the air. Tiny pellets of hail tapped against the roof and hood of the car. His blue Accord was seven years old and already had plenty of dents and dings. He'd bought it used when he moved to Texas and wasn't going to worry if it got some hail damage.

He glanced at Connor's new silver BMW at the far back corner of the small lot. Connor was going to be pissed if he got some hail damage. Despite clinging to his antique cell phone and having a serious aversion to any sort of digital technology (he refused to use the office coffeemaker because it didn't have an actual on/off toggle switch), Connor was finicky when it came to his other personal possessions, always wanting the best. Zoe put it more succinctly, saying, "He's a snob." Connor's idiosyncrasies didn't bother Jack. What Connor did with his salary—what he bought or didn't buy—didn't matter to Jack. Jack handled most of the computer-related aspects of the business anyway, except for the accounting software, which Connor had somehow managed to grasp to relieve Jack in at least one area.

With the heavy downpour, Jack was surprised his business

partner hadn't cleared out of the office early to get his precious car into the garage of his newly purchased McMansion before the storm arrived, but then he remembered Connor had told their secretary, Sharon, he'd cover the office that afternoon during her dentist appointment, an unusually nice gesture, for him. GRS was still a tiny start-up, just the three of them, and they had to cover for each other. However, it looked like they wouldn't stay small much longer.

Jack sprinted from the car to the door but was still drenched by the time he made it inside.

He crossed the small reception area. "Connor, you in there?" There was no answer from behind the closed door to the office on the left of Sharon's desk. Probably on the phone, Jack thought as he loosened his tie. Connor spent more time talking on the phone than he did sleeping. He tended to shout and drop a lot of curse words, which Sharon didn't like. Lately, she'd taken to shutting his door to make a point. Jack crossed behind Sharon's desk where her monitor screen was spinning through a kaleidoscope of abstract shapes.

He stepped into his office, which was opposite Connor's and picked up his gym bag with his clean workout clothes. His suit jacket and dress shirt were soaked, and his pants were wet from the ankles to the knees. He quickly changed into a black Aeropostale T-shirt, gray workout shorts, and Asics running shoes. He dragged his fingers through his damp brown hair, finger combing it off his forehead. He sat down at his desk then went completely still. Something was wrong.

His screen saver, a photo of him and Zoe in front of the fountains at the Bellagio, smiled at him—their honeymoon photo. He'd been out of the office for over an hour. His computer shouldn't be on. It was set to shut down after ten minutes. His gaze raked the room. Nothing was out of place. He nudged the mouse and the screen saver dissolved into a webpage with lines of text and numbers, his bank account.

He frowned and leaned forward, staring at the last line of numbers. "That can't be——" But it was. The balance was over seven figures. *Seven figures?* He wiped a hand down over his mouth.

*Banking error,* he thought. It had to be. The balance had soared late yesterday with a wire transfer from his investment account.

He grabbed the mouse and quickly logged into his investment account. When the numbers came up, he stared at the screen. His balance was zero. The last transactions, dated yesterday, showed that he'd sold all his GRS shares and made a wire transfer. Only, he hadn't sold any shares yesterday. And the number of shares was wrong—it was too high. *Way* too high. He didn't own that much GRS stock. He shook his head in disbelief as he opened his middle desk drawer for a pen and notepad. Straightening this mess out was going to require extended time on hold, he was sure.

He froze. Nestled among the sticky notes, pens, and scattered paperclips, was his gun—the gun that no one knew about, not even Zoe. He'd left it locked in a trunk in the attic. At home.

He scanned the room again, feeling the old mode of alertness settle on him. He was suddenly aware of the complete silence in the office. Outside, the rain lashed the windows, but inside, the quiet pressed down on him. He remained still, controlling his breathing as he listened. Nothing. Absolute silence. Not good. He'd gotten rusty. He hadn't even noticed the stillness of the office when he arrived. Now it seemed to be shouting at him.

The walls weren't thick. He could usually hear something— the whir of a printer, the faint murmur of Connor on the phone, the squeak of Sharon's chair as she swiveled between her computer and printer, but there was nothing now.

Jack stood slowly. He stared at the gun for a moment, debating. Finally, he picked it up and held it with two hands, elbows bent so the barrel pointed to the ceiling. He moved silently until his back was against the wall beside the door. The gun felt good in his hands, comforting. His breathing was slow and even as he listened. He pivoted through the door, arms extended, almost surprised at how easily his muscles transitioned back to the familiar movements.

Still no sound from inside Connor's office. He moved quickly and noiselessly across the low-pile gray carpet. He leaned against the doorframe to Connor's office, waited a moment, and then in one swift movement, he twisted the doorknob and swung into the room.

*Rome, Tuesday, 5:10 p.m.*

AS THE SUN DIPPED TO the west side of the Piazza Navona, shadows crept across the ellipse-shaped piazza toward the Egyptian obelisk that crowned Bernini's Four Rivers Fountain. At the northern end of the piazza, where Roman chariots had swept around the curve when the area was a stadium, a man in an expertly cut black suit sat in front of a café in the shade of a canopy, watching the tourists eat gelato as they strolled across the cobblestones. He sat perfectly still, a subtle tension in his body language separating him from most of the people in the piazza. He had sandy hair tinted with a bit of gray and a round face with flat features. His nose barely broke the plane of his cheekbones, and his lips were small and thin. His light gray eyes constantly scanned the crowds.

Water tumbled through the three fountains of the piazza, magnets for the wandering sightseers. A light breeze pushed at the edge of the white linen tablecloth. The man picked up the phone, checked for messages, then put it back down at an exact right angle to the untouched basket of bread centered on the table.

A waiter hurried through the tables, an antipasti plate of meats, cheeses, and vegetables in his hand.

The phone rang. The man answered with the customary Italian greeting. "Pronto."

An abrasive American voice said, "It's done."

The man switched to English as well. "Excellent." The waiter deposited the plate on the tablecloth, and as the man finished his call, his body seemed to uncoil slightly in the chair as he lifted his wine glass in a silent toast.

# CHAPTER TWO

*Dallas, Tuesday, 6:39 p.m.*

OFFICER TERRY ISLES RUBBED HIS hand across his chest, thinking that he really shouldn't have had that to-go burrito bowl from Chipotle for lunch. He reached into the pocket of his Texas Highway Patrol uniform, pulled out a roll of Tums, and popped one in his mouth. Although, heartburn was a small price to pay so that Stephanie, his fifteen year old daughter, could have her favorite food, a chicken burrito from Chipotle, on her birthday. Add in the fact that she wasn't embarrassed to be seen eating her favorite meal with her cop dad during first period lunch at her packed high school lunchroom and, yeah, he could handle a little heartburn. He spun the steering wheel of his cruiser and merged onto the empty state highway, leaving behind a new suburban housing development, Deep Creek Commons, which had been hit hard by the storm. The flurry of activity—the highway patrol cars, the ambulances, fire trucks, and police cars were in the neighborhood, and now the rhythm of the road had settled back into its normal sleepy state.

Before the storm, the neighborhood of brick starter homes

had neatly trimmed yards dotted with small trees anchored with cords to guide their growth. After the tornado plowed through, it looked as if beaters from a giant mixer had whipped through the streets, flinging wood, flipping cars, and tossing small trees into tumbled disarray. Street signs and light poles angled on the ground, an oversized game of Pick-up Sticks. At least he knew Stephanie had been safe at school during the storm where there had only been heavy rain. The really severe weather had been isolated here.

He was reaching for another chalky tablet when he saw the car parked on the side of the road at the point where the road rose and became a bridge over Deep Creek, the normally small stream of water that the nearby neighborhood had been named after. The car, an older model blue Honda Accord, looked abandoned. He rolled slowly to a stop behind the car, watching for movement, but there was none. He called it in. Nothing unusual came up. The car was registered to Jackson Henry Andrews.

Isles stepped out of the cruiser and approached cautiously. The rain had stopped, but the clouds lingered, tinting the scene gray. The wind was hardly ever calm on the plains of Texas and today was no exception. The stubby strands of grass at the edge of the road were pressed flat from the steady, cool breeze. The fresh scent of ozone lingered in the air.

Deep Creek Commons was the only housing development along this state highway. Officer Isles didn't doubt if the economy ever picked up there would be more. The area was positioned for growth—there was a new shopping center about a mile to the west and the Interstate beyond it—but, for now, his cruiser and the blue Honda were the only cars on the lonely stretch of road. As he neared the car, he could hear the gurgle of swiftly moving water. No one was in the car. There wasn't much to see inside—a cell phone, a few paper napkins, sunglasses, and some playing cards were on the front passenger seat. A pair of golf shoes rested on the backseat.

Isles walked around the car and stood near the bridge's guardrail, looking down into the rushing water. The creek was swollen from the heavy rain and had risen above its normal banks. There were two deep indentions in the wet grass near the road. The curved slashes of dark earth, about the size of the heel of a large shoe, showed through the green. Isles surveyed the horizon, recreating the path of the storm in his mind.

With a grim look, he leaned over, squinting to study the dark recess under the bridge. There were squares of concrete on either side of the creek, supports for the bridge. His visual search widened, taking in the creek. He spotted the jacket first.

It was dark gray and hard to see, almost submerged under the water, but the lining was shiny and stood out from the opaque branches of the small bush it was caught on. The branches clung to the sloping hillside, barely above the water. The creek tugged on the bush, causing the leaves to tremble and pulse.

He stepped over the guardrail and edged down the steep incline, careful to stay away from the footprints he'd spotted. He saw a shoe, a men's dress shoe, caught in a small eddy farther downstream, spinning on its endless track in a bend of the creek.

*Dallas, Tuesday, 9:48 p.m.*

ZOE WAS IN THE KITCHEN when the doorbell rang. Two dozen double chocolate chip cupcakes were cooling on the island while she vigorously stirred a bowl of mint-flavored frosting. Zoe enjoyed baking, especially cupcakes. Helen said it wasn't a hobby, more like a fetish. Helen didn't understand why Zoe would want to spend two hours in the kitchen in the evening instead of watching television or reading a magazine. Of course, Helen never had any qualms about eating any of the cupcakes Zoe made.

Zoe dipped her finger in the icing for a taste before she put the bowl on the counter and headed for the front door, wondering why Helen would come to the front door instead of the kitchen door. With the sharp, minty flavor still slightly stinging her taste buds, she swung open the door. "Decided you couldn't wait until tomor—" Her words died away as she realized that it wasn't Helen standing in the bright glare of the porch light. Instead, there were two men in uniforms, one tall with a ruddy complexion and the other darker and more thickset. The shorter man asked, "Zoe Hunter?"

"Yes," she said, frowning.

"Hello, ma'am," There was an air of tension about them that suddenly made her nervous and worried at the same time as the man said, "I'm Officer Clements with the Texas Highway Patrol. This is Officer Isles. May we come inside? We have some information about Jack Andrews."

"Umm…I don't know why you'd want to talk to me. He's my ex-husband. We're not together anymore."

"Does he have any other next of kin?" Officer Clements asked.

"No," Zoe said slowly. "Only a distant cousin in Vegas." She gripped the door handle. "Is something wrong? Has something happened?"

"If we could step inside," Officer Clements asked again.

"Of course." Zoe nodded jerkily and stepped back. The men removed their hats as they filed into the narrow hallway. Zoe closed the door and they followed her into a small living room. She sat on the corner of the rickety black couch that Jack had owned before they got married. She'd paired it with some chairs upholstered in a black and white patterned fabric and bought two end tables at a garage sale in a burst of newlywed nesting, but no one ever came in the living room, and a thin layer of dust had settled on the tables.

A single black and white print, a cityscape at night, was propped up on the wall behind the chairs. She had taken it down months ago when she started painting the room a robin's egg blue in an effort to brighten up the dull room. Jagged swaths of blue covered half of one wall. The rest were still white. Zoe had never noticed how depressing the print was—the city looked bleak and sort of ominous.

As they sat down, the officer with the ruddy complexion, Officer Isles, spoke. "When was the last time you saw your ex-husband?"

"He was here around noon or twelve-thirty. He was upstairs. He stops by here to shower after his run." She saw the glance they exchanged and she explained their living arrangements.

"Did you see him?" Isles asked.

"No, but that's not unusual. We don't check in with each other."

"When was the last time you spoke to him?"

Zoe shrugged. "A couple of days ago, I guess," she hedged, thinking of the snippy words they'd exchanged about the electric bill. So what if she'd paid her half a day or two late? Just because the electric company said they were going to turn everything off, didn't mean they were going to do it. The first notice was only a warning. She'd paid it. She couldn't understand why he got so worked up. She'd even sweet-talked the customer service guy into removing the late payment notation from their account, so there was absolutely nothing to worry about.

"We don't keep tabs on each other…" At this point in a normal conversation, she would have made some flip remark about their living arrangements. Maybe a joke about how they should have a line down the middle of the house to divide the territory, but this wasn't that kind of conversation. Zoe nervously pressed her hands together in her lap.

Officer Isles said, "We're sorry to inform you that his car was found abandoned after the storm. It was on the side of Highway 375, above a bridge. There was no sign of him, but a men's suit jacket and a dress shoe were found in the creek, which was moving swiftly. Emergency dispatch received a call today, after the storm. A man was spotted struggling in the water downstream."

Zoe felt as if she were listening to a conversation in another language. She heard the words, but couldn't seem to process the meaning. She leaned forward, noticing how tired the officer's eyes looked. "Are you saying it was Jack? He was in the water? I don't understand."

"It looks like he was caught in the storm," Officer Isles explained, his voice gentle. "A tornado touched down near there early this afternoon. He would have been able to see the funnel cloud from the road. We're theorizing that he pulled over and sought shelter under cover of the bridge, then slipped into the water and was carried downstream. We've been searching the creek for several hours, and there's no sign of him. No record of his admission to any local hospital, either."

Zoe lost track of what he was saying for a few moments, thinking of the time she'd spent in the hall bathroom after the sirens sounded. Jack had been out in the storm? Not Jack. Nothing could have happened to Jack. "Are you sure?" she said, not realizing she was interrupting Isles. "Jack's not the kind of person who does things like that…he's careful and so…so safe. He wouldn't be out driving in the storm. He always does everything right. He's got an emergency kit in his car. He always drives the speed limit, stuff like that."

That driving the speed limit trait had annoyed Zoe to no

end. Everyone speeds on the Beltway—everyone, but not Jack. He'd putt along as cars doing eighty or ninety whipped around him.

"We can't confirm it was him, but there haven't been any other reports of missing persons. The search had to be called off because there's another storm moving into the area, but it will resume in the morning." Zoe searched his face then glanced at the other man. Both were solemn and sympathetic.

She took a deep breath, then said, "If that was him in the water, do you think…is there a chance…"

The men exchanged a quick glance. "We can't say for sure right now. We'll know more in the morning." There wasn't even a glimmer of hope in their expressions. Zoe closed her eyes. They thought Jack was dead. A vise seemed to close around her chest.

Isles continued, "Getting out of the car and under the bridge was probably the safest thing to do. You don't want to be in a car when a tornado touches down. Do you have someone you can call to come stay with you tonight?"

Zoe didn't respond right away. He repeated the question.

"What? Oh. Right, um…" She'd almost said, it was okay, Jack would be back later from wherever he was…his dinner or business meeting with Connor. The response was so automatic, so natural, that she opened her mouth to say it, but then realized he wasn't coming home. That thought was like a physical blow that made it hard to breathe. It felt exactly like that time when she missed her footing on the tree house ladder when she was a kid. She'd slipped and fell hard, landing on her back and knocking all the air out of her.

The next few moments were fuzzy and dark spots clouded her vision. But then the smudges evaporated and she was in the dismal front room with its clash of white and blue paint. The officer who hadn't been talking brought her a glass of water from the kitchen. Finally, she tuned back into what they were saying. A friend or relative. Someone to stay with her. "Yes. My friend Helen. She'll come over."

*Dallas, Wednesday, 5:36 a.m.*

IT WAS STILL DARK AS Zoe stood on the shoulder of Highway 375, staring down into the gurgling water below the bridge. Helen was going to be a teensy bit irritated with her when she woke up and found Zoe's note on the kitchen island. Zoe knew it wouldn't last long. Helen was too good-natured, and she would be more worried than angry, but Zoe had to get out of the house. She needed to be alone. Helen had arrived within fifteen minutes after Zoe called her last night. She'd convinced Zoe to drink some tea then ordered her to go to bed. Helen must have slipped a Tylenol PM or something stronger into Zoe's tea because she'd slept deeply.

She'd crept into the living room at five and found Helen asleep on the uncomfortable black couch and the kitchen spotless, all dishes washed and the cupcakes iced and put away. Helen was quite good at looking after people—it was one of her favorite things to do, actually. So Zoe knew if she didn't get out of the house before Helen was awake, Helen would be ordering her to rest and cooking her food all day. In short, hovering over her, which wouldn't do. Helen had a job to go to and Zoe had already kept her away from home all night.

There were voices and activity downstream to her left, but she hardly noticed them. Her attention was focused on the sharp slope of ground and the water. This was where he went to wait out the storm. The island of concrete that supported the pilings of the bridge looked small and steep. It would be hard to keep your footing, especially with the rain and wind lashing around. She searched the grass for marks, tufts that maybe he'd pulled up as he tried to grab for a handhold, but the grass near the water was smooth and bent over from all the rain.

Had it been quick? Had he known what was happening or was he pulled under immediately? Zoe knew he'd fought. If he'd been conscious, he would have kicked and wrestled with the current. Her throat felt tight.

She'd hoped if she saw it herself, she might see something that would give her some optimism, but the water was still high and moving at a rapid clip. If he'd gone in unexpectedly, or hit his head…

A twig swept by, rocking back and forth on the current. Her gaze followed it under the bridge, until she couldn't see it anymore. She let out a ragged breath and turned away from the water.

She swiped at her eyes and realized she was cold. The brisk wind was buffeting her suede jacket and pushing the fabric of her weathered jeans against her legs. She paused to lean down and look in the window of Jack's Honda. There were a few odds and ends—napkins and sunglasses—on the passenger seat, but it was his phone that she focused on. He always had that phone with him. He was constantly connected. He could text faster than she could type. At first, she'd thought his dedication to the business was admirable and his speedy texting was impressive, but gradually the traits became irritating. He was always firing off texts, during dinner, while he was jogging, and even at night. His phone was on the nightstand beside the bed—or at least it had been when they were married. Jack had said it was because they were a start-up business and things would eventually calm down, but when Zoe woke up one night and found him replying to a text at three a.m., she'd decided that day might never come.

She turned away sharply, a wave of sadness breaking over her. She didn't want to look at that abandoned phone. The rush of emotion surprised her. She was divorced. She and Jack had moved on. They weren't even part of each other's lives now, not really. She felt a sharp pain somewhere in the region of her chest as she remembered their last conversation. Utility bills were all they had to talk about.

She went back to her car and watched the movements of the people downstream. As the sun rose, the shadowy figures slowly resolved themselves into men moving along the creek banks, people in boats, and figures in scuba gear. Her phone rang several times. She ignored it. A helicopter circled overhead. Gradually, the searchers moved downstream, farther way from her. She wondered what they would do when they reached the point where Deep Creek emptied into Humbolt Lake. It wasn't that far away. Less than a mile. Would they stop then? Zoe thought a complete search of the massive lake would be nearly impossible. The people receded in front of her almost as if they were being carried downstream, becoming smaller and harder to see. There was no change in their movements, no excited calls or hurried gestures.

She decided to leave when a tow truck rumbled up and parked in front of Jack's Honda. She couldn't watch anymore. She stopped and talked to an officer. She showed him her I.D. and told him she was Jack's next of kin. Zoe wondered how she could feel so numb and detached and yet almost achy at the same time. She told him if they needed to tow the car, they could take it to her house. She found her card from the auto service that Jack had insisted that they have.

Amazingly, it was something she'd kept up even after the divorce. Not her normal style, which was more haphazard, but the annual bill had arrived at a time when she had a little extra cash and renewing it seemed like the smart, responsible thing to do. The tow truck driver said something about impound, so she shrugged and went back to the Jetta. She pulled away from the busy scene, not really caring where the car was towed. She would sort it out later.

She drove aimlessly for an hour, until the sun was completely over the horizon and the roads became impossibly clogged with traffic. She pulled into a 7-11 and bought a coffee. It was too hot to drink, so she held it in her hands, staring at the dashboard. She needed to call Sharon and Connor. She took a cautious sip of the coffee. It was bitter and burned her tongue. She put the coffee down and picked up her phone. Five phone calls and seven text messages from Helen. Yep, she was upset.

Without listening to the messages or reading the texts, she sent a text to Helen. "I'm fine. Will call later. GO TO WORK!" Zoe hit send. Next, she brought up the number for the GRS office, but stopped before dialing. It was too early, and this wasn't a conversation to have on the phone. As much as she disliked Connor, she should go there and tell him face-to-face what had happened.

It was a few minutes after eight when Zoe pulled into the parking lot of the office complex, thinking of the day she'd met Jack. He and Connor looked at one of the office suites she owned. The suites shared the same middle wall, and the layouts mirrored each other. Each suite had two separate offices as well as a reception area. She'd rented the suite on the left to an accountant with the unlikely name of Kiki. Jack and Connor had been looking at the suite on the right. They had been running their business out of Connor's apartment, but it was doing so well they were looking for office space.

Connor had white blond hair, a perfectly tailored suit, was thin to the point of gauntness, and hypercritical. The carpets weren't clean enough, the rooms were too small, and the location was too far away from downtown. He was at least six-five, and he'd looked down his long, sloping nose at her the whole time. Jack, on the other hand, had an upbeat personality and thick, dark brown hair with a bit of a wave to it, and blue, blue eyes. He was all optimistic excitement. The office was fine. Exactly the right size for a start-up and the location was the best part—they wouldn't have to fight the traffic. He'd smiled widely and said, "It's great. We'll take it."

She shook her head to banish those images. So much had happened since then. She scanned the parking lot, but didn't see Sharon's white minivan. She must be running late, but there was Connor's precious Beemer wedged into the last space on the back row to protect it from door dings. She gripped the door handle on the office's front door and pushed, calling out, "Connor? It's me, Zoe."

There was no answer. He was probably on the phone. He always was. While Jack preferred to text, Connor liked to talk. More like, hear himself talk, Zoe thought as she took a few steps toward Connor's office, then her pace faltered. Under-lying the smell of copy paper, ink, and old coffee, there was a funny smell...not a gas leak...something else. Something faintly rancid. Had a mouse or something died in one of the walls? Zoe had seen (and smelled) some pretty gross stuff as a property manager. She'd been called on to remove dead mice from traps and the bathrooms—well, people could be disgusting, especially when they didn't have to clean up after themselves.

She walked to Connor's office door and stepped into the doorway. "Connor," she said uncertainly. His oversized exec-utive leather chair was turned slightly away from her, but she could see he wasn't on the phone. He sat motionless, one arm aligned neatly on the armrest. "Connor?" She repeated, her voice almost a whisper. Her heart began to thump in her chest. She wanted to leave, but forced herself to take a few hesitant steps until she could see his face. His thin blond hair hung limply over his forehead, but didn't conceal the bright red bullet hole between his open eyes.

# CHAPTER THREE

ZOE WASN'T SURE HOW LONG she stood like that, staring at Connor's body, but it was probably only a few seconds before the front door opened, then solid clicks sounded as someone stepped across the small tiled entry area.

Zoe jerked around. "Hey, Zoe, are you in here?" called a female voice. "I saw your car."

Sharon. It was Sharon, her voice reassuringly normal. Zoe pressed her shaking fingers to her mouth then said, "Yes, I'm in Connor's office." It came out breathy and odd sounding. Sharon would know what to do. She was a forty-five-year-old divorced mother of two boys who never took any crap from anyone, including Connor, the most frequent distributor of crap Zoe had ever seen.

"Why do you sound out of breath? Have you taken up jogging, too?" There was the sound of something, paper or files, being slapped down on a desktop, and then Sharon appeared in the doorway of Connor's office. "Am I going to be the only lazy bum around here—" She stopped speaking when she saw Zoe's face, then Connor's body.

"Oh. My. God." Zoe had taken a few deep breaths and expected that she would need to calm Sharon down, but Sharon only shook her head and put her hands on her ample hips. Looking remarkably composed, she said, "Well, I can't say I'm awfully surprised."

"You knew this was going to happen?" Zoe asked.

"Not this exact thing," Sharon said. Her short, dark brown hair feathered against her plump face as she shook her head. "But I knew someday he'd push someone too far."

"Should we check for a pulse?" Zoe asked, reluctantly. She'd always steered clear of Connor, and she wasn't about to go near him now.

"No. He's dead."

"Are you sure?"

"Honey, I worked in a nursing home for two years before I went to work for the boys. He's not going to have a pulse. He's probably been here all night," Sharon said, matter-of-factly. "He was wearing that suit yesterday. Come on, let's get out of here. The police won't want us to touch anything." Sharon ushered Zoe out of Connor's office and pushed her down into the visitor's chair positioned in front of her desk before she picked up the phone to dial 911.

"We should leave. What if whoever did that is still here?" Zoe said, standing up quickly.

"I've already been in Jack's office—I had to drop off some files and," she paused, looked over her shoulder, and said, "I can see there's no one hidden in the bathroom. The door's wide open. You better call Jack while I call the police," she said, her fingers poised over the phone's keypad.

"Jack's missing."

During her rambling morning drive, Zoe had rehearsed several ways to break the news to Sharon and Connor. That bald statement hadn't been one of her choices, but it was all she could come up with at the moment. "The police think he's dead. They're not officially saying that, but I know they're not hopeful. He was caught in the storm yesterday and tried to wait it out under a bridge. He slipped into the water and they're searching the creek now, but…" Zoe shrugged. "Like

I said, they're not hopeful."

Sharon plopped down into her chair, the phone dangling from her hand. "Both of them...gone?" Zoe nodded. She finally had stunned the unflappable Sharon. "Did you see either one of them yesterday?"

"Sure," Sharon said. "They were both here in the morning. Jack left at noon like he always does, and I didn't see him after that. I left early for the dentist and didn't come back. Connor was in there yammering away on some conference call when I left," she said, and then she looked slightly ashamed, as though she'd just remembered Connor was dead.

"Something weird is going on," Zoe said, worriedly chewing on her lower lip. "One business partner disappears and the other is shot on the same day? That can't be a coincidence. Jack came by the house to shower like he always does after his run, but I didn't see him. Do you think he came back here before..." Zoe raised her eyebrows at Connor's doorway.

"I don't know." Sharon slapped the phone down and wheeled her chair to her computer. She moved the mouse then began typing. "I'm the network administrator. I can see when they last used their computers." She tapped a few more keys then leaned back in her chair. "Connor used his computer yesterday morning—just his e-mail, though. Jack used his—Word, e-mail, a few spreadsheets, Internet searches, all normal stuff from seven-thirty until eleven-thirty. Then he logged on to the Internet again around twelve-thirty."

"But he was at home around then," Zoe said.

They stared at each other for a moment then Sharon said. "I better make that call to the police." She picked up the phone and told the 911 dispatcher that there had been a murder.

Zoe asked in a low voice, "Can you think of anyone who'd want to hurt both of them?"

Sharon tilted the phone away from her mouth and said quietly, "You know what Connor was like—he ticked off half the people he met, but murder? No. And Jack? No. No one."

Zoe nodded. "Exactly what I was thinking. But I haven't talked to Jack about, well, anything lately. How was the business going? Did they have anyone who might…want them out of the way? That sounds ridiculous, doesn't it?" Zoe said, amazed she was having this bizarre conversation.

"No. Everything was fine. Fantastic, even. The stock has been through the roof. We'd gotten a lot of good press lately. And we had some interest from a possible new client in Italy."

"But competitors? Someone who'd want Jack and Connor gone?"

Sharon's mouth quirked into a wiggly line, discounting that thought. "No. We don't have any serious competition. That's why we're doing so well." Zoe heard the distant wail of sirens and had an urge to bolt for the door. She wanted away from this crazy situation, but she forced down the desire to escape.

*Dallas, Wednesday 11:26 a.m.*

ACROSS TOWN, JENNY Singletarry looked around Jason's Deli for Special Agent Mort Vazarri. He'd either be here or down the block at Arby's. She hoped he was here because she didn't have time during her lunch hour to make another stop. She spotted him in the back corner eating alone. She hurried to get some food for herself then slid into the booth across from one of her most important contacts. "How's the tuna sandwich, Mort?" she asked.

He shrugged. "Same as always," he said, his voice monotone.

Mort was a burly guy of about fifty, but he looked as though he should be collecting social security checks. His physical appearance hadn't changed much in all the time Jenny had known him: medium height and build with a thatch of thick hair, which had gone gray prematurely when he was in his late thirties. She had once told him his hair made him look like a mad scientist. She'd been seven at the time. She'd had her arms hooked over the backyard fence and her feet braced on the support boards to boost herself up so she could see what their neighbor, Mr. Mort, was harvesting from his garden that ran along the side of the fence. He'd laughed and asked her if her mom wanted tomatoes. He didn't laugh much anymore, not since his daughter's leukemia diagnosis. After two years of treatment, tests, and hospitalizations, she'd passed away.

Unlike his physique, which was unchanged, his face reflected all the stress and grief and pain of his loss. His personality had changed, too. Instead of his normal friendly manner, he was withdrawn and almost listless. The washed-out version of Mort worried her, not because she was afraid he'd quit or move away and she'd lose a source, but because she'd known him forever. She'd been fascinated with him when she was a kid.

The FBI agents she saw on TV or in the movies were always young and handsome or they were slightly older and troubled, but still handsome. They were nothing like her middle-aged neighbor who told great knock-knock jokes and gave away tomatoes. In fact, Jenny thought that her incessant drive to discover the truth—her aspiration to be a reporter—could be, partially at least, traced back to her desire to find out the truth about Mort—was he *really* with the FBI?

She'd spent long hours observing him on weekends from the safety of her upstairs window, which overlooked his house. She kept careful notes. He mowed his grass, weeded his garden, and had conversations with her dad about the brown patches in their lawns. It seemed too mundane for a real FBI agent. Then one day, his wife Kathy had invited her inside their house and Jenny had seen proof: his badge. And she'd also seen the pictures lining the hallway. Sequenced in a timeline, the photographs traced his time in his military uniform, then in a tuxedo for his wedding, and later in his police uniform. At that point, the pictures shifted to their daughter. Walking slowly back down the hall, turning back time as it were, Jenny realized she'd learned her first lesson in truth. The truth of Mort belied all those television stereotypes. Mort was real and the truth was more surprising to her than the made-up stuff.

During college she'd kept in touch with Mort and Kathy in a distant way, dropping in to see them for a few minutes during Christmas or spring break when she was home. She always took a mystery novel for their daughter, Ellen, who was several years younger than Jenny. Ellen had been a surprise baby who had arrived when they were in their late forties, long after they'd given up on having a family so it seemed especially devastating when she was diagnosed with an aggressive cancer. She fought for two years, but died when Jenny was in her senior year. It was only after Jenny returned home with her new journalism degree that she realized how bad off Mort was.

She didn't know much about clinical depression—the health sciences were about as far away from journalism as you could get—but she was willing to bet that Mort was seriously depressed. His partner of fifteen years retired and moved to the Alabama Gulf Coast, and his new, younger partner tended to rub him the wrong way, to put it mildly. Kathy seemed to find a vocation at the cancer society. She immersed herself in fundraising, patient education, and cancer prevention awareness. She would never be the same after her daughter's death, but she seemed to find solace and support in her volunteer work. Mort, on the other hand, seemed adrift, removed, and almost indifferent, which was such a contrast from the usual spark and verve that characterized him before Ellen's illness and death.

Jenny knew from experience not to ask how he was. She'd only get his standard answer: fine. She dipped a spoon in her tomato soup and stirred. "So I hear you and Mr. G.Q. are working on a new case."

The corner of his mouth turned up. "You throwing around that non-existent press pass again?"

She raised her chin. "I'm a legitimate employee of the *Dallas Sentinel News*."

"Yeah, but last time I checked, the obit writer didn't need to know about on-going FBI cases." He grinned briefly before finishing off the last bite of his sandwich.

"All I need is one good break to move up to News," she said, then steered the conversation away from her rather unfulfilling current job. "Is G.Q. around?"

"Nah," Mort wiped his mouth with a paper napkin. "He's over at Nordstrom's perfume counter. New girlfriend—Alana, I think—works there."

"How long do you give it?"

"Let's see, this is the first week…probably two more weeks. A month tops."

"I give it less than a week."

"You're on. Twinkies or Twizzlers?"

"Twizzlers, no question. Well, either way, it's good to know one of Dallas's top twenty-five eligible bachelors isn't going off the market."

Mort tossed his napkin onto his plate with a bark of laughter. "Not anytime soon."

"It's good to hear you laugh, Mort," Jenny said and then immediately regretted it because his face shut down. She'd committed the cardinal sin—she'd mentioned his emotional state, something he avoided at all costs. "So about this case," she said quickly, pulling her notepad from her bag. "I hear that GRS stock holders aren't happy."

"Where did you hear that?" Mort asked, his arms folded

across his chest.

"My friend Hank works in Local News. He mentioned it."

"Is someone working on a story?" His face was neutral, but Jenny knew he wanted to know if the paper would throw a spotlight on one of his current investigations.

"Yeah, me," Jenny said pertly. Mort shook his head, and she continued, "No one's really digging into it yet. They're short-handed as it is, after the lay-offs, and it's still local election season. Almost everyone is covering the primary run-offs and the local school board elections." She leaned forward. "This is my chance."

"Are you sure you want to work for that editor?" Mort asked. "I hear she's a real piece of work."

Jenny lowered her voice. "Word is that it won't be long before she'll be at a local television station." The newsroom editor at the *Dallas Sentinel News*, Anna Thessanta, was a twenty-five-year-old shrew who could shout anyone down and seemed to survive on a diet of Starbuck's lattes, carrot sticks, and a few almonds thrown in for protein.

"Why don't you do that—work in TV? That's where all the action is, right? Newspapers are dying."

"I'm not TV material. I'm too plain." She lifted a strand of her lank, brown hair and pushed her glasses up the bridge of her nose. "That's not for me," she said with a shake of her head. "And I see what you're trying to do—distract me. But I'm not falling for it. The rumors about GRS sound pretty bad."

"Well, it sounds as though your, what-do-you-call-it, blog, website thing is going pretty good. Kathy reads it everyday," Mort said, sidestepping the GRS topic.

"That's terrific. I'm glad she likes it," Jenny said, adding, "It's a blog. *The Informationalist* is great, but it's not real journalism, you know?" The number of unique visitors to the blog was growing steadily, and she was surprised that what had started as a lark had grown into something of an underground sensation. Her friend Toby, who worked as a doorman at a swanky hotel, sent her some photos of a shoving match between an NFL quarterback and the paparazzi. She'd posted the photos with Toby's description of what had happened and added her own slightly sarcastic commentary. The blog was a hit. The blog stats proved it, but she felt an edge of discomfort. *The Informationalist* was tabloid news, "infotainment." She wanted to be a respectable journalist with serious articles below her byline. "So about GRS ... what do you know?"

Mort shrugged. Jenny stifled a sigh. He was clearly more interested in discussing her writing career than GRS, but if she was right, if the research she'd done pointed to what she thought it pointed to...well, this might be the case that would hold his attention, maybe spark his interest and help him shake off some of the hopelessness that seemed to hang on him like an oversized coat. And the story could be her break, too. She finished her soup then moved her bowl aside so she could spread a stack of papers on the table.

"What are those?"

"Press releases from GRS." Jenny handed him one. "This is from February."

He scanned it. "GRS to revolutionize the e-waste sector. Yeah," he said, his voice bored. "Hot topic now, with the fast turnover of computers and cell phones. They want businesses to outsource e-recycling to them. They guarantee a secure disposal and that components will be broken down, using proper environmental precautions. Appealing to everyone's environmentally conscious side and all that."

"Right," Jenny said. "Until I researched this, I had no idea that e-waste was shipped to China and India and broken down by hand. And that toxins and pollutants can be released."

Mort tilted his tall, red glass for the last sip of his drink then looked toward the soda dispenser.

Jenny fanned out more press releases. "They've announced partnerships with C-Tech Recycling, Trans-Global Recycling, and Guahzouh Inc., a disposal company in China." Mort edged toward the end of the booth with his glass as she continued, "None of which have actually happened. In fact, I can't find records that the last two companies even exist. C-Tech Recycling does exist, but it isn't a partner with GRS. C-Tech signed an agreement to receive recyclables from GRS for six months."

He glanced at her. "Just six?"

"Yep." She had him. She could see it in the sharpness in his gaze. She dropped a sheaf of printouts at least half an inch thick on top of the press releases. "These are message board posts at investment websites. Beginning in January, there's increasing chatter about GRS. It's an 'innovative company,' a 'fast burner,' and 'investors should get in quick.' Some of the messages are copied verbatim from one message board to another, always anonymously, of course. I have no way of figuring out if the same person or group of people has been talking up GRS, but...."

Mort had been leafing through the message board posts, but he stopped and looked at her. "And in return for all this legwork, you're expecting some inside info on the investigation. We have people who do this, you know. You've probably duplicated their work already."

"I have to do all this research myself—to make sure. I'm not taking anyone's word for anything, not even the FBI's. I'm writing this story, Mort," she said firmly.

He sighed, stared at her for a moment. "Off the record..."

"Of course."

"None of this is for publication. Not yet. The SEC has had some complaints."

When he didn't say anything else, Jenny raised her eyebrows. "About..."

"Irregularities, possible stock price manipulation, question-able investor information." He glanced pointedly down at the papers.

"Anything on the partners," she asked as she consulted her notebook for names. "Connor Freeman or Jack Andrews?"

"Nothing I can say. We've interviewed some local investors. Freeman and Andrews are next up."

"Okay. Thanks, Mort." It wasn't a lot, but Mort was on-board now and would keep her in the loop. "I have to get back to work. I'll call you." She left him hunched over the papers, his empty soda glass forgotten.

)(

HALF an hour later, Special Agent Gregg Sato, smelling so overpoweringly of flowers that Mort had to roll down the window a few inches, turned the car into the parking lot of the business complex where the office of GRS was located. "What the—"

Mort didn't look up right away. Sato tended to whine about everything from the traffic to the wrinkles the seatbelt put in his suit coat. But when Sato didn't follow up with a moan about the parking situation, Mort glanced up from the pages he'd been reading then let them drop into his lap. "Well, well, well. What do we have here?"

Yellow police tape ringed one of the buildings, and a police officer stood outside the tape, waving incoming traffic toward the next set of offices. Two technicians were combing the small island landscaped with ivy and low-growing bushes that jutted out into the parking area in front of the sealed off building. When the police officer saw their car, a brown four-door Chrysler with tinted windows and special plates, he motioned them to a park beside a crime scene van.

"No idea, but I'm sure it's not good for our case," Sato said.

# CHAPTER FOUR

*Dallas, Wednesday 12:32 p.m.*

ZOE WISHED SHE HAD FLED the office when she had the chance. She was seated in a miniscule park area on a stone bench at the center of the office complex. The day had begun cool, but as the sun rose, the humidity began to build along with the temperature. It felt as if the sun was steaming the moisture from yesterday's rain out of the ground. She'd long since taken off her suede jacket and now she pushed the sleeves of the batik print cotton shirt above her elbows. She'd grabbed whatever she could find in her closet this morning and hadn't been thinking about dressing for the heat of the day when she left the house in the pre-dawn hours.

She twisted around to watch several guys in suits huddling at the edge of the park. Zoe had already answered copious questions from the police officer who arrived on the scene first. Shortly after his arrival, the parking lot had filled with a fire truck, an ambulance, and more police cars. They separated her and Sharon, taking Zoe into the small park area to answer questions. Sharon leaned against her minivan.

Zoe sat nervously watching as the quiet office park buzzed with activity. Zoe assumed the people photographing things and gathering small items in bags were crime scene investigators, and two men in suits had to be the police detectives. A scruffy man toting a large camera climbed on the roof of a nearby building to film the scene until a police officer made him stop. Soon, crime tape blocked off the office and encircled Connor's BMW. Zoe watched as Sharon finished talking with a suited man, climbed in her van, and drove out of the parking lot, passing several vans with television station logos positioned at the exit.

Zoe shifted on the bench. Her car was only steps away. It wasn't blocked off by the crime tape. She could slip away right now. Zip out of the parking lot, just like Sharon had. No one was watching her right now. She reached into the hip pocket of her jeans to slip out her keys, but froze when she heard a deep voice behind her. "Got anything for me?" It was Detective Martin. He'd been asking her questions in that bass voice a few moments ago until he was called away. She twisted her head slightly to look over her shoulder. He was on the other side of a hedge. She could just see his pale yellow crew-cut and his eyebrows that sloped down to form the base of a "v" at his nose. Zoe half stood, ready to make a break for her car.

A woman answered him, but the hedge blocked her from Zoe's view. Snippets of her words filtered through the foliage, "…death … yesterday around noon."

Zoe sat back down as abruptly as if someone had pushed her. Sharon's stats showed that Jack had used his computer at twelve-thirty. If Connor was dead at that time, why wouldn't Jack have called the police? Was it possible he hadn't noticed? Zoe bit her lip. She supposed it was possible Jack could have returned to the office and not noticed Connor's dead body. Possible, but not probable—that's what the police would think, Zoe was sure. And why would he leave and drive to Highway 375 with a storm on the way? None of it made sense.

She dropped her keys into her lap and rubbed her temples. She just wanted to go home. So much had happened in the last day.

"So, Jack Andrews is your ex-husband."

Zoe looked up. There was a new guy in a suit seated on the bench that was at a right angle to hers. This guy didn't look like the other law enforcement people she'd been talking to. They'd looked like average folks. This guy looked like he should be staring out from a billboard in Times Square. He was in his late twenties and had glossy black hair, a tan complexion, and sharp black eyes. The cut of his charcoal suit over his broad shoulders shouted designer. He smoothed down his chartreuse tie. "Ma'am? Andrews is your ex?" he repeated, smirking a bit at her confused stare as if he regularly had a befuddling effect on women.

"I'm sorry, who are you?" Zoe asked sharply. She was hot and tired and stressed. She didn't need this guy's condescension. "I'd really like to go home. I've answered all these questions with Detective Martin. Is he still around?"

"No idea. I'm sure he'll be along soon," he said as if Detective Martin were a dog that had wandered away but would return home on its own. "You haven't answered our questions, yet. I'm Special Agent Greg Sato." He pulled out a badge. "FBI"

"FBI?"

"Yes, ma'am," he said as he put his badge away. "Now, you're Zoe Hunter, correct?" He asked, his tone implying she couldn't handle anything more than simple sentences.

She sat up straight. Her pulse thumped, and the spurt of irritation she felt at his self-satisfied expression burned away some of the lethargy she'd been feeling. "Yes, I am. I don't know what happened to Connor. I found him like that this morning. And, before you ask, he's made plenty of people mad. I couldn't even *begin* to give you a list. He wasn't the most accommodating person around, if you know what I mean. And as for Jack," she shrugged, "I can't tell you. He's missing."

Sato's dark eyebrows arched. "Missing?"

"Yes. Missing." His mildly amused tone irritated her. "The Highway Patrol informed me last night. There is a search going on for him right now."

Sato, who'd been lounging back with his arm draped over the bench, sat forward and glanced back at an older guy with a lined face and a head of gray hair, who stood off to the side of the small park. He leaned toward Detective Martin, who was talking, but he was watching Zoe's conversation. His suit jacket was off, his sleeves were rolled up, and he was moving one hand down over his mouth in a contemplative gesture. Sato looked at the older man inquiringly. He nodded his head, which Sato seemed to take as confirmation of Zoe's words.

Sato blinked and turned back to her, his whole demeanor thrown off. He was no longer smooth and arrogant. "We'll discuss that...later."

"Then I can go?" Zoe said, picking up her keys again.

"No, not yet," Sato said, with more surety. "How many shares of GRS do you have?"

"None."

He scoffed. "None?"

"Yes, zero. What does that have to with anything?"

He pulled on his cuffs, and Zoe could see the arrogance rising again. "You expect me to believe that you haven't jumped on the GRS bandwagon? Even if he is your ex, surely you got in on it." Zoe shook her head, and he said, "The stock has risen from a dollar-nineteen to twenty-five dollars in the last few months, and you don't own *any*?"

"No. Not one share." She could see Sato still didn't believe her, so she added, "My aunt is a very smart woman. She's the only one in my family who's ever made money—and hung on to it. She told me to invest in real estate. That's what I do. Stocks are too volatile."

"The housing market hasn't been exactly booming lately."

"No, but you know what? Even if prices go down, I still have those offices over there. If I wanted to sell them, maybe I wouldn't be able to sell them for what I could have a few years ago, but they still have value. They'll never be worth nothing. With stocks," she made a movement with her hand like she was throwing something away, "it can all be gone in a day."

"Interesting theory." Irony laced his words.

Zoe frowned. "Why are you asking about GRS stock?"

"Routine inquires," he said. "Did you help Andrews with his business?

"No," she said. "Office work is not my thing."

He tugged at his cuffs again as he said, "Do you own a gun?"

"No."

"How about your ex-husband?"

"No."

The older man came over. He nodded to Zoe and leaned down to speak quietly to Sato. Sato stared at him a moment, then turned back to Zoe. "Where would your ex-husband go if he was in trouble?"

Zoe laughed. "Nowhere—he doesn't get in trouble. He's a boy scout."

"A relative? A friend? A vacation home?" Sato persisted.

Zoe's eyebrows knit together as she realized he was serious. "What are you saying?"

He ignored her question. "Where would he go?"

"He'd come home. He doesn't have anywhere else to go," she said quietly.

"Any relatives nearby? A parent, maybe?"

"No. His dad died years ago in a car accident—drunk driver. His mom died the next year. He doesn't really have anyone else."

"Old college roommate?"

"No," Zoe said, shaking her head and thinking for the first time that it was a little odd how disconnected Jack had been when she'd met him. "He's not really a 'joiner,' I guess you'd say. He keeps more to himself." She supposed she hadn't noticed because she'd always had plenty of friends.

Sato handed her a business card. "If you hear from him, it is very important—urgent—that you contact us."

"What are you saying? The Highway Patrol thinks he'd dead. How could I hear from him? Do you know something—"

He stood up quickly, and cut her off. "Thank you for your time. We'll be in touch."


*Dallas, Wednesday, 3:05 p.m.*

ZOE CALLED HELEN ON HER way home and apologized for skipping out.

"Oh stop," Helen said. "Your life is a tad crazy right now. You're forgiven."

It took almost the whole drive for Zoe to tell her about Connor and the aftermath with the police. After a beat of silence, Helen said, "That's terrible, but you know, I'm not that surprised. Dang, here comes my supervisor. Got to go. I'll call you back."

Zoe finished the drive automatically, moving through the familiar routine without thinking about it. The gnawing unease that had been with her since last night had grown into full-blown anxiety that made her sick to her stomach. The sight of Jack's beat-up Honda sitting at the curb jerked her out of her daze. For half a second, she thought maybe—

Then she remembered. The tow truck guy. She'd given him

this address. She parked in the garage then walked back down the driveway to pluck the envelope from under the windshield wiper. It contained a note that their auto service would be billed for the tow.

Zoe was leaning against the passenger side door of the Honda when the generic brown car with two men in the front seat rolled to a stop behind her neighbor's MINI Cooper parked on the other side of the street a few houses away.

She stood for a few moments, looking down into Jack's car. Was it only this morning that she'd looked into the car, wondering about Jack? So much had happened and she only had more questions. Zoe sighed in frustration. She wanted to know what had happened to Jack.

The police or highway patrol or whoever she'd spoken to this morning—she was a little fuzzy on who exactly had been in charge—had obviously released Jack's car and allowed the tow truck driver to return it to his home instead of impounding it, but from all those questions that Sato had asked, she had a feeling it wouldn't be long before the FBI might want to look at it, too. The gnawing in her stomach kicked up another notch.

As she opened the car door, her neighbor with the blonde pageboy who always wore yoga pants and tank tops drove by in her MINI. She tooted the horn and waved. Zoe waved back. She had no idea what the woman's name was, but they waved to each other when their paths crossed. Zoe glanced at the four-door brown car that had been parked behind her neighbor, but didn't think anything of it because she was focused on picking up the phone and the rest of the things that had fallen on the floorboard.

She sat down in the passenger seat with the door open. She hit the display on Jack's phone. He'd made several calls yesterday morning. Nothing since noon yesterday. He had one missed call between then and now. There was also a voice message from the same number as the missed call. She tried to log into his voicemail, but didn't know his code, so she dialed the number.

"Dental Associates, how may I help you?"

"Sorry, wrong number," Zoe said and hung up. She looked through the rest of the phone's screens, but couldn't find anything that she thought was important, so she turned her attention to the car.

From the floorboard, she picked up three napkins and some playing cards. She went through the console and the glove compartment, but apart from a few gas receipts, sunglasses, and the normal detritus of maps and phone chargers, she didn't find anything that helped her figure out what had happened yesterday. She sighed and moved over to the driver's seat to pull the car into the garage, using the spare key that was still on her key ring. She turned off the car, then picked up the sunglasses by one earpiece and twirled them around. They had reflective lenses and she never could see his eyes when he wore them. Feeling at a loss, she stuck them on top of her head, which, for some reason, made her feel slightly better. She gathered the phone and bits of paper and went inside.

*Dallas, Wednesday, 3:50 p.m.*

FORTY-FIVE MINUTES LATER, MORT ELBOWED Sato. "There she is."

Sato struggled up from his slouched position and blinked rapidly, trying not to look as though he'd drifted off.

It was easy to recognize Zoe Hunter, even from a distance, because of her red hair. She walked briskly down the drive-way, stopped at the mailbox, which was located near the street in a bed of geraniums, and deposited several letters. Then she crossed to the house directly opposite hers, where she unlocked the front door and disappeared inside. Sato looked at Mort.

Mort shrugged. Sato's hand inched up to the ignition key, but before he could start the car, Zoe emerged with a small white dog on a leash. She set off down the street with the dog pulling at her arm. Mort said, "She won't go far. If we follow her, we'll stand out. Better to wait here."

Sato frowned, but transferred his hand to the steering wheel. They watched her turn the corner at the far end of the block, the dog flopping around her feet like an energetic mop. "We should have stopped her before she got into his car."

Mort flipped to a new page in the file he held in his lap. "It would have tipped her off. Besides, we don't have a search warrant for it." Without looking up he said, "Don't be sour—just because she didn't fall for you."

"You think she's clean?" Sato demanded. "You buy that innocent act?"

"Didn't say that," Mort said, easily. He stared through the windshield. "I don't know what I think yet." For so long, he'd felt as if a deep, black cloud had engulfed him, overshadowing everything. He walked around with the constant feeling that something was about to go wrong, something was off, which was crazy. The worst thing in the world had already happened—he'd lost his child, watched her fade away as the disease took over her body, and he'd been powerless to do anything to help her. And now he couldn't do anything to ease Kathy's pain or his own. It couldn't get worse. But that ominous feeling left a miasma over everything, dulling and diluting life.

Today, watching Sato talk to the Hunter woman, he'd felt a spark of curiosity. Was she telling the truth? Was she as naïve as she had seemed when she looked at Sato with those wide hazel eyes? Probably not. She'd been savvy enough not to fall under Sato's spell when he turned on the charm. That had been entertaining. But there was something there...her denials had a ring of truth, he just wasn't sure if they were completely true or only partially true.

Mort's phone rang. He identified himself, listened, and then hung up and immediately began redialing.

Sato twisted toward him. "What?"

"That 911 call with the sighting of someone in Deep Creek? Well..." he paused to punch in an extension.

"Yeah?" Sato said impatiently.

Mort considered making Sato wait until after he left a message—tormenting Sato did make the time go by faster—but he decided he better not push it. For the year they'd been partners, Mort had pretty much let Sato lead their investigations. He was clearly annoyed that Mort wasn't playing his usual backseat role. "It was made from a cell number—looks like a burner. In any case, it's no longer in service."

"What about the name of the good Samaritan who called it in?"

"Didn't have time to give it—connection was lost before dispatch was able to get it."

"That's a little too convenient, isn't it?"

For once, Mort agreed with his partner.

# CHAPTER FIVE

*Dallas, Wednesday, 5:10 p.m.*

ZOE STOOD UNCERTAINLY IN THE kitchen. She had six new phone messages, thirteen e-mails, and a stack of mail to open. She put the snail mail down on the island and picked up Jack's phone. Nothing. No messages. Zoe sat down on the barstool with a thump.

She had moved through the rest of her day as if nothing had happened. She'd shut off her mind, ignoring the questions that were playing in a never-ending loop, and set about taking care of the things that had to be done. She'd made the changes to the spreadsheet that her client requested. A quick trip around the block with her neighbor's dog had completed her dog-walking gig for the week. All her jobs were finished, and she had nothing on her schedule except the new travel book, which wouldn't arrive until next week. She was reluctant to come out of her Zen-like focus, but she knew she had to. She cut open the envelopes with her butterfly letter opener and separated the junk.

She paused over the last letter, which had a check enclosed in the envelope. It was from Kiki Compton, the accountant who rented the other office. Kiki never paid her rent by check. She always sent an electronic transfer. Zoe realized she hadn't seen Kiki today then remembered she was away on her annual spring vacation.

The typed paragraph was formal notice that Kiki wouldn't be renewing her lease when it expired at the end of next month. A note scrawled in blue felt-tip marker at the bottom read, "Sorry to drop this on you, but Joe got a new job in Houston, and we're moving as soon as school is out. You've been a wonderful landlady, and I hate to go, but it's an opportunity we can't pass up."

Zoe leaned against the counter as it dawned on her that she would have two empty offices to rent in the next few weeks. The rent was a large chunk of her income, and a hefty portion of it went to make her half of the house payment. And Jack wasn't around to make the other half of that payment, either. What would she do? Apply for that job at the county? She frowned at the thought.

She shook her head and straightened up, mentally scolding herself for even thinking of her finances at a time like this. Connor was dead and Jack…she forced herself to think about what she'd been avoiding for the last several hours. Jack was gone, too, she thought, remembering the solemn faces of the Highway Patrol officers who'd brought her the news about Jack.

There had been no news from the search team, and she'd heard on the radio on the way home that afternoon that cadaver dogs were now part of the search. She knew what that meant—the chance of finding him alive was very slim.

She cleared her throat and blinked rapidly. Stay busy, she lectured herself. Keep moving. She cleared away the mail then poured herself a glass of ginger ale. The fizzy bubbles tickled her nose, and she debated adding a splash of something stronger to the drink, but instead she turned away from the kitchen. She was already sad enough.

She paused at the bottom of the stairs, looking up thoughtfully, going back over what the FBI guy had asked. If they'd called in cadaver dogs, then why had that guy, Sato, asked her where Jack would go if he were in trouble? That suave FBI guy had been jerking me around, Zoe thought. She watched enough police shows to know that investigators sometimes manipulated suspects and witnesses.

*And why hadn't they asked more questions about Connor?* Not that Zoe would have been able to help them. She wouldn't have been able to tell them who to call to notify of his death. She knew he wasn't married, but beyond that info, she didn't know anything about his personal life. Once she'd discovered what a jerk he was, she'd pretty much steered clear of him.

The words "notify them of his death," so formal and dismal, seemed to ring in her ears. She supposed she really should call her mom and tell her what had happened. No, she decided, definitely not. Her mom would be on a plane in hours, the travel schedule conveniently sent to any and all bottom-feeding paparazzi who might be interested in snagging some camera time with her at the airport. No, something like this would bring out the absolute worst in Donna. Good thing she was closed away at that spa for her serenity treatment.

At least, Jack's parents had already passed on. How awful would that be—to get a call with the news that your son had died? She shuddered at the thought.

Then she remembered Eddie. She rubbed her hand over her eyes. Jack's cousin Eddie was the lone family member who Jack kept in touch with. She supposed Jack had other distant relatives, but he'd only ever mentioned Eddie. She should call him. Not should, she had to. Eddie should know. Her mom was optional, but Eddie was all the family that Jack had. She really wished Jack had introduced her to him when they were in Vegas. Of course, they'd been a little busy getting married on the spur of the moment.

Zoe set down her glass on the hall table and pulled Jack's phone from her back pocket and scrolled through the names in the contact list. She didn't find an entry for Eddie. After picking up her glass, Zoe walked up the stairs slowly, feeling odd. It had been months—a year maybe?—since she'd been on the second floor of the house. She went in the master bedroom and looked around. It looked plainer, more streamlined, without the gauzy mosquito netting she'd had draped over the brass four-poster bed. She'd taken the comforter, a patchwork of rich fabrics in ruby, caramel, amethyst, and turquoise that had covered their bed.

During one of their arguments, Jack had declared that he hated it. It was now on the bed downstairs in her room. She shook her head. Why had they been arguing about the *comforter*? Now there was a dark blue comforter trimmed in chocolate brown on the bed. It looked good in a masculine, understated way, and she wondered when he'd bought it. The rest of the room was unchanged—black contemporary dresser and treadmill angled toward the small TV in the corner. The only additions Zoe could see were a small black desk and a mini-refrigerator that was humming away in one corner.

Through the two windows that looked out over the front of the house, the leaves of the large cottonwood tree, vibrantly green with new growth, swayed in the faint breeze. Zoe had always loved the view—it was the one thing she missed about the room. She walked to one window and pushed the curtain to one side so she could see better. She looked out at the dancing leaves and smiled faintly, thinking of all the times she had fallen asleep listening to the wind whistle through the leaves. She missed that sound. The only thing that lulled her to sleep downstairs was the clatter of the loose screen on her window.

Out of the corner of her eye, she saw that brown car she'd noticed earlier, pulling away from the curb. It moved down the street, slowed in front of her house, then sped up again once it passed her house. That was odd, Zoe thought. She looked back to the house where the brown car had been parked. A young couple lived there. They both drove tiny compacts. Maybe they had company? She didn't know her neighbors intimately, but she did know that no one else in the neighborhood drove that kind of car. She moved to the desk, feeling uneasy.

"Let it go," she muttered. She set her ginger ale on a coaster, plopped into the rolling desk chair, and slid over to the refrigerator. It contained small cartons of orange juice and milk and a few white take-out boxes. A box of Raisin Bran Crunch sat on top of the refrigerator beside a stack of plastic bowls and cups. A four-cup coffee pot was wedged on top of the fridge next to a hot plate.

She swiveled the chair back and forth, contemplating the clean desktop. Jack's laptop and a desk lamp were the only two things on the desk. The laptop was in hibernation mode. A few clicks brought it to life. His mail program wasn't password protected and she logged into it and ran a search for Eddie. A few e-mails popped up with the address "Eddie@ murano.com."

Feeling a bit weird and intrusive, she clicked on the most recent e-mail, which was over a year old. It was short, only one line. Eddie confirmed that he would meet Jack in the lobby of The Venetian. GRS business had taken Jack to Vegas a few times, and she supposed he and Eddie had gotten together then.

Eddie's contact information, including a phone number and store location—inside the Venetian Hotel in Las Vegas—was listed in an automatic signature at the bottom of the e-mail. Zoe printed it out, absently folding it and sticking it in her back pocket with the phone as she looked at the e-mail that had arrived since yesterday. Most of them were junk e-mails announcing sales. She'd been hoping there would be something from Connor that would help explain what had happened, so she went back through the e-mail, but found nothing except the normal day-to-day communication of people running a business.

She sighed and hit the button to check for new mail, more out of frustration than anything else. A new message popped up from Star Bank. Zoe clicked on it. It was from the local bank manager. They were urgently trying to reach Jack regarding a transaction that took place yesterday. The phone number they had on file was out-of-service, and they wanted Jack to contact them right away.

Zoe hoped he wasn't overdrawn because there was no way she could cover his account and hers, too. She chewed her bottom lip for a moment, undecided. Then she opened a web browser page. She'd just check his bank account and see what had happened. There were a couple of places she knew Jack jotted down login information for his online accounts. She checked his desk drawer. No helpful scraps of paper. She lifted the lamp with her left hand.

"Bingo." She tilted the lamp so she could read the sticky note attached to the bottom and typed in the numbers.

She was lowering the lamp back to the desk when Jack's bank account loaded and the screen filled with numbers. She lost her grip, and the lamp banged down to the desk with a crack. She hardly noticed because all her attention was focused on the computer. The bank balance was huge. Enormous, in fact. *So many zeros.*

Where did Jack get that much money? And if he had that much money, why did he make his portion of the mortgage payment five days late last month? Heck, with that balance he could pay off the house. The majority of the money had been deposited yesterday. Before the deposit, the account balance was six hundred dollars and ninety-two cents. Now that looked more normal, Zoe thought. What was going on? She clicked on the deposit to get the details on where it came from, but she only got an error.

She swiveled the chair back and forth, lost in thought. Had Jack been lying to her about money? She stared at the bank balance, counting the zeros to make sure she was actually seeing what she thought she was seeing. Yep, she was. Twelve million dollars. Twelve *million* dollars.

What would it be like to have that much money? There would be no worries about paying the bills—any bills—that was for sure. For just a second, she thought about transferring a couple hundred dollars into her checking account, but almost instantly, she shook her head—she couldn't do it. It would be a stupid thing to do and flat out wrong. Besides, it had to be a mistake—one of those crazy computer things that happen once in a blue moon. There was no way Jack had twelve million dollars.

She quickly closed the lid of the laptop and stood up. Another thing to add to her list—call the bank. Too late to do it today. Would they even talk to her? It wasn't her account, after all. Even though she also banked there, she doubted they would give her any information about Jack's account.

She reached for the lamp that was now in two pieces. The base had completely broken off from the stand. There was no way to fix it, she realized, as she examined the break. There was something in the base, some sort of paper.

She could just see the edge of it through the hole where the stand attached to the base. She put down the stand and tried to work the paper out of the base with her finger, but the hole was too small. She flipped the base over and examined the bottom. Jack's login paper was attached to the thick felt glued on the base. She pried a corner away and a fat roll of twenties encircled with a rubber band fell into her hand and another thumped onto the desk. She stared at them for moment, then ran her finger over the edge of the bills.

They were *all* twenties. She had no idea how much money she was holding, but it had to be several hundred dollars.

"Whoa," Zoe whispered. Had she ever actually touched this much money? She rubbed her finger across the edge of the bills again and slowly turned in a circle, trying to take in the room with a different perspective. Had she known Jack at all? He had never been one to hide money—at least, she didn't think he'd been like that. As her gaze ran over the master bath, she stopped, and focused on the shiny silver towel rack, just visible through the doorway.

Slowly, she put the lamp base down on the desk with the two rolls of money beside it. She walked to the bath doorway, her head tilted to the side. The towel racks were bare. She flipped the hamper open. Empty. No used towel tossed casually over the shower door either. Zoe thought back to yesterday. Jack had dumped his load of dirty towels in the laundry room on his way to work. She'd seen them. They'd sat there all day, unwashed. The only towels in this bathroom were neatly folded and put away in the cabinet under the sink.

The hairs on her arms prickled as she remembered the footsteps she'd heard yesterday. Jack hadn't been upstairs showering—no one had showered here yesterday afternoon.

But she knew she'd heard someone upstairs.

This was too weird.

And scary.

Zoe liked to live life on the fly, so to speak, but this was too far over her comfort line. A quick circuit of the upstairs—the other bedroom, bath, and hall closet—revealed nothing out of place. Of course Zoe hadn't been upstairs in a long time, but nothing looked disturbed or was obviously missing. There wasn't that much upstairs to attract someone—a thief?—aside from rolls of money and they had been well hidden.

Zoe returned to the master bedroom and stared at the fat

cylinders of money lined up side by side on the desk, thinking fleetingly of calling the police. She quickly shook her head at herself. None of the windows were unlocked, and she couldn't name anything specific that was missing—except for her ex-husband, of course. And, oh yeah, his business partner had been murdered. Nope. Definitely not calling the police to report hearing someone upstairs yesterday.

Back in the bathroom, she took another look around, but didn't find anything except soap, deodorant, razors, shaving cream, and Jack's citrusy cologne. As she leaned against the bathroom counter and crossed her arms, the paper in her back pocket crinkled, reminding her she should call Eddie. She fished the paper out of her pocket along with Jack's phone and dialed.

A masculine voice answered, "Murano Glassworks, how may I help you?"

She took a deep breath, already dreading breaking the news of Jack's situation to his only relative. "May I speak to Eddie, please?"

"She's not available. Can I take a message?"

# CHAPTER SIX

*Dallas, Wednesday, 6:04 p.m.*

T HERE WERE A FEW BEATS of silence, then Zoe said,
"Ah—did you say *she*?"

"Yes. Eddie is out, but she will call you back…your name?"

"She …" Zoe muttered under her breath. Jack's cousin was
a guy. At least Zoe thought he was a guy. Had Jack ever actually *said* Eddie was a guy?

"Pardon?"

"Oh, sorry. Yes, I'll leave a message," Zoe said. She gave her
first name and cell phone number, then stood there for a
few moments in bewilderment after she hung up. A rhythmic pounding sounded from downstairs, Helen's distinctive
knock. Zoe glanced at her watch and hurried downstairs. It
was a little after six. Helen must have stopped by on her way
home from work to check on her, Zoe thought.

"Meals on Wheels," Helen announced as she stepped in the
door, a takeout bag from La Cuisina in her hands.

"Is that their spaghetti?" Zoe asked. She hadn't even thought
about food all day, but with the scents of garlic, oregano, and
warm bread wafting through the kitchen, she realized she was
starving.

"Yes, it is," Helen said as she unloaded large cartons, a long loaf of bread, and a bottle of wine.

"You really should start charging for delivery, you know." Zoe gave her friend a quick hug on her way to get glasses and plates.

"Don't worry; I'll take my fee in cupcakes."

Zoe paused with her hands on the stack of plates. "What about Tucker?"

"Working late. He's got a big case," Helen said, then pointed to another bag. "There's more for him." She pulled open the silverware drawer and asked, "Any word?"

"No. Nothing. The radio news said they are using cadaver dogs."

"Oh. That's…" she trailed off, a look of sympathy in her eyes.

"I know. Not good."

"And Connor. That's unbelievable," Helen said.

"Well, not really. He wasn't a nice guy."

Helen handed silverware to Zoe. "So you think the two things are unrelated?"

Zoe broke off a piece of the crusty bread then spoke slowly, "I don't know. Connor was such a jerk that I could see him pushing someone to the brink and then getting himself shot, but Jack…I don't think I really knew Jack at all."

By the time they'd consumed the last noodle and all that remained of the bread were crumbs, Zoe had told Helen everything that happened.

Helen took a gulp of the wine, then said, "So you're saying Jack was a secret millionaire?"

Zoe picked up her empty plate and Helen's as she said, "No, I don't think so. It's probably just some mix up at the bank, but the cash upstairs…that bothers me. I didn't think Jack was the type of person to hide cash around the house, and now I find out his cousin Eddie is a girl, not a guy…it's just strange."

"Did he talk about Eddie a lot?"

"No, only a time or two and, now that I think about it, I don't think he ever said Eddie was a guy. I assumed that was the case because of the name. But why wouldn't he correct me when I got it wrong? I'm sure I said something like, *tell him I said hello*, before he left on one of his trips. And once, I said I wished I'd been able to meet him."

"What did Jack say to that?" Helen asked as she helped Zoe transfer the dishes to the dishwasher.

Zoe looked at the gap in the drywall of the kitchen ceiling. "Something about it being better if I didn't because Eddie was the eccentric of the family, the modern-day equivalent of the crazy aunt in the attic. I thought he was joking."

"Well, I'm sure she'll call you back and explain. Maybe there are two people named Eddie who work there."

"Helen, I don't think—" Zoe broke off as the doorbell sounded. She grabbed a towel and dried her hands on the way to the door with Helen following close on her heels.

Zoe checked the peephole. "It's the two officers who came to tell me about Jack," Zoe said, her heart suddenly pounding double time. Did they have news?

She opened the door and Officer Isles nodded to both of them. "Evenin', ma'am. We don't have any news, but we'd like to ask you a few questions, Ms. Hunter."

"Of course," Zoe said releasing a breath she hadn't realized she'd been holding.

Once they were seated in the uncomfortable front room, Officer Isles asked, "Were you aware your ex-husband's company was about to be investigated by the SEC and the FBI?"

The question was so different from what she'd expected. "What?"

He repeated the question and Zoe realized that both officers' looks of compassion had been replaced by something else, something harder and more guarded.

"No. GRS is doing great. Sharon, their secretary, told me today that their stock is up, and they have gotten some really good press. Things are going really well, apparently."

"So how much involvement did you have in the day-to-day running of the company?" Officer Isles asked as his partner's gaze bored into Zoe.

"None. I had nothing to do with GRS. That was all Jack and Connor."

"That would be Connor Freeman? Your ex-husband's business partner, correct?" Officer Isles asked.

Zoe nodded and wondered if her face looked as strained as Helen's. She had that look she used to get in school when she'd step on Zoe's foot to keep her from making a smart remark to the teacher.

"What can you tell us about him?"

"Not much," Zoe said, then shrugged. "I didn't really like him. He was rude and thought insulting humor was funny for some reason…" she trailed off when she realized that Helen looked as if she'd been punched in the gut. She was doing something weird with her eyebrows, a look that Zoe hadn't seen since sixth grade when their history teacher caught them passing notes during class.

"So you didn't like Mr. Freeman?"

Zoe's heart rate kicked up another notch. *Stupid. Stupid.* Here she was thinking they were still investigating Jack's disappearance, but this conversation was about more than that. She licked her lips and forced herself to slow down before she answered. It wouldn't do her any good to backpedal or try to change her answer now. "No, I didn't really like him. I don't know of anyone who did, actually."

"Then why was your husband in business with him?"

"Ex-husband," Zoe said firmly. "Connor had the start-up money. Jack had the concept. Necessary evil and all that." Helen widened her eyes, and Zoe had the distinct feeling that she was stifling a groan. "That's what Jack said, anyway. All that happened before we were married, so I only know what Jack told me."

"And have you ever known your ex-husband to lie to you, Ms. Hunter?"

Zoe glanced from Officer Isle's impassive face to his partner, who was still engaged in staring her down. Had Jack lied to her? She didn't know. He'd never mentioned a couple million dollars squirreled away in his bank account, but it looked as if the money only appeared there yesterday, and the bank was trying to contact him about a transaction, which indicated that wasn't the normal situation in his bank account. But Eddie...what Helen said could be right. There could be two Eddies at Murano Glassworks. "No, Officer Isles," Zoe said, raising her chin just a bit. It was true. She didn't know— *for sure*—that Jack had never lied to her.

A little of the tension went out of Helen's posture, and Zoe thought she must have answered that one correctly. Before Officer Isles shot another question to her, Zoe asked, "What's the situation with the search? Any news?"

Officer Isles shifted on the couch and sighed in a way that conveyed his disappointment with Zoe. "Ms. Hunter, over a hundred people have been involved in the search for Mr. Andrews. The only things that have been found are his suit jacket and a shoe. Divers were called in this afternoon to search the riverbed and the lake. They found nothing. Cadaver dogs were used as well. Again, nothing."

Zoe swallowed and tried to think of something to say. Helen spoke for the first time. "Is that unusual? At this point? It's only been one day."

Officer Isles tilted his head from side to side slightly. "There is no typical timeline in a disappearance, but considering the topography and the fact that the water level in the creek has receded rapidly...I'd say we would normally have a resolution in a case like this within twenty-four hours. But when you add in the fact that the missing person's business was facing investigation as well as the fact that the business partner was murdered on the same day...well, this isn't the typical missing person case."

"I see," Zoe said quietly.

"In fact," Officer Isles continued as if she hadn't spoken, "because this is such an unusual case, we'd like your permission to look around...see if we can find anything that will help the investigation."

Zoe thought of the two rolls of money and the broken lamp upstairs. That would look odd, if nothing else. She flicked through possible answers. She didn't want them looking around her house. Things had shifted. They weren't viewing her sympathetically anymore. Instead, they viewed her suspiciously and Zoe didn't want to risk them finding anything that would look as though she was somehow involved in whatever was going on. After all, if Jack had hidden rolls of money upstairs, who knew what else he'd hidden around the house. Zoe wouldn't have any proof that she didn't know about the money...or anything else they found.

"No." The two officers and Zoe swiveled toward Helen, who'd stood up as she spoke. She looked a little flustered. She was turning one of her bracelets around and around her wrist, but she swallowed and said, "I mean, unless you have a search warrant?" She raised her eyebrows.

"We can get one." It was the first time the other officer had spoken. He had a mulish look on his face.

"Then I suggest you do that," Helen said.

"Your friend doesn't have the right to push you around," Officer Isles said to Zoe.

She stood up, too. "Oh, I think she's right. Her husband is an attorney."

# CHAPTER SEVEN

*Dallas, Wednesday, 7:02 p.m.*

MORT VAZARRI USED HIS ELBOW to open the door to a bedroom at Connor Freeman's home in an exclusive neighborhood. Sato was downstairs at the foot of the curving staircase, working his smile for all it was worth as he talked with Chloe, a good-looking brunette crime scene technician. Sato liked to work the people angle in their cases. Mort knew the value of working contacts and dissecting interviews, but he'd always preferred objects to people. Physical things could tell you a lot about a person. Their medicine cabinet, trash, books, magazines, and mail showed how people really lived no matter what they said.

Objects were more reliable than people, too. Get three eyewitnesses together and you're likely to get three conflicting stories. Things like pill bottles and paper documents were hard evidence and couldn't be discredited nearly as easily as witnesses. Interviewing suspects…well, every tiny detail had to be checked and rechecked. People lied. Their stuff didn't.

Of course, there would be no interview with Jack Andrews… at least not right away. All they had at the moment was an unproductive interview with Andrews's ex-wife and the remnants of Connor's life. What would his place tell them?

Not a heck of a lot.

Mort's gaze ran over the empty room, which was almost exactly like another bedroom down the hall. He moved to the last bedroom. At least this one looked lived in. A Mission-style double bed, two nightstands, and matching dresser, all in cherry wood, filled the room. A black and white comforter and a silver lamp with a black shade were the only decorative touches. There was a clock on the nightstand, along with a glass with an inch of water. The connecting bathroom was white throughout. Several black towels lay crumpled in the corner near a clothes hamper. A razor with a dried blob of shaving cream rested on the counter. The closet and drawers contained a jumble of clothes—well-cut suits, expensive ties, and a few casual shirts and jeans. Was Freeman messy or was something else going on here, Mort wondered as he nudged some of the clothes aside to check the back and sides of the drawers.

His wife would recognize the brands, but Mort knew quality when he saw it. Connor Freeman had spent more on one shirt than Mort had spent last weekend when he took Kathy out for a nice dinner at Outback. Other than a few sticky notes, a couple of receipts, and a discarded wrapper for a bar of soap in the trash, Mort didn't find anything interesting. Even the medicine cabinet was a bust—Tylenol, toothpaste, deodorant, razors, and a couple of Band-Aids.

Mort met up with Sato in the great room, an expanse of open space that combined a family room, a gourmet kitchen with a huge granite-topped island, and a dining room area with a pool table under an ornate chandelier with little lamp-shades. Twin leather couches formed an "L" around a massive flat-screen television in the family room portion. "This whole set up has the personality of a hotel room," Mort said to Sato. "No pictures on the walls, no snap shots on the fridge."

"Too much house and not enough life here," Sato said, and Mort raised his eyebrows.

"Single guy doesn't need this much space," Sato said, raising one shoulder. "Just saying." Sato lived in a one-bedroom condo within walking distance of several Dallas hotspots and his twenty-four hour gym. Mort opened the stainless steel double fridge, which contained Chinese takeout, pizza, a bottle of wine, and a questionable lump that might be cheese. There were ten glasses and some silverware in the sink, crusted over with remnants of food.

On the far side of the wide room, sat a large desk with a rich leather inlay. Mort headed for the desk, "Now this is more like it." He rubbed his hands together, surprised to feel a little kick of anticipation. The desk was messy. This was where Freeman had spent his time.

A few steps from the desk, he stopped abruptly. "This has been searched." Up close, he could see that empty drawers hung open. Their contents had been stacked haphazardly on the desk top.

Sato joined him, pulling on gloves. "You get her phone number?" Mort asked, glancing at the brunette crime scene tech who'd waved at Sato before leaving through the front door.

"Of course."

"In case you have any follow-up questions," Mort said.

"Follow-up is crucial. You know that," Sato said.

"Right. Anything else useful come out of your chat?" Mort asked.

The smile dropped off Sato's face. "Yeah, neighbor says she saw the garage closing around three o'clock yesterday."

"Did she recognize the car?"

"Didn't see it, just heard the door going down as she was walking her dog and glanced over as it closed."

"And the M.E. put the time of death between twelve-thirty

and one-thirty," Mort said thoughtfully.

Sato and Mort exchanged glances. "Desk first, then garage. My money is on the desk."

As he examined papers, Sato said, "So, who do you think? The partner's ex-wife? Maybe she had something going on with Freeman?"

"Love triangle gone bad?" Mort said, squinting at the tiny print on a document. "Possible. 'Course, if we can find what the person was looking for or find an obvious gap in the files, then we'll have something concrete to go on."

*Dallas, Wednesday, 7:30 p.m.*

"SO WHAT DO YOU THINK I should do with this?" Zoe held up the rolls of money.

Helen shifted her lips to the side as she considered. "Well, Tucker says you've got two options." Before Zoe closed the door behind the two officers, Helen had already been calling her husband. "One: you go with the 'my life is an open book play'—give them access to everything and tell them you knew nothing about anything Jack had going on."

"Tried that, at least the second part, and it didn't go over too well."

"I know. Option Two, which Tucker says is your safest move, is to stall them as long as you can. And get a good attorney. Tucker's calling a friend who does criminal law."

Zoe clinched her fist around the wad of bills. "I don't have the money for that."

Helen tilted her head toward the computer. "Looks like Jack has plenty of money."

Zoe's shoulders sagged. "That's not Jack's money. It's some computer error or something. Besides, I can't draw money out of his account. We haven't had a joint account in ages."

Helen shrugged. "Just saying. I don't think you should worry about paying an attorney right now."

Zoe closed her eyes. She didn't have a choice. "I've got to find out what's going on. Who knows what they might find, and then they could assume I knew about it…"

Helen nodded, her big brown eyes expressing her sympathy. "Sounds about right."

Zoe plunked the rolls of money down on the dresser. "Okay. Here's what we're going to do. The broken lamp goes downstairs—not in the trash, in the extra room, I think. The trash would look suspicious. Anything we find goes here," Zoe said, slapping her hand down on the dresser. She dug in her pockets, pulled out a rubber band. As she pulled her hair back into a ponytail, she said, "And now we take this room apart."

They worked for three hours, going over every inch of the room. Helen took the desk and copied Jack's laptop files onto a memory drive, saying "In case they take it before we can look at everything."

Those words made Zoe hurry more as she went through every drawer, shaking out each piece of clothing. Helen clicked away on the mouse, reading files as Zoe moved through the room, checking the bed, the nightstand, the desk, the closet, even the small fridge. She looked everywhere she could think of—the underside of the drawers, between the mattress and box spring, under the bed, behind the pictures, in the back reaches of the bathroom cabinets. She found nothing but clothes, dust, and a few odds and ends—faded dry cleaning receipts in the back corner of the closet, used pens and stray paperclips in the desk, and ketchup and mayonnaise packets in the fridge.

It was after ten when Helen closed the last file and leaned back in the chair, rubbing her eyes. "Nothing on here but business stuff, and none of it looks as though anything strange was going on at GRS. It all sounds very straightforward and typical."

Zoe shoved the fridge back into place against the wall and said, "Just like this room. It's just a bedroom." She threw her arms out then let them drop back to her sides in frustration.

"That is a good thing," Helen reminded her.

"I know, but I wonder if I've made it worse. When Officer Isles comes back with his search warrant, he may not find anything, but my fingerprints—and yours—will be all over this room."

"Oh, we should have worn gloves, shouldn't we? Didn't think of that," Helen said, her eyebrows knitted together in a frown. "Should we wipe everything down?"

"Wouldn't that look worse? No fingerprints at all? Besides, we opened all the files on his computer…they'll be able to tell we poked around. Yeah, we're not exactly good at this stealthy search thing."

Helen's phone buzzed. "It's Tucker," she said before answering.

After a short conversation, she hung up and said, "He's got a lawyer for you."

Zoe didn't want to think about a lawyer. Instead, she said, "You should go home."

"And you should come with me. I don't think you should stay here."

Zoe smiled at her friend. "I knew you were going to say that. It's sweet of you, but I'm staying here."

Helen stood up and stretched. "I knew you were going to say that, too."

"Right. So don't even bother arguing with me. It will only get you home later. I'm staying. I want to look around the extra bedroom and hall closet before I call it a night."

Zoe was able to get Helen to leave only after Helen made three more attempts to talk her into going to her house for the night. Zoe watched Helen back out of the driveway with Tucker's dinner and extra cupcakes, then she checked all the locks downstairs before returning upstairs.

In the extra bedroom, she did the same sweep as she had done in Jack's room, but it didn't take nearly as long because there wasn't much in the spare bedroom. Now the extra bedroom downstairs—the flea market room, she called it—that would take some time. She stifled a gigantic yawn and looked through the hall bathroom and the linen closet, again finding only what you'd expect in those places. She returned to Jack's room, flopped down onto the bed, and stared at the ceiling fan, which was turning lazily overhead.

She'd done everything she could, short of ripping up the carpet or checking behind the vent and outlet covers, which seemed a little extreme. Another yawn set her jawbone cracking. She supposed it was a good thing that she hadn't found anything. It meant that in a cursory search the police wouldn't find anything either. She watched the slow spin of the fan blades, and her thoughts drifted to the flea market room…she really should go down there and look around, just to make sure. But there was so much stuff she felt overwhelmed.

She didn't realize she had drifted off until a jolt ran through her body, jerking her from the dregs of a deep sleep. It took her a second to work out where she was.

*Jack's room?* Then it all came rushing back. Jack missing. Connor dead. Search warrants and rolls of money.

Yeah, all problems still present and accounted for. She stretched. Reluctant to move, she watched the fan blades rotate above her. Then she blinked and focused on the ceiling fan.

She wasn't sure what brought back the memory. Maybe it was because she was lying there staring at the ceiling fan, still groggy from sleep. Or maybe it was a fragment of a forgotten dream that kicked up an old memory. Whatever the reason, she suddenly remembered that one time she came into this room and found Jack on a ladder with his head tucked up to the ceiling, the fan blades in an awkward embrace around his chest. For a second, when Zoe walked in the room she thought he looked startled, but then he'd smiled and asked how her meeting went. This was back in the early days of their marriage. In fact, it had happened shortly after they moved in, probably within the first few weeks. Jack had said the ceiling fan rattled and he was adjusting it.

She struggled onto her elbows and tilted her head back to study the ceiling fan. She hadn't remembered it ever rattling, and his expression when he first saw her…he'd looked almost…guilty.

She surged up and stood on the bed, but ducked down so the blades didn't knock her in the forehead. She pulled the chain to turn off the fan. The blades whispered over her fingers a few more turns until she stopped the rotation with her palm. Her head was slightly below the level of the housing that covered the fan's motor. A light layer of dust coated the metal. She patted and tapped the exterior, but it was solid. Nothing was loose.

She hopped down off the bed. Ten minutes later, she was on Jack's ladder unscrewing the housing around the motor. It was warm near the ceiling, and she felt beads of sweat on her forehead. She removed the cover and poked gently inside the fan. Wires. Lots of wires.

Zoe wiped her forehead with the back of her hand and set to work, replacing the cover, feeling a bit silly—silly to think that if Jack had hidden something else in this house that she'd be able to find it. There were a million hiding places, and just because he'd been surprised to see her that day didn't mean anything. Neither did the fact that she'd seen him on a ladder "working" on a seemingly functioning fan. She gave the screw a final turn and was about to step down when her gaze ran up the short rod that dropped from the ceiling and held the fan suspended a foot or so from the ceiling. At the top of the rod there was a small cone-shaped cover attached to the ceiling.

She was up here with a ladder and had a screwdriver in her hand. She might as well look there, too. She moved up a step on the ladder. It only took a few turns of the screwdriver to loosen the cover. She gave it a twist and it dropped down, exposing more wires curled into a tight ball. *Okay. There you go. Nothing. Now you can go to bed and sleep easy…after you figure out where to stash the rolls of money.*

She shoved the cover back into place, but it stuck. It wouldn't slide into the grooves so she could replace the screws. She pulled the cover away and ran her fingers along the inner rim. Instead of the smooth metal she expected, her fingers touched something with a slightly bumpy texture. She ran her fingertips along the uneven surface until she found an edge, then slid her finger under it and pulled it out. It was a small book.

She recognized it even before she flipped the dark blue book over and saw the gold lettering on the front. It was a passport. The face in the picture belonged to her ex-husband, but the name didn't.

# CHAPTER EIGHT

*Dallas, Wednesday, 11:22 p.m.*

"BRIAN KENNETH MCGEE," ZOE WHISPERED as she read the name off the passport, shaking her head. "What have you gotten me into, Jack?"

Almost fearfully, Zoe reached back up and felt around inside the rest of the cover. Sure enough, on the other side there was another passport, this one with a woman's picture. Irena Anna Whitehead. In her thirties, she had dark hair, cut in a shoulder-length bob, which framed her pale face. She wore severe rectangular dark-framed glasses and had a wide face and a delicate mouth. Not a beautiful face, but striking. There was a confidence that showed through even in the personality-erasing identity photo.

Still perched on the top of the ladder, Zoe repositioned her hip and leaned against the top step of the ladder. Her whole world had been thrown out of sync in the last twenty-four hours, and she felt a little unsteady. Why did this passport for Brian have Jack's picture? Who was Irena? Why did Jack have her passport? Were the passports fakes?

They certainly looked authentic. When she angled the page with the photo to the light, a film of embossed seals glittered.

She made sure there was nothing else unusual inside the cover of the ceiling fan, then replaced it. It slid easily into the track this time. She quickly replaced the screws then scrambled down the ladder. Downstairs in her room, she pulled open her top dresser drawer and pushed aside a tangle of jewelry along with a pile of notebooks. She found her passport under a twist of scarves. She'd only used it once, for Helen's destination wedding in Cancun.

Zoe compared the passports and couldn't see any difference between the two she'd found in the ceiling fan and hers, except that the passports for "Brian" and "Irena" had never been used. Zoe stacked all three passports and tapped them against her chin. Why have a passport with a name other than your own? A thought struck her, and she felt as if she'd been punched in the gut. What if Jack wasn't his real name—what if it was Brian? She felt slightly sick at the thought. Had he deceived her for years? Who was he? And this Irena person, who was she?

Zoe opened the Brian passport. No one looks good in their passport photo, but Jack's squared off jaw and blue eyes insured that he looked passable, despite the horrible lighting that gave his skin a yellow cast. His hair was different, longer around the ears, and it was a bit darker than it was now. He looked…younger, more fresh-faced and eager than he did now. The issue date of the passport was four years ago. What had he been doing four years ago?

She sat down on the edge of the bed and looked up at the ceiling. Jack had never been one to talk about his past. She hadn't pressed. His dad died during his senior year of college. His mom had been fighting cancer for years and died a year later, so Zoe had always assumed that talking about his past was too painful.

Jack had graduated from college in Georgia with an engineering degree, then gone to work for a pharmaceutical company right out of college, but he'd hated it. She squinted up at the corner of the room. What had he said? Something about a friend from school had helped him get a federal job. He'd moved to D.C. and lived in a condo in Georgetown, he'd said. Cubicle work, he'd called it. Boring. So boring that he'd quit after a few years and put every penny he had into GRS with Connor. Had he ever traveled outside the U.S.? And why did he have a passport for Irena?

"You're not going to get any answers sitting here," she muttered to herself and went to get the ladder. There were three more ceiling fans in the house. By the time she'd worked her way downstairs to the flea market room, she'd found two more thick rolls of cash. Her short nap had rejuvenated her, and she was wide-awake, almost jittery, as she climbed down the ladder into the debris of the flea market room after replacing the cover of the last ceiling fan.

She surveyed the chaos, thinking this would be a great place to hide something. It was a life-size Where's Waldo puzzle. She began in the corner by the door and worked her way though the room. The only interesting thing she found was her polka dot flip-flops that she had lost. One hand on her hip, she surveyed the room and considered what to do next.

Look through the kitchen? Her gut reaction told her that Jack wouldn't have hidden anything there. It was the room she was in the most of the time. The island was basically her office, and since she worked from home it was her default location. There hadn't been anything hidden in the ceiling fan in her room either, so it appeared that Jack avoided areas that they had designated as her space.

She had looked through his car, his room, and his computer files. Had Helen checked his e-mail? Zoe absentmindedly pushed her hair off her forehead as she rewound what Helen said. No, she'd said she checked his documents. Zoe had only glanced at the recent e-mail. There might be something in his sent mail folder…

Fifteen minutes later, she'd changed into a tank top and silk pajama pants and was lounging in her bed with Jack's laptop balanced on her legs. Her hair, damp from her quick shower, was twisted up in a clip on top of her head. She'd placed the passports and rolls of money in the envelope with the pictures Connor had sent. It was on the bed among the scattering of throw pillows.

As she opened Jack's computer, she felt none of the qualms she had earlier. Clearly Jack was involved in something and, with his disappearance, he'd pulled her into it, too. She opened the e-mail program. The more she knew, the better she'd be.

Her burst of energy burned off quickly, and by the time she'd worked her way through a week's worth of boring e-mails about routine GRS business, she could barely keep her eyes open. Discussions about how much copy paper to buy and whether or not they should upgrade their printer did not make for thrilling reading. *This is why I don't want to work in an office,* she thought to herself as she rubbed her eyes. Across the room, her phone buzzed. Zoe shifted the computer to the bed and lunged for her jeans that she'd dropped over the back of a chair in the corner. Both her phone and Jack's were in the pockets of her jeans. She grabbed the hem, reeled the jeans to her, and pulled the ringing phone out before the call could go to voicemail.

"Zoe Hunter, please," said a rich, languid female voice with a trace of a Southern accent.

"Speaking," Zoe said. She hadn't checked the incoming call and didn't recognize the voice.

"This is Eddie with Murano Glassworks, returning your call. How can I help you?"

"Oh, right." Zoe thumped back onto the bed. She'd forgotten about the call to Eddie. How to break the news? She fiddled with a strand of her hair that had escaped from the clip. "I called about Jack...I have some bad news."

"What was that? The connection isn't good."

How had the Highway Patrol said it? What words had they used? Zoe scrambled to remember, but she couldn't recall their exact phrases. Better to just come out with it, she decided. "I have some news about Jack, Jack Andrews. I'm really sorry to tell you this, but Jack is missing."

The line went silent.

After a few beats, Zoe asked, "Are you still there?"

"Ah, yes, but you must have the wrong number. I don't know a Jack...what did you say his last name was?"

"Andrews." Maybe Helen was right and there were two people named Eddie at the business?

"No. Sorry," the woman said, her voice indicating the call was over.

"Wait! Don't hang up. Is there another Eddie there?"

"No."

"But there has to be," Zoe insisted. "Jack's cousin Eddie works at Murano Glassworks."

"We have exactly four employees, including myself and there's no other Eddie. I'm the owner—I should know."

"Then it's got to be you," Zoe said. "Jack talked about his cousin in Vegas, even met with you on his business trips out there."

"I don't know what this Jack guy told you—"

"He's my ex-husband, and I have an e-mail he sent you," Zoe's free hand dug into the comforter, twisting and wrinkling the lush fabric.

"I wish I could help you, but I don't know him," the woman said and hung up.

Zoe pulled the phone away from her ear and stared at it, checking the number. Yes, she recognized the pattern of the last four numbers. It was the number she'd dialed earlier, the number from Jack's e-mail to this Murano Glassworks place.

"What is going on?" she asked aloud, rubbing her forehead.

*Dallas, Thursday, 8:37 a.m.*

THE SUN HAD BARELY CLEARED the treetops, and the humidity was already building, but Zoe barely noticed as her feet pounded the asphalt. She had awoken with all the questions still buzzing around her brain and decided a run might clear her head. It felt good to focus inwardly, settling into the comforting rhythm of her breathing and the pulse of the music in her ears. On her tight budget, she couldn't afford a gym or the martial arts classes that she and Jack had briefly taken together during the early months of their marriage. Any kind of fitness classes were out of her reach financially now, but she didn't mind. She had some kickboxing and yoga videos for when the weather was too bad to go outside, but running was her most frequent workout—cheapest, too. She splurged on a pair of Asics running shoes once a year, and she was set.

She made the turn in the cul-de-sac near the end of her run at Whispering Wind Court, her cue to crank up the speed. She loved her sprint home, and she shot out of the short cul-de-sac, her ponytail beating against her shoulders as her arms pumped. She glanced left and right before she dashed across the street and that was when she caught a glimpse of the brown car again. She stumbled, regained her balance, and automatically returned to her quick pace.

*That can't be a coincidence.* Her thoughts raced as quickly as her feet. It was the same car she'd seen yesterday, doing the slow roll by her house, and now it was back again. She made the turn onto her block, and instead of running home, she dodged into her neighbor's yard and slipped behind the tall hedge that bordered their house.

Breathing noisily, she crouched, wishing she hadn't worn a hot pink tank. At least her running shorts were black. She waited, her heart hammering and her calves tightening from the abrupt halt in exercise and her awkward position. She shifted on the balls of her feet. The street remained empty and quiet, except for the chatter of a squirrel. *Maybe I am losing it.*

Then she heard the low purr of an engine and the brown car slid past. The older FBI guy, the quiet one, was on the passenger side, and his gaze scoured the street.

Zoe leaned back against her neighbor's house. The rough brick bit into her bare shoulders. They were following her. Watching her. The thought made her heart rate climb more than her jog had.

Zoe quickly shadowed the hedge and slipped into her backyard. She slammed into the kitchen, grabbed a paper towel, and wiped the sweat from her forehead and the back of her neck as she sprinted upstairs. In Jack's bedroom, she stood to one side of the window, careful not to let her sweaty back touch the gold curtains. Her breathing had returned to normal, and she was doing some calf stretches by the time the brown car eased up to the curb a few houses down and parked.

Zoe bit her lip as she stared at the car. No one got out. Why were they following her? What did they have to gain from watching her? She knew nothing about GRS and after her discoveries last night, it was apparent that she didn't even know Jack that well. Heck, they probably knew more about him—the real Jack—than she did. She stepped away from the window and went to shower, hoping it would be a blazing hot and humid day. Maybe that would send them on their way.

After her shower, she placed another call to Murano Glassworks. She'd called before her run, but they hadn't been open, so she was relieved when a human answered. It was a woman, but she didn't have Eddie's sultry Southern accent.

"Eddie, please," Zoe said, crisply.

"Who should I say is calling?"

Zoe gave her name and listened to the Black Eyed Peas singing about how it was going to be a good night. Zoe didn't share their optimism. The same woman came back on the line. "Sorry. Eddie can't take your call, and she would like for you to stop calling." The dial tone sounded before Zoe could form a reply.

"Of all the…" Zoe muttered, hitting redial. Eddie had answers. Zoe knew she did. Jack had gone to Las Vegas. Zoe had seen the travel confirmation messages in his e-mail, and he'd mentioned Eddie plenty of times. Zoe even had the e-mail they'd exchanged.

The call rang, then finally went to the store's voicemail. They obviously had caller ID. She needed another phone. She dialed on the home phone and asked for Eddie, but the same woman sighed with exasperation. "I recognize your voice. I'm not going to put you through, so you might as well stop calling. If you persist, it's harassment, you know. We'll contact the police."

"Listen, I've got the FBI practically camped out on my doorstep—"The woman hung up on her. Zoe let out a growl.

# CHAPTER NINE

*Dallas, Thursday, 10:12 a.m.*

WHEN THE PHONE RANG, JENNY Singletarry was chewing on the cap of her pen as she proofread an obit for an eighty-nine-year-old woman who'd written a book on birding and was a ballroom dance champion. She recognized the number and considered letting it go to voicemail. Victor was in a primo spot—the county offices—but the last couple of times he'd called her it was with the news of a DUI arrest of a local hockey player and another time with a tidbit that a D-list celebrity had been arrested for punching a photographer outside the Anatole. They were great tips, but entertainment news was not where she wanted to make her mark. Unfortunately, she had to take what she could get right now, she thought as she picked up the phone.

"Victor, who's misbehaving now? Wait, let me guess. Professional golfer? Or is it the child of some local politician? Too much to drink before they pulled onto the Tollway?"

"No, nothing like that," Victor said as he chewed something crunchy. Jenny heard the crinkle of a wrapper in the background. Probably Cheetos, his favorite. "I think you'll like this one. It's hard news, like you want. It's about that tech guy who disappeared on the same day his business partner got whacked."

Jenny dropped her red pen and swiveled to the corner of her desk away from Brenda, who shared the other half of the cubicle. "And…"

He swallowed noisily. "There's a joint investigation—local police are handling the business partner's homicide and…," he paused as if waiting for a drum roll, "the FBI is investigating the company. Looks like a pump and dump scheme."

Jenny had been hunched over her phone. Now she sprawled back in her chair. "I already knew that," she said. *There goes my exclusive,* she thought. If Victor knew about the FBI and GRS, then the word was out.

"So, no new galleys? John Black has a new book out in two months."

As fond as he was of Cheetos, Victor loved books even more. He had a textbook Pavlovian response to the thought of getting his hands on a galley or advance reading copy of one of his favorite author's upcoming books. Jenny kept him happy with discarded review copies from the Arts and Living Section. Despite the fact that the newspaper's book reviewer was a victim of budget cuts last year, review copies still arrived from major publishers and piled up in a corner of the newsroom. "I'll check the stack for you anyway," Jenny said. No sense in irritating him, just because he had old news.

"You're a star," Victor said. "So, you already know about the search warrant and the person of interest? I swear the judge signed the search warrant not two minutes ago."

"You are sly—holding that until the end," Jenny snatched up a pen. That was Victor. He loved the drama of being an "informant."

If she could get a jump on everyone else…she scanned her stack of work. She could probably palm off the last few obits on Brenda, especially if she threw in the spa gift card she'd gotten for her birthday. "Go."

"The search warrant is for a home in Vinewood, the missing guy's place. Person of interest lives there, a Zoe Hunter."

Jenny frowned. "That sounds familiar."

"She's the ex of the missing guy. Apparently, they still live together."

"Interesting. Any idea what they're looking for?" Jenny asked as she looked up Mort's number on her cell phone.

"I didn't see it myself, but I heard it was something about papers and a gun."

"This is great, Victor."

"Don't forget...Black. Look for John Black."

"I won't forget. And if this pans out, I'll bring you a boxful of review copies." Within five minutes, she was in her car sitting at a red light, anxious to merge onto the Beltway. But when her light turned green, brake lights flared ahead of her on the overpass. She quickly changed lanes to take another route.

Forty-five minutes later, she parked at the curb and double-checked the house number, her heart sinking. Yep, it was the right address. She was too late. The street was too quiet. No activity at all. She'd missed it. She dropped her head back on the headrest and blew out a sigh. *Great. I gave away an hour massage so that I could get a "no comment" and a door slammed in my face.*

Nothing she could do about it now. She straightened and dug her camera out of her purse. She wanted a picture of uniformed officials knocking on the door or agents carrying sealed evidence out of the home, but it didn't look as though that was going to happen. She clicked off a few boring shots of the exterior, then went to the front door.

*Dallas, Thursday, 11:57 a.m.*

ZOE GLANCED OUT THE PEEPHOLE, saw a young woman with straight brown hair and glasses on her doorstep holding some paper, and assumed it was the new assistant for the realtor she often did contract work for.

Zoe opened the door. "Hi, I'm Zoe. You must be Candice's new assistant. Got something for me?"

The woman frowned. "Ah...no."

"You're not with Realty One?" Zoe's glance swept the street behind the woman.

"No, I'm Jenny Singletarry with the *Sentinel*."

Zoe quickly stepped back and swung the door shut, but the woman put her hand out and braced it open. "Wait. Please, wait. Wouldn't you like to tell your side of the story?"

"What are you talking about?"

"About you and Jack Andrews and this pump and dump scheme. All the police are going to tell me is that you're a person of interest in the fraud case, but you know what that means...most people will think you were involved—whether that's true or not."

Thoughts flew through Zoe's mind, but no words came out. The woman on the doorstep seemed to sense how truly stunned Zoe was on hearing the words "person of interest" and pressed closer to the door as she said sympathetically, "It must have been awful to have them invade your house and take your things."

Zoe realized the woman was inching her way inside. "What?"

"The search warrant. Did they find what they were looking for today?" The woman asked, again with the solicitous tone of voice.

Was this some strange scam? Was the woman just plain loony?

The woman faltered. "You don't know what I'm talking about, do you?"

Zoe shook her head, and the woman backed away from the door and retreated down the steps. "They're not here yet." Zoe was able to catch the whispered words as the woman swung around to survey the street. "I beat them here," she said in amazed tones, then she groaned. "They're caught in the traffic on the Beltway."

Zoe's heart began a steady thump in her chest. *They were coming back—the police. And this time they'd have a warrant.*

The woman spun back toward Zoe, pushing her glasses up on her nose and gripping the paper in her hand tighter.

"What—"

"No comment," Zoe said and quickly closed the door, then slammed the deadbolt home. She paced into the kitchen in a daze and walked in a circle, her hand lightly tracing along the top of the island as she muttered, "Person of interest. I'm a person of interest." In Jack's disappearance? In Connor's murder investigation?

It didn't really matter, she decided as she made another circuit, this time her hand over her mouth. Whatever had spurred the search warrant, whether it was related to Jack's disappearance or Connor's murder, it was for this house, and they were interested in her.

She scanned the exposed rafters of the kitchen ceiling and the cabinets lining the walls. She hadn't even looked around in here. Had Jack put something deep in one of the cabinets? She had searched, but what if she'd missed something?

Who knew what else Jack had hidden around the house? She never would have thought he would hide money and passports. What if he had hidden a gun? What if it was the one used to kill Connor? She hadn't seen a gun at the office. Where was the gun the police had asked about, presumably the gun that was used to kill Connor? If the police found a gun here…her heart skipped up another notch.

She whirled around and sprinted out of the kitchen to her bedroom where she grabbed the pile of passports. She hesitated for a second, her hand hovering over the envelope with the rolls of money and photos. The money wasn't hers…but she couldn't leave it out and she didn't think she had time to put it back before the police arrived.

She stuffed the passports into the envelope and put it in her leather messenger tote, then dumped the contents of her purse into the bag. She wiggled her feet into a pair of strappy tan sandals with a low heel, the first pair of shoes she came across, and threw on a loose-weave turquoise sweater that dipped over her shoulder, revealing the white tank she already wore. She tucked her phone into the back pocket of her jeans, picked up her keys, and Jack's sunglasses. At the kitchen door, she stopped abruptly and backtracked to her bedroom where she pawed through the pillows and comforter, then shoved everything on her dresser in different directions until she spotted Jack's phone behind her perfume bottles. She snatched it up and hurried to the door.

She backed out of the driveway into the quiet street. No sign of the reporter and no official-looking cars were closing in on her house, but she still swallowed hard. Her hands were slippery on the steering wheel as she drove down the tree-shaded street through the flickering patches of sunlight and shadow. She almost missed the brown car as she cruised past it. It was parked on the opposite side of the street from her house, tucked up under a droopy mimosa tree behind a large black van. She kept her gaze focused forward, but couldn't help slouching down a little in the seat. Out of the corner of her eye, she saw a woman on the sidewalk, bent down to the open passenger window. Zoe transferred her gaze to the rearview mirror and saw that it was the reporter. She held her cell phone in her hand and was shaking it as if making a point.

The car's brake lights flared and Zoe realized they had seen her. The woman stepped away, and the car surged backward, then forward in a half arc, but a slow jogger picked that point to trot across the street and interrupt their U-turn. The brown car rocked as the driver slammed on the brakes. Zoe licked her lips as she made a sedate right turn, then stepped on the gas as she exited the neighborhood and merged onto a major road, which was busy with traffic, but not clogged. She slipped in and out of the cars, never going over the speed limit despite an urgent longing to press the accelerator to the floor, until she reached the Beltway, the road that encircled Dallas and Fort Worth.

No brown cars in sight behind her. She pressed down on the gas and switched to the far lane, twisting her tense shoulders to work out the kink that seemed to be tightening the muscles into a knot. She drove for twenty minutes with no sign of the brown car or flashing lights in her rearview mirror. The intense need to get away had receded, and she could breathe easier, but she had no idea of where to go. Helen's house had been her immediate thought, but she passed Helen's exit without even changing lanes. She couldn't go there and involve her. Besides, it would only delay the encounter with the police. Friends and family were the first places they'd check.

She whipped by another exit, this one for 35, an Interstate Highway, and a thought slipped into her mind. What if she kept going? Just stayed on the road until she was out of Dallas? Out of the state, even?

The thought bloomed into a plan. What if she kept driving…all the way to Las Vegas? Eddie was never going to talk to her over the phone, but maybe face-to-face she could get some answers. If she went home now…well, she could imagine the reaction of the police if she stated she'd found the passports and money. The FBI agents clearly hadn't thought she was clueless about Jack's activities, and that reporter person was talking about fraud. Did it have something to do with all that money in Jack's account? She felt her heart rate jump as she gripped the steering wheel tighter. What if they turned up something incriminating during their search...no, it had to be Vegas, Zoe thought as she hit her blinker and took the next exit for Denton.

# CHAPTER TEN

*Las Vegas, Friday, 12:42 p.m.*

ZOE PULLED INTO THE PARKING garage of the Venetian Hotel early Friday afternoon. She spun the wheel,
maneuvered into a slot near the door labeled "Casino," and
stretched her arms over her head, running her fingers over the
fabric that lined the roof of the car.

She let her arms fall back to her side and closed her eyes for
a moment, reveling in the fact that she'd made it. And in good
time, too. She'd only stopped a few times, including once in
Amarillo to fill up with gas and grab a cup of coffee. She'd
hesitated over using the fat rolls of money for her purchases.
It wasn't her money.

Instead, she'd dug in her purse and used her last two twenties. She'd found an ATM at another gas station and, with the
wind whipping her hair around her face, she'd cashed the
last rent check from Kiki. Zoe had used that cash to pay for
other times she'd filled up the car. One gas station had been
located next to a Cozy Choice Hotel, a mid-range national
chain. Zoe strolled into the hotel, took a seat at the computer
tucked in a corner of the lobby, and used the complementary
Internet access to set up a free Gmail account, from which she

e-mailed Helen a note that only she would understand.

"Heading out for my own serenity break. May join mom." The e-mail would clue Helen in that Zoe was out of town, but Helen would know that Zoe would never go on a serenity break in the first place and joining her mom at the spa would never happen either. Later, Zoe caught a few hours sleep at a rest stop in the mountains near Flagstaff where the air was crisp, then drove the rest of the way, a short four hours, straight through.

The dry heat, so different from Dallas' sticky atmosphere, hit her as soon as she stepped out of the car. It seemed as if she could almost feel her lips beginning to chap and her skin wrinkling. Chilly air swept over her, making her break out in goose bumps as she pushed into the casino where she could hear the constant ding of the slot machines. Marble columns lined the hallways, richly colored frescos edged in heavy gilt decorated the ceiling, and intricately patterned marble tiles created geometric patterns on the floor. Like everything else in Vegas, it was over the top—excessive grandness and opulence to the extreme. It was too much, especially after twenty hours on the road.

Zoe blinked and rubbed her eyes. The patterns of the floor tiles were making her eyes cross. She'd been in The Venetian before, but she had been much more interested in Jack than in the casinos during that trip. Besides, they'd spent most of their time in their room. She flinched away from thoughts of those heady days—almost embarrassed to think how naïve she'd been. She'd fallen for Jack hard and had believed everything he'd said.

She ignored the lavish décor and picked up her pace, moving by the people hunched at slot machines and the circulating waitresses. She bought a coffee at a snack area in the casino, then made her way to the second floor with its simulation of a Venetian canal and St. Mark's Square. Lined with shops,

Zoe figured the canal with arched bridges and gondolas was a good place to look for "cousin" Eddie's store. Zoe didn't spare a glance at the strolling, costumed Venetians decked out in Renaissance finery, the singing gondolier, or the unmoving, yet human statue dressed head to toe in a white nun-like getup, who posed on a small dais and stared impassively into the distance as tourists with fanny packs snapped pictures of themselves beside her. Zoe strode briskly along the canal with its Aqua Velva–tinted water, the caffeine reenergizing her until she spotted Murano Glassworks and halted so abruptly that a woman with gray curls above her sun visor bumped into her.

Zoe apologized and moved to lean against a barrier that enclosed the "outdoor" tables at one of the restaurants. Murano Glassworks was a small storefront in a prime location, just off the replica of St. Mark's Square. She sipped her coffee. Customers filled the store, but it looked as though most of the people were browsing. Two salespeople circulated through the store, one a tall, lean guy who couldn't be more than twenty and a slightly older, petite woman with dark blond hair cropped in a pixie cut.

Zoe tossed the empty cup in the trash and went into the store, her heart beating a little faster. She strolled by the blond woman and saw her nametag: Eddie. Zoe picked up a translucent dome-shaped glass paperweight, which encased colorful geometric patterns that looked like flowers. They were similar to the paperweights GRS gave to clients. She stole a glance at the woman. With her pointed chin and the long bangs of her boyish haircut brushing her brown eyes, she was nothing like the person Zoe had mentally pictured when she'd spoken to Eddie on the phone. Zoe hadn't realized she'd made some assumptions about Eddie, but she had. She'd expected Eddie to be like her voice, full-bodied and curvy, probably with masses of dark hair.

"That's an excellent example of a vintage millefiori," Eddie said, gesturing to the paperweight Zoe held.

"Oh. Yes…I suppose so," Zoe said. She had been studying Eddie so closely that she'd forgotten she was holding the paperweight. She tilted it, caught sight of the price tag, and hastily replaced it on the shelf. She couldn't afford a seventy-five dollar paperweight.

"The small shapes inside the paperweight are actually glass. It's shaped into long tubes and cut into tiny pieces, which reveals the interior pattern. We also have millefiori jewelry as well as more vintage paperweights, if you're interested." Her gaze skimmed over Zoe, and she was sure Eddie was noting the dark circles under her eyes and the crumpled clothes that didn't have designer labels. "Or," Eddie continued as she tidied the display, aligning the paperweights, "we have some nice contemporary paperweights at a lower price."

"No, thanks. I'm interested in Jack Andrews."

Zoe had to admire the woman's poise. She didn't falter or show any surprise. She continued to neaten the table. As she leaned across Zoe to straighten the last few items on the table, one eyebrow shot up, disappearing under her fringe of bangs. "You must be Zoe."

"Yes." Zoe crossed her arms. A customer, a stout woman, breathed out an impatient sigh, clearly wanting to move through the narrow aisle, but Zoe planted her feet and stared at Eddie.

Eddie's gaze flicked to the woman, then back to Zoe. "Let's step outside."

They walked across the prefab piazza to the canal. Eddie rested her elbows on the balustrade running along the canal and looked into the turquoise water. "Your area code, two-one-four, that's Dallas."

Zoe gripped the decorative iron. "Yes. I drove straight through."

"I can tell how important this is to you," Eddie said as she turned her head to look at Zoe over her shoulder, and Zoe noticed how long her eyelashes were. "But I don't know this Jack guy."

"I have an e-mail from him to you. He traveled here regularly," Zoe said, wishing she'd brought the e-mail. "You don't understand—this is incredibly important. I have to get some answers. I'm in trouble because of him, and you're the only link I have to finding answers. He's missing. He could be dead."

Eddie was shaking her head. "I really wish I could help—really. You seem sincere but," she shrugged, "I can't." Zoe started to speak, but Eddie cut across her words and said quietly, "I don't know anything. Please don't make any trouble. I don't want to call security and make things worse for you." With her lips pressed together, Eddie gave Zoe a regretful half-smile and pushed off from the balustrade. She walked quickly to the store and immediately went to help a customer.

Zoe sagged against the iron, suddenly feeling every minute of lost sleep. Her eyes felt gritty, and the coffee had left a bitter taste in her mouth. A gondola floated by, the gondolier in his striped shirt and round straw-hat singing *O Sole Mio* over a bride and groom snuggled together.

Zoe felt that disoriented feeling she got in the fun house at the fair when she was a kid. What kind of crazy place was this? This recreated, reconstructed reality was just a rip-off of another tourist destination. They had a river on the second floor of the building with water the same color as the painted sky (complete with wispy clouds) overhead. Zoe shook her head and pushed away from the balustrade and wandered through the casino aimlessly for a while.

Eventually she came to a bar and hoisted herself up on a high table in the corner. The waitress, a thirtyish woman with jet-black hair that matched her heavy eyeliner, asked what she'd like. At this point, alcohol would wipe her out, so

Zoe ordered a ginger ale and an appetizer of fried mozzarella cheese off the bar menu. She moved her glass around on the napkin, creating concentric rings as she contemplated what to do. Driving back to Dallas was at the bottom of her list, but where else could she go? Not to her mom. No help there. Her mom would issue a press release and begin setting up interviews with all the 24-hour cable news channels.

Aunt Amanda was a possibility. She was sensible and smart. The fact that she was in Sarasota, Florida depressed her. Zoe was about as far away from Sarasota as she could be and still be in the United States. Her food arrived. She didn't realize how hungry she was until the aroma of fried mozzarella wafted up from the plate. The marinara sauce was excellent. By the time she scooped up the last of it, she'd nixed Aunt Amanda from her list.

If Zoe showed up on her doorstep, she'd pull Aunt Amanda into this investigation, and she didn't want to do that. The FBI would eventually find Aunt Amanda and ask her what she knew. There was no need for Zoe to hurry things along. She pushed her plate away with a sigh, realizing that going to Helen was out, too. Investigators probably knew about Helen already since they were watching Zoe's house. They probably would have tracked down anyone who came inside, so the less contact Zoe had with Helen, the better. Zoe could hear Helen's voice arguing with her in her head, but she ignored it as she removed some of the debris from her messenger bag and set it on the table, digging some cash out of the bottom to pay the bill.

As the waitress slid the money off the table, she said, "Oh, that's not a good sign, honey."

"What?" Zoe looked up from the depths of her bag. The waitress was pointing to the mess of lip gloss, sunglasses, and receipts on the tabletop.

A shiny red fingernail touched one of the playing cards

that Zoe picked up from Jack's car. "An eight of Spades—that means danger. And this," she lined up the other card, "A two of Spades. That's deceit."

"Really?"

"My mom taught me," she said with a half shrug.

Zoe flipped the card over. The sturdy bell tower from St. Mark's Square filled the space over the words THE VENE-TIAN HOTEL. Zoe checked all the cards. They were the same. "Are these from the casino?"

"No, I used to work the floor. That's a souvenir deck from the shops." She removed the plate. She hesitated, her head cocked to one side, "You look really familiar. Have you been on TV or something?" Before Zoe could reply, she snapped her fingers. "*Smith Family Robinson.* You were the girl on that reality show, the one about an average family surviving on a tropical island."

"I get that sometimes," Zoe said with a little shrug. "I just have one of those faces, I guess." Sometimes people did recognize her, but she tried to brush off any interest the show generated. She *especially* didn't want someone recognizing her here.

"Oh, okay. Well, you be careful," she said.

Zoe stacked the cards carefully, trying to remember exactly how Jack's car interior looked when she stood on the road above the bank of the river. She closed her eyes and ran her fingers over the glossy coating on the cards. Everything had been jumbled up after Jack's car had been towed to the house, but that first time she glanced in the window the cards were on the passenger seat, laid out in a row, face up, with their edges tucked under the phone, as if someone had placed them there and used the phone to anchor them. Had Jack done that? Or someone else? Or was it a coincidence?

Zoe opened her eyes and tapped the edge of the cards against the table, her eyes narrowed. She'd eaten and was feeling more clear-headed. Eddie had seemed sincere, as though she really didn't know Jack, but surely it wasn't a coincidence that these specific cards were in the car and that they were playing cards from The Venetian. It *could* be a coincidence, but after the last day or so, the coincidence seemed...unlikely, to say the least.

She'd go back to Eddie's store and watch. It was all she could think of to do at the moment. She sure wasn't hitting the road back to Dallas, and since she couldn't come up with another destination, watching Eddie seemed to be her only option. Zoe heaved her messenger bag onto her shoulder, ducked into a gift shop, and paid an exorbitant amount for a travel toothbrush and a microscopic tube of toothpaste, then walked along the corridors until she found a bathroom. She emerged a few minutes later feeling almost normal. It was amazing how much better food, caffeine, and a little primping could make you feel.

She made her way back to Eddie's store through the increasing crowds. As the day wore on, the number of strolling tourists grew, but Zoe decided that was a good thing. She wanted to observe without being noticed. She browsed in a store, featuring T-shirts, key chains, and Venetian playing cards that was located directly across from Murano Glassworks, until she was sure that Eddie was still there. Zoe worked her way around the shopping and dining area, keeping the store and Eddie in sight.

She settled against a balustrade and tried to look as though she were waiting for someone. She had to move on after about an hour when a woman with blunt bangs and a short pageboy took an interest in her. Zoe figured she was hotel security. She moved, pacing along the canal, then moved to a new vantage point and watched from a distance as Eddie flittered among the customers, restocked shelves, and cleaned the fingerprints from the glass doors and display counters. After two hours of cruising the shopping area like a teen on Friday night, she took a table at one of the restaurants. She ordered a panini and told the waiter she wasn't in a hurry. Of course, the moment her food arrived, Eddie waved to the other employee and slipped her purse onto her shoulder.

Zoe threw the last of her twenties from Kiki's rent money on the table and wrapped her panini in a paper napkin. She followed Eddie out of the hotel into the glaring sunlight of The Strip where people crushed together on the sidewalks in a slow moving parade. Zoe took a few hurried bites of the panini—so good—then ditched it in a trashcan and merged into the crowd, trying to keep Eddie's fair head in sight. It wasn't easy because the crowds shifted and swirled like water.

Zoe dodged around people handing out flyers for shows and other more exotic entertainment. She sidestepped slow-poke tourists gawking at casino exteriors or slurping colorful liquids from straws attached to enormous plastic cups. The vehicles on The Strip weren't moving much faster than the pedestrian traffic, and a constant blare of horns filled the air. Zoe barely noticed the dry, scorching afternoon heat that seemed to make the air waver when she looked into the distance.

They came even with Caesar's Palace, which was on the other side of the street, and Eddie stepped onto one of the escalators that lead to a bridge to cross to the other side of the street. Zoe took the steps two at a time and reached the top in time to see Eddie take the stairs on the other side down to street level.

Pushing through the crowd, Zoe hurried to get to the street. Eddie headed away from Caesar's and took another trip up and over a second pedestrian bridge. Cool air washed over Zoe, chilling her as she followed Eddie through the cool, sumptuous setting of the Bellagio Casino. But apparently this was only a short detour because in a few minutes, Eddie went back outside toward The Strip.

The fountains of The Bellagio danced in front of her. Water sprayed in time to the voice of Frank Sinatra singing *Fly Me To The Moon* as Eddie headed for the shady stretch of sidewalk in front of the fountains. Zoe stopped abruptly as Eddie's pace slowed in front of the fountains. She gazed at them for a few seconds, her hands resting lightly on the balustrade, then she turned and walked back toward Zoe. Zoe turned her back to Eddie and tried to blend in with a family pushing a stroller. Zoe shadowed the family, trying to keep out of Eddie's line of sight. Water shot into the air with the music's crescendo, and all eyes were on the fountains, except for Zoe's. She watched Eddie, who was making tracks back the way she'd come.

Zoe frowned, glancing back at the place where Eddie had paused to watch the fountains. She'd come all this way to watch them for a few seconds? There was a heavy-set guy with vintage style Ray-Bans, a baseball cap, and a T-shirt with the classic Welcome to Las Vegas sign standing where Eddie had stood. A short grandma elbowed the man out of the way, so she could get a clear photo of the fountains. Zoe gazed out over the palm trees lining the median of The Strip and up to the replica of the Eiffel Tower and was overcome with an Alice-in-Wonderland kind of feeling.

Zoe turned her attention back to Eddie's blond head. Zoe gave Eddie a few more paces, then merged back into the crowd and followed her.

*Well, that was useless*, Zoe thought as she trailed behind Eddie all the way back to the square brick clock tower that was reproduced on the cards in her messenger bag. Eddie disappeared inside the casino. Zoe swept in through the glass doors and walked along the edge of the corridor, keeping a few paces behind Eddie.

A hand gripped her elbow. A low, male voice whispered in her ear, "Don't make a sound."

# CHAPTER ELEVEN

*Las Vegas, Friday, 3:35 p.m.*

ALMOST IN THE SAME INSTANT that the man spoke, he steered her through a nearby door. Instinctively, Zoe fought him, writhing as a rush of adrenaline kicked through her body, but he'd grabbed her so suddenly, she was through the door and into the small room almost before she'd realized what had happened.

*Bathroom* registered in her mind. *Empty* bathroom.

*Not good.*

The door hissed closed behind them. Zoe caught a glimpse of the man in the mirror. Baseball cap and black Las Vegas T-shirt—the guy she'd seen at the fountains.

His grip on her elbow loosened slightly. Zoe took half a step forward with her right foot and thought of all those drills they'd done in martial arts class. She leaned forward, then delivered the hardest back kick she could, aiming low.

The heel of her foot connected with his abdomen.

Thank you, Master Paul, Zoe thought, as he tumbled backward and crashed into a trashcan beside the door. The impact had vibrated up her foot and into her leg. A real live person was much more solid than all those pads they'd used in class.

And it had been years since she'd practiced those kicks. She rushed to the door.

He wheezed something.

Zoe paused, her hand wrapped around the door handle. Had he said her name?

He had one hand braced on his stomach as he fought to get his breath back. "So I take it…" he paused to suck in a breath, "you'd rather I was dead." He pulled off the baseball cap and sunglasses.

Zoe, breathing hard from the adrenaline rush, frowned at him. The body was wrong—too soft and fat, but…dark, wavy hair. Silver-blue eyes. And through the stubble on his squared jaw, she could see a tiny white scar slightly off-center on his chin. She gripped the door handle. "I'd hit you, if you weren't already on the ground," she said, a wash of relief and fury surging through her.

"Got that message already," he said.

She tried to sort through her emotions. She was mad, but there was something else, too. Could she really be glad to see him? After this stunt he'd just pulled? And after he'd deceived her so thoroughly? "What were you doing," she asked, settling on fury. It felt better. "Were you trying to scare me out of my mind?"

"What are you doing here, Zoe?" he asked, standing up slowly, his tone calm.

"What are *you* doing here?"

"Trying to find out why someone killed Connor, framed me for it, and then tried to kill me," he said, leaning down. He picked up the trashcan, but checked his movement, wincing and favoring his left side.

"Are you hurt?" Zoe asked dispassionately, crossing her arms and leaning her hip against the sink.

"Nothing that won't heal."

They stood for a few seconds looking at each other, finally

he said, "You should go home. Forget you ever saw me."

"Can't."

"Why not?"

"I'm a person of interest in the investigation into Connor's death, and I need some answers from you about GRS stock for the FBI."

He dipped his head. "I see."

The door opened and a woman in a blazer cautiously checked inside. A plastic wire ran from her plain white shirt collar to an earpiece almost hidden behind her short curly hair. "Have we got a problem in here?" she asked.

Jack settled the baseball cap on his head. As he slipped on his sunglasses, he shot a glance at Zoe over the frames. Zoe could turn him in right now. A few words would bring more security, and eventually he'd be on his way back to Dallas. There was something in his jaw, a set firmness that told her he was braced for the worst. He pushed the sunglasses up. She couldn't see his eyes, but she felt his gaze on her.

Zoe licked her lips and said, "No, just one too many cocktails. Come on, honey, let's get you home." Zoe moved to him and took his arm.

The security woman stepped back and held the door for them.

"Thanks, *darling*," Jack said in a loud voice and swayed against Zoe. His side felt squishy against her arm. As they retraced their steps and exited the hotel, he lowered his voice so that only Zoe could hear, "Thanks."

"I only did it because I want some answers. If I turn you in, I doubt I'll get them."

He nodded. "Is she following?"

Zoe glanced back. "No."

"No one else in a blazer like hers?"

"No," Zoe said as they threaded their way through the valet parking. Jack kept up his slightly unsteady gait as they walked through the shadow cast by the brilliantly white Rialto Bridge. Jack stopped leaning on her so heavily, but he was moving in a way Zoe had never seen. Instead of his easy long-legged gate, he'd shortened his stride and slumped his shoulders. "Where are we going?" she asked.

"Anywhere away from here," he said.

"Thanks for letting me know you're not dead, by the way," Zoe said.

"You were worried?" His tone was heavy with skepticism.

"Of course I was worried. We were married once. What did you expect me to do when the police showed up at my door and said you were missing, probably dead? Shrug my shoulders and say, not my problem?"

"Well, yes. That's about how I thought it would go."

Zoe stopped walking and stared at him. "You're not serious?"

He gripped her arm and pulled her along. "It's wonderful to know you care, but right now we've got to keep moving."

Zoe planted her feet. "No, Jack. Not another inch until you tell me what happened."

He pulled on her arm. Zoe stood firm. She eyed the crowds and said, "I can yell. We're still on the casino property. I'm sure there's security around here, too."

"Fine." He leaned close, moved his sunglasses to the bill of his cap, and fastened his gaze on her. Despite the crowds swirling around them, Zoe felt as if she and Jack were encapsulated from them. The noise of people talking, the honk of car horns, the wind rattling through the dry palm fronds overhead, all seemed to fade as Jack said quietly, "I came back from lunch and found Connor dead in his office. I was about to do the good citizen thing and call the police when a man came through the front door with a gun aimed at me."

His face was as earnest and as open as she'd ever seen it. "What did you do?"

"I took the gun away," Jack said as if that was the most logical thing in the world.

"Okay. Then why the disappearing act?" Zoe asked, flinging her hands out in frustration. "All this mess could have been avoided. That guy probably killed Connor—"

"Because," Jack cut in, "I didn't see the other guy behind me. He hit me over the head and knocked me out. Never saw it coming," he said. "Stupid on my part."

"So there were two men, not just one?"

"Yes, two," he said tightly. "Now that I've had time to think about it, the second guy must have come in the window of the bathroom because I looked there, and I hadn't seen anyone earlier. It's the only way he could have gotten in."

A woman in three-inch heels and a tight pink tank top stumbled into them. She apologized and backed away as she giggled and slapped her companion, a lanky guy wearing a baseball cap turned the wrong way.

Jack pressed on Zoe's shoulder, and they rejoined the ebb and flow of people. "When I came to, the two guys were standing over me, discussing what to do with me—specifically where they should leave my body and how I should be posed to realistically portray a successful suicide attempt."

Zoe's steps tangled. "Suicide?"

"Yes," Jack said, catching her elbow. "Apparently, I killed Connor and was immediately overcome with remorse and killed myself."

Zoe's steps slowed again, and she struggled to take it all in. "But…that's…" Words failed her.

"Crazy? Improbable?" Jack said. "I know. My thoughts exactly, and if my ex-wife is asking herself if what I'm saying could really be true, you can see why I was reluctant to go to the police with the story."

"It is rather…far-fetched, but if it's the truth—"

"Of course, I never was able to fully weigh the pros and

cons of that course of action because they were going to kill me."

Zoe looked at him doubtfully.

"Zoe," Jack spun her toward him and gripped her upper arms. "They were going to kill me. *Kill me*." His hands tightened on her arms, emphasizing his words. "Not rough me up a bit and walk away. I was their job. Their assignment. I heard it all while I had my face planted in the carpet under Sharon's desk while they argued."

Zoe stared at him, processing his words. Finally, she said, "But you got away."

"Yes." He released her, and they walked again. "Barely," he said, his hand moving to his side.

"And the two guys…what happened with them?" Zoe edged away slightly. She didn't know this man. It wasn't only his physical appearance that had changed. Under the stubble and the weird clothes, he had a hard edge, an intensity that she'd never seen. He'd always been focused, especially when he was working business deals, but his manner then seemed mild compared to the single-minded concentration radiating off him now.

"Don't look at me like that. They were breathing when I left. Unconscious, but breathing."

"I only ask because there was no one else there when I found Connor," she said, slowing her pace.

He glanced at her quickly, frowning…with concern? Zoe wasn't sure about his expression. "You found him?"

"The next morning. I went by the office to tell him and Sharon about you—that you were missing. At first glance, every thing looked normal—aside from Connor, that is."

"Sorry you saw that," Jack said quietly.

"Sharon was there almost as soon as I found him."

"Odd that they'd tidy up," Jack said. "They didn't seem the type."

Zoe wasn't too interested in what the men did. They could have waxed the floor for all she cared. "So after you left the office, you what? Decided to disappear? Make it look as if you were dead?"

"It was the only thing I could think of. They weren't leaving Dallas with me alive—that was clear from their conversation. They'd already used my gun to kill Connor. It had my fingerprints on it. And there was the money—I saw the transfer into my account before I found Connor."

"You own a gun?" Zoe said incredulously and so loudly that several people on the sidewalk gave them curious looks. She'd told the police he didn't own a gun. It was the one thing that she'd been so sure of, but now that seemed like a long time ago.

"Yes."

"Why didn't I ever see it?"

"I kept it in a safe place. It just never came up."

Zoe stared at him a few seconds, then blinked. "Okay," she said, drawing out the syllables. "Forget the gun for now. Let's get back to your disappearance. Your 'death' wouldn't fool them—or the police—forever." Zoe glanced back involuntarily as they followed the curve of the sidewalk and joined the procession of tourists moving up and down The Strip. No blazer people.

"No, but it protected you. If I'd gone home…"

She gave him a long look. "Really. You did it all for me? The whole disappearing act was to protect me?"

He gave her a small smile in concession to her mocking tone. "And it bought me time, which is what I needed to clear up any…misunderstanding, shall we say, that the police might have about my involvement in Connor's death. I suspected that I wouldn't have the freedom of movement to figure out what Connor had gotten into if I went to the police."

"So you're going to figure out why someone—not you—

killed Connor and present it to the police in a tidy package. They'll appreciate that."

"Something like that."

Zoe felt the back of her neck prickle and looked over her shoulder. The crowds swirled around them.

"What is it?" Jack asked.

"I don't know. I just had that weird feeling someone was staring at me," she said as she scanned the sea of faces behind them.

"There's thousands of people here," Jack said, wearily.

"There," Zoe said, her gaze locking with a man in a silver sedan a few feet behind them. "The guy in the silver car." He was driving, creeping slowly as he exited The Venetian in their wake. There was something about the intensity of his gaze that made her walk faster. "Why is he driving so slowly?" Zoe asked. There weren't any cars in front of the silver car. "Do you think he's hotel security?"

Jack glanced at her, then over his shoulder. A screech cut through the air, then the deep rumble of an engine. *He peeled out*, Zoe thought, her mind moving much faster than her body. She felt Jack, who still had a firm grip on her arm, yank her to the other side of the white waist-high pylons that studded the sidewalk. They stumbled and fell in a tangle of limbs. Jack's breath hissed out. An explosive crash sounded, seemingly inches behind them.

Zoe disengaged herself from Jack and looked behind them. The car's grill was squashed into a pylon, which was almost horizontal. Fluids dripped out of the engine, sending up hisses of steam as they hit the hot pavement. The airbags had deployed and Zoe couldn't see the driver.

Jack used his elbow to roll into a sitting position then stood up, pulling Zoe with him. His sunglasses were gone. They'd skittered across the sidewalk. She reached out to pick them up. "Leave them," he said, as people closed in around them.

"Are you okay?"

"Should we call an ambulance?"

"Lord, almighty. Did you see that? He must be drunk as a skunk."

Jack pushed through the people, waving off their questions and offers of help. "We're fine. No harm done," he said, cutting a quick glance over his shoulder as they shoved through the crowds, moving north toward the Treasure Island Casino.

"Speak for yourself," Zoe said, checking the raw, pink skin on her elbow.

"You're fine," Jack said. "I know. I broke your fall."

"Well, my elbow is on fire."

"I'm sure it's less painful than being flattened like that pylon. Come on. The driver is on his feet."

"What?" The driver, a short man carrying a little too much weight for his size with thin black hair, cut close to his head, was scanning the crowd, squinting his dark eyes in an intent way, as if he were hunting for something. Zoe spun away from him. "Let's go."

The outdoor pirate show at Treasure Island was in full swing.

Jack gripped her hand as they melted into the throng. They threaded their way through the tourists and emerged on the far side of the crowd. Jack walked faster, but maintained his slouchy stride as they hurried along the street that ran at a right angle to The Strip. They hurried along, passing a huge mall.

Zoe glanced back, but couldn't tell if the short guy with the scary eyes was following them.

"Is your car parked around here?" he asked.

"Back at the garage in The Venetian," she said.

"We'll take mine," he said as they crossed another street and suddenly they were out of the tourist district. They were in a quiet, industrial area with low warehouses and few cars. No flashing lights, no pressing crowds, no high-rise hotels.

Just flat, dusty terrain, a few scraggy palm trees, and the occasional whoosh of cars as they accelerated up a nearby freeway entrance ramp.

Amazing to think that only a few blocks away The Strip vibrated with activity. The sudden quiet was creepy. Jack transferred his grip to her elbow as they scrambled over a set of railroad tracks.

Zoe felt a curl of self-doubt. This was a man she didn't know. *What am I doing, walking away into a deserted area with him?* Sure, his story explained what had happened—sort of—but he'd lied to her about so many things, the passports, the money, and...she hadn't even known he owned a gun.

She twisted her arm, and he let go. He didn't notice that she'd stopped walking. He continued on to a black hatchback. He slipped a set of keys out of his pocket, unlocked the doors, and slid into the driver's seat. He glanced around and saw her standing behind him. He put one foot on the ground as he leaned out and called back. "You coming?"

"That's not your car."

"It is now."

"Where did you get it?"

"I don't think we have time for this right now."

A metal sign a few feet in front of the car pinged and swiveled back and forth as if someone had thumped it. Zoe frowned and looked at it. It read, NO OVERNIGHT PARKING.

There was a hole in the "o" of the word "overnight." Zoe looked back the way they'd come and saw the short man standing at the railroad tracks, his arm extended, pointing a gun at her.

# CHAPTER TWELVE

*Las Vegas, Friday, 4:10 p.m.*

JACK REACHED ACROSS AND OPENED the passenger door. She dove for the car as the sign vibrated again. Jack threw the car in reverse as Zoe tumbled into the floorboard, then the car surged forward, and the momentum shut the passenger door with a solid thud. Zoe flailed around, trying to get herself upright and in the seat.

"Stay down." Jack shoved her shoulder, and she slid back to the floor. She didn't hear any more shots, but it was hard to hear anything above the engine noise. Jack scrunched down in the seat, his head and shoulders tucked low. She decided the floorboard was an excellent place to be. After a few quick turns, that tossed her around like the abandoned flyers flittering around The Strip in the wind, Jack's foot pressed down on the accelerator, and he straightened in his seat. The road was smooth, a freeway Zoe saw as she eased into her seat and quickly fastened her seatbelt. "Is he following us?"

"No. He was on foot. I don't think his car is drivable, so we should be okay," he said as he passed a truck and slipped neatly in front of it.

Zoe brushed some strands of hair out of her eyes, tucking

them behind her ears. "What is going on? Who was he?"

"No idea," Jack said, his gaze switching quickly from the road to the mirrors and then back to the road. "I didn't get a good look at him, but my best guess is that he's one of my friends from the office."

Maybe because her heart was still racing and her legs felt like she'd just finished a half marathon while he looked like he had nothing more important to do than set the cruise control, his cool response and expressionless face riled her. "How can you be so calm? What is going on? That man was shooting at us, no—at *me*," she said, her voice rising. "Why was he shooting at me?"

"Taking your questions in order," he said as he squinted into the sun at a green billboard listing exits, "I'm rather freaked out myself, but someone has to drive, don't they?" He flashed her a quick smile. "So I'll wait until we find a nice quiet rest stop to have a panic attack. Next, I have no idea what's going on. And last, he shot at you, presumably, because you were with me. He couldn't get a clear shot at me."

Zoe gave him a long look, trying to assess if that comment about a panic attack was a dig, but he seemed to be more concerned about who was on the road with them, than about shooting verbal barbs at her. He'd always been a reserved person. Early on, his very closed-off nature had been a bit of a turn-on for her. It was a challenge, breaking through that reticence. She flushed, remembering a few times when "reticent" would be the last word she would have picked to describe him. But there were only a few times like that. More often than not, he'd been emotionally shut away from her, locked in his own world. But there was something about that smile that he'd flung so casually at her, something unguarded and vulnerable in his face—something that she hadn't seen in a long time. She gave herself a mental shake. That smile of his was dangerous. She'd fallen for that smile before and look where it had landed her: squarely in a murder and fraud investigation, not to mention the fact that someone was shooting at her. And what was she doing…thinking about his smile right now?

She turned sideways to face him. "So you're as confused as I am?" He opened his mouth, but Zoe continued, "Because I'm pretty confused, Jack. Let's start with my first hint that you've been lying to me: *cousin* Eddie—not a cousin and not a guy, by the way—why did you let me think that?"

"There are certain…things about me that you don't know." He switched on the blinker and moved to the exit ramp. Zoe noticed that when he reached up to adjust the rearview mirror, his hand trembled slightly.

She was glad to see he wasn't completely unfazed by everything that had happened. "I arrived at that conclusion all by myself." Jack winced. "Why don't you fill me in on these… things?"

"I can't," he said. "I would have liked to have told you before, but I couldn't."

"Why not?"

"Confidentiality agreement."

Zoe rolled her eyes. "You expect me to believe that?"

"It's the truth," he said, mildly as he guided the car into a busy eight-lane road lined with a mix of big box stores, low-slung shopping centers, and apartment complexes.

"So leading me to believe that Eddie was a man was part of the confidentiality agreement—that must be one specific document."

"I didn't *lead* you to believe anything. I mentioned the name and you assumed it was a guy," Jack said.

"That's still deception."

"Omission," he countered.

Zoe shook her head impatiently. "Okay, forget that. *She* is not your cousin. She says she doesn't even know you."

"She's not my cousin," Jack said.

"So what is she? An old girlfriend? And why did she lie to me?"

"Careful, it almost sounds as if you're jealous."

Zoe's eyes narrowed. "I don't care what she was…or is…to you. All I care about is that you lied to me about her and she lied to me. I want the truth. I want to know what is going on—what have you got me involved in, Jack? Or should I say Brian?"

His reaction was barely perceptible. He continued the smooth movement of his hands on the steering wheel, but she saw the tightening around the corners of his eyes. He stopped at a red light and swiveled toward Zoe, his arm angled over the steering wheel. "Look, Zoe, there are some things I can't explain. I can't tell you why I lied to you. Eddie lied to you because I told her to tell anyone who asked that she didn't know me. She's an old friend from work."

"From your boring pharmaceutical sales job or your boring government job?"

"The government job."

"I can't quite picture it—you and Eddie talking over the cubicle walls, running out for a sandwich, and chipping in for the monthly birthday cake."

"How do you know that's what office workers do? You've never worked in an office."

"You forget, I have Helen. And I did work in a claims department one summer."

The light changed and Jack focused on the road. "I bet that didn't last long," he said, a shadow of a smile crossing his face.

"Fifty-four days. I couldn't stand it," Zoe said.

"Exactly how I felt. Of course, I stuck it out quite a bit longer than you."

"I'm sure you did. So you know Eddie from…where exactly was it again?"

"Policy and Plans Division."

"God, just the name makes me want to yawn," Zoe said, and he grinned, but when he didn't say anything else, Zoe waved her hand in a circular motion. "Go on."

Jack raised his eyebrows. "You want to know more about policy and plans? So few do. It can be quite fascinating, if you look at the big picture—"

"Eddie. More about Eddie," Zoe said, sharply.

"Oh, Eddie. Well, we worked together. I quit and moved back to Georgia. We kept in touch sporadically."

Zoe frowned. "I don't remember anything like that—not even a Christmas card from her."

Jack shrugged one shoulder. "Through e-mail. She got married and moved to Vegas. Her family owns the glass store. So when I came out here the first time, I went by to say hello. I introduced her to Connor later. It was when he and I went to one of those business expos."

"And she's the supplier for the paperweights you give to clients."

"Yes. Connor insisted, you remember that."

"Yes, I do," she murmured. Zoe had been involved periph-erally in a few business discussions early on in their marriage. She remembered how Connor swore that the paperweights were exactly right for the business to giveaway to clients—"a signature item that was unique and memorable." Zoe hadn't really seen it that way. She'd suggested something more cutting-edge because GRS was a *green technology* company. Connor had insisted, and Jack had said he didn't care. Jack had been more concerned about developing business contacts and wrangling appointments with CEOs to pitch their services.

Zoe waved her hand as if swishing away the paperweight tangent they were on. "So she sells glass."

"Murano glass," Jack qualified. "It's quite sought-after."

"I don't care if she sells diamonds. You went to her when

you were in trouble."

"Yes," Jack said simply.

Zoe raised her eyebrows.

"More? Okay. Well, she was an old friend. I knew I could trust her, and she happened to live in the same city where Connor still had an apartment."

Zoe frowned. "Connor has an apartment? Here? In Vegas? But he has a house in Dallas. He never said anything about living here."

"Apparently, there were quite a few things he never said anything about."

"And that's where we're going now?" she asked, noticing that in the space of a few miles the neighborhood had deteriorated. Aging, low-slung strip malls spotted with graffiti and gang tags lined the road. "That's your plan? I know you have one. You've always got one."

As they passed a small residential area of tired ranchers with patchy grass and dirt yards, Jack said, "You're right. It's not much, so I'm open to any other suggestions you might have, other than impulsively running in a random direction."

"I didn't run off on a whim. Besides, there's nothing wrong with following an impulse," Zoe said heatedly. "Just because you make a decision quickly doesn't mean it's wrong. You don't always need a lot of time to make a good decision. Sure, I decided to come here on instinct, but I found you, didn't I?"

Zoe thought she heard him murmur something under his breath about lucky breaks, but she chose to ignore it. After a beat of silence, Jack said, "There appears to be no answer to that question which will further my argument, so I will wisely avoid it and ask instead, do you have a cell phone?"

"Yes," Zoe said as they drove by two skinny kids who were riding bikes in wide loops around the deserted parking lot of a boarded-up grocery store.

"Let me see it," Jack said. Zoe reluctantly handed it over.

"You're not going to throw it out the window are you?"

"No," Jack said with a small smile. As he drove, he flipped the casing open and removed the battery and SIM card, then handed everything back. "Just to make sure," he said. He didn't say what they were making sure of, and Zoe didn't ask. She didn't want it put into words. She dropped everything into her messenger bag as Jack pulled into the parking lot of the Oasis Apartment complex.

The three-story units were pressed close together, and a few spindly palm trees strained for the open sky above the rooflines. Stucco flaking from the exterior of the buildings littered the cracked sidewalks as if the whole complex was a giant reptile sloughing off its old skin.

"How did you find out about this place?" Zoe asked, stepping over a broken glass bottle near the stairs of building C. It wasn't the kind of place that Zoe wanted to visit, but she wasn't waiting in the car alone either. Jack cut her a look. "Right," Zoe said. "That's probably another thing I don't want to know."

The apartment was situated in a breezeway under an open-air stairway, which smelled rank. She kept her hands in her pockets as she followed Jack into the alcove under the stairs. She noticed he didn't hesitate. He headed unerringly in the right direction. "Been here before?"

"Yesterday. Before that, I had no idea about his little hideaway, such as it is." He bent over the door handle. Zoe said, "Great, you're picking the lock. Well, I suppose we're already in so much trouble, what's a little breaking and entering?"

He twisted the handle, pushed the door open. "No need to worry—no further black marks on our records," he said. "I have a key," he said, holding one up.

"Another thing I probably don't want to know about," Zoe said.

"Found it under the flower pot," he said, nodding to a

foot-tall prickly pear cactus in a medium-sized terracotta pot beside the door.

"Yet, you're wearing gloves," she said, eyeing his pale blue hands.

"You can never be too careful. Probably best to keep your hands in your pockets. After you," he said with a wave of his gloved hand.

Zoe stepped inside. The apartment was airless and dark. Jack closed the door and hit the light switch. "This is Connor's apartment?" Zoe asked. The soles of her sandals made a sucking sound as they clung to some invisible sticky substance on the entryway tiles. She moved onto the spotted brown carpet of the living area where an orange tweed couch was positioned in front of a heavy dark wood coffee table littered with game controllers. A boxy twenty-five inch television perched on two cinderblocks. A high counter separated the living room from the kitchen on the far left side of the room, and Zoe could see stacks of take-out containers and pizza boxes tilting on the kitchen counter beside discarded cups from a variety of fast food chains.

"Are you sure?" she asked, exchanging a glance with Jack. They'd both been to Connor's empty house in Dallas with it's leather couches, chandeliers, and stainless steel kitchen. Formica countertops and dirty commercial-grade carpet weren't his style. This whole place wasn't his style, except for the ancient computer. Despite his flashy car and latest digital appliances in his kitchen in Dallas, at his core, Connor was a Luddite. If he'd built that house in Dallas, Zoe was sure the sound system would connect to a boom box with a cassette player. Ever suspicious of new technology, Connor avoided upgrading, always insisting that the newest electronic gadget or computer or software wouldn't be as good as what he had.

"As strange as it seems, yes," Jack said, heading for the area at one end of the kitchen that a realtor would have called a breakfast nook, except that there was a hulking computer on a cheap pressboard desk instead of a dining table. Jack moved to the computer and turned it on.

"So you think you'll find some answers on the computer?"

"I should—now that I'll be able to get into it."

The computer had been whirring and chugging, but a window popped up asking for a password.

"How are you going to do that? Do you know his password?"

"I don't need it," he said, plugging a small gray flash drive into one of the USB ports. "Password breaker," he explained as he typed a few letters. The screen filled with numbers, which continued to scroll as Jack picked up a pencil and absently drew on a scrap of paper. The spray of the Bellagio fountains materialized on the paper. A window popped open on the screen, drawing his attention back to the monitor and he murmured, "Hello," then pulled a memory drive from his pocket and plugged it into the computer.

Zoe stared at Jack's profile, working it out. "Eddie got that for you, didn't she? You came here yesterday and couldn't get in Connor's computer, so you asked her to get that password breaker thing—I'm sure it's another thing I don't want to know the finer points on."

He ignored Zoe's last comment and merely said, "It wouldn't be wise for me to head out on a shopping trip. I am trying to keep a low profile. Besides, these things aren't easy to find."

Zoe walked a few steps into the kitchen, her gaze focused high on the ceiling as she thought. "It had to be this afternoon at the fountain—that's what you were doing there. Why else would Eddie walk all the way down there, then come back? And you did take her place, right after she moved away from the balustrade. It was a—what do they call it?—a drop!"

Jack glanced up at her, then focused back on the computer. "Fine. Don't respond. I can tell from your face—your deadpan, no expression face—that I'm right."

The silence continued, so Zoe said, "I'm looking around."

He didn't look up. "Go for it. I sure as hell didn't find anything around here. Not that I looked too hard."

"I can see why you wouldn't," Zoe said, pacing to the short hallway that led to a bathroom and a bedroom. The door to the bathroom was open. A quick glance inside was plenty for Zoe. For a second, she wondered why Connor would choose a shower curtain with black flowers—it seemed a little girly, but then she realized the flowers weren't a pattern. It was actually mold.

With a shiver, Zoe moved on to the bedroom. There was a mattress on the floor with a tangle of sheets and a thin blanket flung to the side. A cardboard box served as a nightstand with a small lamp and clock. Issues of *Money* and *Entrepreneur* and a few books were scattered around the floor. "This is so...*not* Connor," Zoe called, looking down the short hallway that opened into the living area.

Jack had his back to her as he worked on the computer. "Makes you wonder who he really was, doesn't it?" he said without turning around.

"Yeah, it does," Zoe murmured, walking to the closet, which she edged open cautiously with her foot. A few thin shirts hung above several pairs of crumpled shorts on the floor. "It just doesn't fit," she said stepping back from the closet. "Connor wore Armani suits and Hugo Boss ties. And he was so fussy about his car. It was always spotless. He'd wash it right after it rained so he wouldn't have any water spots on the windshield. He wouldn't live in this place."

"And yet, he did," Jack said, gesturing to a pile of envelopes on the counter. Zoe walked back into the living room and studied the envelopes addressed to Connor Freeman. "Those were in the trash," Jack said.

"Strange," Zoe said, shaking her head. "Give me one of

those gloves."

"What?"

"Your glove. You're not doing anything except pointing and clicking. Give me your left-hand glove. I want to look at the books in the bedroom."

"I don't think Connor's reading material will hold a vital clue," he said, but he stripped the glove off. Zoe ignored his tone. He didn't think she could find anything, but she was willing to bet that Jack took a quick look around yesterday and when he couldn't get into the computer, he'd headed out. Poking around the dirty apartment was not high on the list of things she wanted to do either, but if there was anything here that could help them, it was worth digging through the layers of dirt and grime. It couldn't be worse than cleaning up after that renter who kept his motorcycle and pet iguana in the duplex office, she thought as she marched down the hall.

She moved the lamp and clock off the box serving as the nightstand and opened the flaps. It was filled with smaller, white boxes with a winged lion imprint on the top of each one. She recognized the boxes. These were the paperweights GRS gave to clients. Jack had brought some home when they first ordered them. Moving awkwardly, she used her gloved hand to pull out a box and remove the lid. A heavy glass paperweight rested in a square of foam. Zoe replaced the lid and rubbed her gloved thumb over the smudged imprint, wondering why Connor would have a box of paperweights here. She replaced the white box and reassembled the make-shift nightstand.

She went through all the pockets of the clothes, which took some time. The closet smelled of sweat, and the tiny room was hot. By the time she finished with the clothes, she was covered in a sheen of perspiration, and she had nothing more to show for it than two fast food receipts.

She skipped over the magazines and considered the books.

There was a battered copy of a *Bathroom Reader*, a few paper-back political thrillers and, strangely, a cookbook. Zoe couldn't picture Connor whipping up beef bourguignon, especially in this apartment, but then again, she couldn't actually picture *Connor* in this apartment. She moved on to the last few books, which were oversized and heavy. Yearbooks, she realized, opening the glossy-pages. She found Connor Freeman's photo. His white blond hair was cut shorter, and his face was thinner, but he had the same slyly superior grin that had irritated Zoe. She closed the book, then immediately felt guilty. No matter how annoying Connor was, he didn't deserve to die the way he did. She put the yearbooks back as she'd found them, surveyed the room once more to make sure it looked as it had, then went back down the hall to the living room.

The memory drive was blinking and Jack was stuffing a stack of papers in a garbage bag. "Papers that Connor didn't get around to shredding," Jack said, then glanced at the computer. He added the paper with his drawing of the fountain to the stack. "I'm copying everything I can. About ten more minutes and we're out of here."

"Do you want any help with that?" Zoe asked. Jack actually looked a bit harried. His hair sagged over his forehead on one side, a sight Zoe recognized. He'd run his fingers through it, which was usually a sign of exasperation with her. It had occurred frequently when she'd have a perfectly wonderful idea like going out for ice cream on the spur of the moment and he'd point out that no one went out for ice cream at ten-forty-five at night.

But it seemed he wasn't exasperated with her. "No. The other glove would be helpful," he said sharply as he glanced out the window. "Find anything?"

Zoe worked the glove off and handed it to him. "Besides that he was a slob and had eccentric reading tastes? No, nothing."

Jack handed the bag to Zoe, then shot a quick glance at the sliding glass doors before he took a seat in front of the computer, his gloved fingers rapping out an impatient beat on the mouse.

"Nervous?"

"No, just ready to get out of here. We've been here long enough."

"I don't think this is the type of neighborhood where people call the cops very often."

"I'm not worried about the police. The Dallas police don't even know this place exists, and I doubt the Las Vegas police are aware that Connor had any connection to this city. Eventually, they'll make the connection, but I don't think they'll be busting the door down any minute. It's one of the few times bureaucratic sluggishness is actually a positive thing."

That could only mean he was worried about a visit from someone else—someone shady. "I see," Zoe said.

He grunted as he stared at the screen, his right heel tapping out a quick-time rhythm. Zoe was tempted to say, "A watched download bar never fills," but she bit her tongue. Jack was antsy, and she doubted he would appreciate her humor. Instead of staring at the back of Jack's head, she moved into the living room, but didn't sit down on the couch. The cushions looked as if a layer of Doritos and Cheetos had been ground into the fabric. The center cushion had a permanent indent, and Zoe supposed that was where Connor had spent most of his time when he was here.

How long had Connor lived here? Did he come back here "to visit?" He was out of town frequently, and Zoe had always assumed it was on business trips to visit clients, but maybe he came here instead? Zoe shook her head. Why would he come back here when he had a beautiful—all be it almost empty—home in Dallas? To pig out on fast food and play video games? Zoe just couldn't imagine it. She glanced back at Jack. He hadn't moved. Zoe sighed and leaned against the arm of the couch. The cushions shifted and she saw something shoved down between the sagging middle cushion and the next cushion. She used her knuckle to work it out.

It was a small black Moleskine journal. *Now this looked more like something Connor would use,* Zoe thought as she slipped the elastic band off the cover and opened the book. About half the lined pages were filled with notes: phone numbers, dates, and names. It was a gold mine of information.

She turned the pages. She recognized some airport codes and dates near the end. There was an odd list, too, with random words. She looked up to tell Jack what she'd found. A man with a gun was moving swiftly across the living room toward Jack.

# CHAPTER THIRTEEN

*Las Vegas, Friday, 5:22 p.m.*

ZOE DIDN'T KNOW A LOT about guns, but she knew that the long narrow extension attached to the barrel was a silencer. Jack was still seated at the computer with his back to the room. The man didn't glance around. The sight of the man with the gun was so unexpected and he moved so silently that Zoe almost wondered if she was seeing things. It only took a second for the thought to register and for her to realize how absurd it was.

She must have made some sound—an inward hiss of breath—or a sudden movement. She wasn't sure what she did to draw the man's attention, but he glanced her way, his dark eyes under wiry eyebrows registering her presence. It was the man who'd tried to run them down, then shot at her.

Zoe jumped up from the couch and scrambled backward, dumping the journal. Jack heard her, too. As he stood, he spun toward the man, who was small with stubby legs, a round face, and a bit of a gut. If Zoe had seen him on the street, she wouldn't have given him a second thought, but with the gun in his hand and the determined look on his face, she felt as if she were almost mesmerized and couldn't look away.

Her shoulder blades hit the wall, stopping her backward progress.

The stubby man's dark gaze flicked from her to Jack who stood, arms held out at his waist, palms down. The man waved the gun back and forth a few times almost as if he was reciting "Eeny, meeny, miny, moe." He must have ended on Zoe because he pointed the gun at her, then motioned her over to Jack's side of the room with two tiny flicks of his wrist.

As Zoe inched away from the wall, there was a blur of movement as Jack heaved a kitchen chair at the man.

"Run," Jack shouted.

Zoe swiveled on her heel and made for the door. The chair crashed into something—a wall or the floor. As she fumbled with the door lock, her fingers thick and clumsy, she glanced over her shoulder.

The dining nook was empty. Jack must have ducked down behind the kitchen counter.

The man kicked the chair away. It skidded into the leg of the flimsy desk, which collapsed, causing the desktop to tilt. The computer slid off the desk like a boat going over a waterfall. It slammed into the floor in a spray of plastic.

The lock finally released and Zoe flung the door open. Zoe backed through the door, watching as the man rounded the counter that divided the living room from the kitchen, his gun pointed down at the floor.

*He's going to shoot Jack. Right here in front of me,* Zoe thought.

Jack popped into sight and tossed the contents of a takeout container at the man's head, then placed both hands on the counter and vaulted feet-first into the living room.

The man swiped at his face with his free hand, wiping away some sort of goo. He was too heavy-set to follow Jack over the counter. He had to reverse course and go around the other way. His gun swung wildly back and forth as Jack zipped around the couch. He looked surprised to see her. "What are you doing? Run! Get out of here!"

Zoe stepped outside, then remembered the black journal. She knew it was important. All those names and dates and numbers. They had to have it. She spotted it on the floor and ducked under Jack's arm.

"Zoe," Jack yelled as she scooped up the journal and felt the man surge toward her. She didn't look at him. She twisted around and sprinted for the door behind Jack, but she could swear she felt the short guy's presence behind her. She expected to feel his hand yank at her hair or shirt any second.

She shot through the open door and ran out from under the steps into the sunlight, feeling as if her legs were moving at Roadrunner cartoon-like speed, but her steps faltered as she scanned the parking lot.

*Where was Jack?*

Not at the car.

Not on the sidewalk or the parking lot.

Zoe took off again, cutting through the landscaped portion of the ground, her feet slipping on the white gravel. She'd gone two steps when she heard a crack. She looked back and saw the man laid out on the ground, flat on his face, Jack standing behind him. Pieces of the flowerpot that had been outside the door were scattered around them like candy from a broken piñata.

"That's the craziest thing I've ever seen you do," Zoe said, astounded.

"Is that a compliment?" he asked, a smile creeping into the corners of his mouth.

"Definitely."

*Dallas, Friday, 4:55 p.m.*

JENNY HAD HER ANKLES CROSSED and tucked onto the base of her rolling office chair. She swung her knees from side to side and gnawed on the lid of her blue Bic pen as she contemplated the stacks of paper spread across her desk that represented everything she knew about Zoe Hunter.

Jenny glanced at her phone, willing it to ring. She'd left three messages with Mort. He was furious. She'd pointed out that it wasn't her fault if the police weren't smart enough to listen to traffic reports. That probably hadn't been her best move, she thought with a sigh.

It was her fault that Zoe had gone to ground. No one could find her, and Mort was upset—rightfully so—that his number one source of possible information had dried up. Jenny did feel guilty for tipping Zoe Hunter off. Well, sort of. There had been something in Zoe's face, a look of fear and disbelief that struck Jenny. It made her think of a small animal trapped by a predator. That look made her want to dig into this story and find out if Zoe was as innocent as she appeared or if she was only an excellent actress.

Her gaze switched to the newspaper clipping that she'd thumbtacked to the fabric of her cubicle wall. "Vinewood Man's Disappearance Draws Questions as Business Partner Found Murdered." It had run this morning. She ran her finger over her byline, the corner of her mouth twisting down on one side. She didn't have that sense of accomplishment— that charge—that she'd imagined she would feel with her first published news story.

She sighed. It really was the worst possible start to a journalist's career. You didn't *become* part of the story. You reported on it. Of course it was her first person account of her inter-action with Zoe that had interested the news editor. "Lead with that," she said. "And keep that boring financial stuff to a minimum," she'd instructed after hearing Jenny's pitch for the article.

She was still in obits, of course. There were no openings for a reporter, but she had the inside edge on this story, and she wasn't about to give it up. And there was Mort. Jenny thought it was probably good for him to get worked up about something—it had been so long since he'd shown any emotion—but she really wished he wasn't furious with *her* for blowing his investigation. So, besides pursuing the story for herself, she was also trying to make up for her blunder. She was spending every spare minute she had searching for Zoe.

She hadn't gotten very far, despite scraping in every possible source she could think of. The police and Mort were holding things tight. Even Victor had drawn a blank.

Jenny shoved the "childhood reality star" stack to the side. Her gut told her this situation had nothing to do with Zoe's time on a "deserted" island with her mom and step-dad. That left her with the stack of info about GRS, which she'd already been through and could practically recite by heart.

The final stack was much smaller: the personal life. Jenny crunched down, leaving another indentation in the pen lid as she flicked through the papers. Zoe's name came up on the tag line of a few photos that had appeared in the paper: she'd participated in a breast cancer 5K run, and she'd obviously taken classes at Greenly University because she was pictured in a group of students participating in a campus cleanup day. She'd run ads in the newspaper for her business, which looked like a virtual assistant business, but she called herself an "Information Specialist." She specialized in copy-editing and listed several popular Smart Travel Guides as her credentials, but it appeared no job was too small or too off the wall for her. In her experience section, she listed everything from dog walking to property management.

She'd married Jack Andrews in Vegas. The divorce paperwork was filed about a year later, and despite the divorce, both their names were still listed on the property in Vinewood.

Jenny swiveled her knees some more and switched her attention to her computer monitor. The Internet was a God-send for research. The official documents and public records were like a sketch or outline. It was a person's Internet foot-print that provided the color and brought the sketch to life. Zoe probably didn't realize it, but her photos she'd posted on-line, her Facebook account, and her business website all gave glimpses into her private life.

Jenny rotated the lid of the pen as she clicked on Zoe's Face-book profile picture. Posed in front of an outdoor fountain, she was smiling widely, her arm thrown around someone's shoulder who had been cropped out of the photo. Bright sunlight glinted on her red hair and highlighted a few freckles on her pale skin. She looked like a relaxed, fun person with just a glint of mischievousness in her hazel eyes.

The business website photo had the professional gloss of special lighting and a muted background. While her long, red hair was arranged smoothly behind her ears, her casual oxford shirt and jeans along with her relaxed stance seemed to announce she didn't take herself too seriously. Her short bio seemed to confirm it. "Jill of all trades. Digital problem solver. A runner with a serious dessert addiction."

Jenny flicked through the pictures Zoe had posted on-line. There were a few of her among friends at dinner or events like 5K runs or parties, but most of the photos were vacation photos of Las Vegas—there were shots of several famous spots along The Strip, including the iconic "Welcome to Las Vegas" sign and the Bellagio fountains.

Jenny's cell phone buzzed and she lunged for it. She had a text message from her hair stylist. "Did you come through for me, Sheila?" she asked, as she pulled up the message. Sheila worked at The Salon, which was pricey for someone like

Jenny—someone on an entry-level salary—but she managed to swing a few haircuts there because Sheila cut and highlighted the hair of several important people. Not people who were famous or wealthy, but people who worked for famous and/or wealthy people. It's amazing how much your personal assistant or your housecleaner knows about you, Jenny thought. Sheila liked being "in the know," and she liked to show off her knowledge, which worked out great for Jenny because Sheila also liked to pass that info on to Jenny.

The text message was a series of exclamation points, which meant Sheila had big news. Yesterday, after Zoe Hunter skipped out on her and Mort, Jenny had considered cancelling her haircut appointment, but she'd gone, and the whole tale of how she'd messed up had come pouring out. Jenny dialed Sheila's number and gnawed on her pen lid until Sheila answered, waiting as she went outside of The Salon for a break. "Okay," Sheila finally said, "now I can talk. You're not going to believe this. That woman you told me about, the one who ran off? She used an ATM in Amarillo yesterday."

"Wow...how did you find that out?" Jenny asked, scribbling down the info.

"The bank manager's personal assistant was in today to get her highlights touched up. She said there was a huge uproar at the bank this morning with the police wanting to know if she'd used her ATM card. She had." Sheila sucked in a breath. "But this is even better. Her ex-husband's account got a huge deposit at the beginning of the week. Millions of dollars. *Millions.* And now it's gone. It was all my client could talk about. Her office has been overrun with bank officials and the FBI."

Jenny thanked her and made a mental note to up her tip next time she went for a haircut.

Jenny chewed her pen and clicked back and forth between some of the open windows in her screen. She enlarged the profile photo and studied the background. Yep, those were the Bellagio fountains behind Zoe. She was married there, had vacationed there, and she'd driven to Amarillo…which would be on the way to Vegas. It wasn't much to go on. Lots of people got married in Vegas, Jenny reasoned, but there was something tugging at her, a gut feeling. She reached for the phone.

The reporter from the Las Vegas newsroom wasn't incredibly helpful. "You can't look up the crime report yourself?" Jeff McCord asked with a long-suffering sigh.

"Sure, but I wanted to see if there was anything that stood out—from a local angle."

There was silence for a few seconds, and Jenny thought he'd hung up, but then she heard his chair creak, and he said, "Damn computer. They're great, except—"

"When they don't work," Jenny finished.

"Yeah," he agreed, and she heard a small smile in his voice. "Finally. Okay," he said, drawing out the word. "I'll send this to you, but it all looks routine. A couple of burglaries, a few DUIs, a house fire up in Henderson. That's about it. Pretty quiet for a Thursday in Vegas, actually. What were you looking for, specifically?"

It was Jenny's turn to sigh. "I don't know…something unusual," she said, thinking that short of calling every hotel in Vegas, there was no way to know if Zoe had gone there, and Jenny was sure that wherever Zoe was, she was taking pains to avoid interacting with the police.

"In Vegas, unusual is normal," Jeff said. "Like this one. Guy drove onto the sidewalk today and ran into a barrier in front of The Venetian. Wasn't even drunk. No one hurt, but the car was totaled."

"Well, thanks for looking," Jenny said.

"Sure. E-mail is on the way to you—and if you find anything, you'll send me an e-mail, right?"

"You don't even know what story I'm working on," Jenny

said with a laugh. At the beginning of their conversation, he'd been too busy to listen to any details.

"Hey, for all I know, you might be the next Bob Woodward."

"Unfortunately I'm feeling a bit more like Bob Hope right now, but I'll call you if I find anything," she said before hanging up.

He sent the e-mail, and she saw it was all routine stuff, just as he'd said. She grabbed her peanut butter and jelly sandwich and headed for the break room. When she returned forty minutes later, her phone was ringing. She answered, and a reedy, masculine voice announced, "My name is Chris Felty, and I saw your story in the online edition of the *Sentinel*." He stopped to clear his throat, but his voice still sounded thin as he continued, "I'm on vacation, but I always check the paper for the comics and the word puzzle."

She'd heard from other reporters about their encounters with wacky readers, but she hadn't expected an oddball to contact her after her first story. He rambled about his blog and how he traveled three to five times a year, writing online reviews for hotels and travel websites. "So anyway, I was taking a video of the hotel with my phone when it happened. It was the darndest thing. The car hopped the curb and headed right for them."

"I'm sorry, who?"

"The redhead and that guy they thought was dead."

There was a beat of silence. "Really?"

The man was tapering off. "Yeah...so anyway, if you're interested...I posted the video on my blog and on YouTube. Any chance you could link to it? Will there be a follow-up story?"

Jenny pulled the tooth-marked cap off her pen. "Oh, I think so."

*Las Vegas, Friday, 6:14 p.m.*

"CHOW MEIN?" ZOE ASKED AS she and Jack stood over the stubby man's inert body. The gooey film of the sauce covered his face. A red gash on his chin showed where he'd hit the concrete after the flowerpot connected with his head.

With his still-gloved hands braced on his hips, Jack shrugged. "You use what you've got."

Jack had rolled the guy onto his back, and they'd pulled him back into the apartment, Jack lugging his shoulders and Zoe lifting his feet. He was still out, his head lolling to one side. A few noodles clung to the man's neck. Zoe looked away. She had the same feeling she'd had when she was fourteen and went ice-skating with Helen for the first time. Unlike Helen, who had clung to the waist-high barrier and inched her way carefully onto the ice, Zoe had stepped confidently on to the ice, pushed off for the center of the rink, imagining herself skating for a gold medal, and promptly felt both feet fly out from under her. She had that same disconnected, out of control feeling.

"*You use what you've got?* Since when do you use what you've got? You're a by-the-book kind of guy, not a make-things-up-as-you-go-along kind of guy."

"Surprised you, have I?" Jack said, as he placed a hand under her elbow. She let him steer her to the couch. She plopped down on the dirty cushions without cringing, which showed just how unsteady she felt.

"Feel okay?" Jack asked, squatting down so that he was at eye level with her. She blinked and focused on his silver blue eyes. He was so close she could see each dark eyelash. She noticed he had a few new crinkles at the corners of his eyes that hadn't been there before. The stubble of his beard was darker than his hair and she had the strangest urge to touch the scar on his chin.

"If you feel like you're going to faint, put your head between your knees," Jack said matter-of-factly.

"I'm fine," she said abruptly, leaning back. "Fine."

"Okay," Jack said. Obviously hearing the sharpness in her tone, he stood up.

"Fight or flight—pretty strong instincts. You're coming down off the adrenaline high." Was there a trace of a grin at the corners of his mouth? Zoe stared at him, but his face was serious as he picked up the gun from where he'd kicked it inside as they were dragging the stubby guy back over the apartment threshold.

With a few quick movements, he'd removed the silencer, emptied the bullets, and tossed them under the couch. Zoe doubted they'd ever be found. No one in their right mind would look under the disgusting couch in this trashed-out apartment. He tucked the gun into the back of his waistband, then leaned down and began to methodically search the stubby guy's pockets.

"One thing to keep in mind," he said conversationally, "don't freeze. When something like this happens," he nodded his head at the man stretched out on the grimy carpet, "it's like that poem. If you can keep your head when everyone is losing theirs...well, you're more likely to be okay."

"How do you do that? Not freeze? All I could think about was the gun and what could happen."

Jack gave a half shrug as he struggled to remove the man's wallet from his back pocket. "I don't know. You just don't let the fear paralyze you. You think about what options you have, not about the worst thing that could happen."

More than ever, Zoe wondered who Jack was. Body snatchers seemed to be the only explanation for his cool aplomb as he took whatever came his way in stride. She would have thought Jack would be freaked out in a situation like this without his precious calendar and a to-do list to work through. She took a deep breath and tried to shake off her questions about Jack and, instead, focus on the guy laid out at their feet.

"Do you recognize him?" Zoe asked. Despite the sticky coating of chow mein on his face, Zoe knew him. "He's the guy who had tried to run us down outside the casino, then shot at us in the parking lot."

Jack nodded. "He held a gun on me at the office, too."

"But you said in the car you didn't know him." Zoe edged forward on the cushion. She felt better. Her legs were hardly trembling at all, and she didn't feel as though she couldn't get a deep breath.

"I didn't get a good look at him outside the casino—there was a glare on the windshield, and he was too far away to see his features in the parking lot. I was more focused on driving than making a positive ID at that point, too."

"So he followed you here from Dallas?" Zoe asked.

"He followed someone," Jack said a bit grimly.

Zoe frowned. "You think he followed me? How would he know who I was? And how would he know I'd take him to you?"

Jack merely raised his eyebrows. "I don't know. I don't know how he knew who I was or where I worked, or how to get in there, or that I had a gun. There's a lot I don't know."

Zoe ignored the sarcastic sting of his words, thinking of only one thing. "Where's the other guy? You said there were two in the office. Where is he?"

"I don't know that either, but I got the impression that this guy—the older one—was in charge and the other guy—he was a teenager—didn't like the way things were going. Apparently, he wasn't informed that murder would be involved. He was okay with assault—he was the one who knocked me out—and armed robbery, but not killing. Maybe he's gone."

Another possibility hovered in Zoe's mind, but she didn't

voice it. She didn't want to think about the likelihood of another death. She picked up the black Moleskine journal and shoved it in her pocket. She didn't want to lose it again.

"What's that?" he asked.

"Connor's journal. It was in the couch cushions. It must have fallen out of his pocket. It's got all sorts of notes about dates and people. We're taking it with us."

Jack had opened the wallet and was looking through it as she talked. "Okay," he said.

Zoe gave him a long glance. He was only half-listening. His attention was focused on the cards he'd pulled out of the stubby guy's wallet.

It was her turn to ask, "Are you alright? You look kind of gray. If you feel faint, put your head between your legs."

Jack shot her a fleeting look, acknowledging her joke, but there was a strained look about his face that almost made Zoe regret her words. He ducked his head, rubbing the part of his wrist that wasn't covered with the latex glove across his forehead, as he muttered, "We've got to get out of here."

# CHAPTER FOURTEEN

*Las Vegas, Friday, 6:37 p.m.*

"SO YOU WANT TO TELL me about it?" Zoe asked.

Jack took his time, carefully wiping his mouth with a napkin as he glanced around. They were sitting in a restaurant attached to the deli section of a Von's grocery store near UNLV.

Before they left the apartment, Jack grabbed the pile of un-shredded papers. The computer and memory drive were useless. The fall from the desk had broken the drive into pieces and the computer wasn't much better. Zoe said something about it being possible to repair it, but Jack said, "No time." They left it on the floor.

Jack had pulled a trash bag from under the kitchen sink, filled it with some of the fast food debris covering the counters, then dropped the gun inside. "No need to leave this where he can find it," Jack said, nodding to the stubby guy who was still out cold on the carpet, his feet and hands tied with cords from Connor's extensive gaming setup.

On the way to the car, Jack casually tossed the trash bag with its lethal contents in one of the apartment complex dumpsters. Zoe had been amazed. With his relaxed stride, he'd looked as if he had nothing more on his mind than getting back inside to watch basketball. Zoe wondered how much of his life with her had been spent in this weird altered state with reality pushed below the surface.

But up close in the car, Zoe could see that whatever he'd seen in Stubby Guy's wallet had impacted him. He was quiet, and there was a "don't talk to me" vibe coming off of him, so Zoe had left him alone. She skimmed through the papers from Connor's shred pile, which were mostly spreadsheets, while he drove.

Zoe took a sip, then set her can of ginger ale on the table with a firm click. "Let's not play the silent game any longer, Jack. I can tell whatever you saw in that guy's wallet was a game changer."

A smile flicked across his face. "Never go on the run with your ex. You can't get away with anything. She knows you too well."

Zoe stared at him a moment, then said, "Not as well as I thought."

Jack ran his thumb over the label on his bottle of Snapple Peach Iced Tea. "This whole thing—this situation—may be connected to my old job."

He stopped as though he didn't know what to say next. Zoe said, "Jack, I'm pretty sure that you didn't work in Policy and Plans."

"That's what's funny. I did—work in Policy and Plans, that is. At least, for about five months, and yes, it was insanely boring. Then I was transferred to Italy. Same department at the consulate in Naples. Still boring."

"So you worked for the State Department?" Zoe asked just to confirm. "Officially?"

He nodded. "It wasn't like you think. Nothing like the movies."

"You didn't wear a tux and drive a sports car?"

He smiled with his whole face this time. "Suits, yes. Tuxedo, no. And I drove a moped—everyone does there. The idea was to blend in," he said then took a bite of his sandwich.

"I see," Zoe said, but she didn't. She couldn't picture him zipping around a foreign country on a moped.

"It was pretty routine stuff. I had my work at the consulate. I had the cocktail party circuit, dinner parties. I tried to meet people, establish friendships. It went on like that for almost a year before there was a change. A friend of mine…" He paused, and the way he seemed to search for words to describe what he was thinking made her think he was telling the truth. His words weren't smooth and glib, and he was clearly uncomfortable talking about this topic.

He cleared his throat, then said, "My friend, he worked in the same department." Jack sent Zoe a significant glance, and she nodded that she understood. "He got a new assignment. He had several assets."

Zoe raised her eyebrows. "Assets?"

"Contacts. Resources," he said. "One of them was handed off to me. For about six months, everything went fine." His chin wrinkled, and his lower lip went up, forcing the corners of his mouth to turn down. "At least, it seemed fine." He put his sandwich down. He looked nauseous, reminding Zoe of the time he'd had the stomach flu. "The asset didn't show for a meeting, and I couldn't make contact. I went through the protocol, made preparations. The Irena passport was for her, to get her out of the country, if I could find her…" his voice trailed off, and he ran his hand over his mouth. "Her body was found a week later."

She searched for words. "That's…terrible," Zoe said. "I'm sorry, Jack."

"Unfortunate. That's what they called it. I was reassigned. They told me to move on, to keep working." His tone was subdued as he said, "I couldn't do it. She was my responsibility."

He carefully rewrapped his sandwich and set it aside. "I couldn't take it—the guilt, the thought that someone had died on my watch. I resigned, got out." He blew out a breath and seemed to mentally comeback to the present. He focused on Zoe's face. "Decided to do something nice and safe—like open my own business," he said, lightly.

When his eyes crinkled up on the corners, it was nearly impossible not to smile back at him. He leaned forward over the table, his fingers laced. "I never told you about it because it was in the past. Over and done. And there was that pesky confidentiality agreement as well."

"Really? There is a confidentiality agreement?"

"Yes. And they're very serious about it, too."

Zoe shifted in her chair, mentally reviewing what he'd told her. "So you think Connor's death and Stubby Guy's visit is connected to her death somehow?"

"Stubby Guy. I like that," Jack said with a hint of a smile, then he turned serious again. "Stubby Guy, as you call him, had an Italian drivers license on him along with euros. It's got to be connected. Italian thugs don't randomly show up at your place of business and murder your partner for no reason—at least not in America," he added.

Zoe sat up straight. "Connor's pictures," she said and pulled her messenger bag into her lap. "Connor mailed these photos to me. With everything that's happened, I forgot to show them to you. That could be Italy, couldn't it?" Zoe asked as she passed the photos to him.

He skimmed through them. "Could be anywhere in Europe. There's no distinctive landmark or readable sign. Cobblestone squares are a dime a dozen over there. And we don't know when these were taken. Just because he mailed them recently doesn't mean they were taken recently."

Zoe sipped her ginger ale. "It's *likely* they were taken in

Italy. GRS has connections with Italian business—the paper-weights are imported from Venice."

He waved that thought aside. "Coincidence."

When Zoe frowned at him, he leaned farther over the table. "The woman who died, her name was Francesca. Her husband was in the Naples mafia—very high in the Camorra, that's the organization that controls Naples and the Campania region. Francesca was providing information on her husband. He must have found out who I was and come after me."

"Back up. Why would the CIA be interested in a mob guy in Naples in the first place? I thought the CIA was more into terrorists in the Middle East, stuff like that."

"Organized crime is a very sophisticated operation in Naples, practically mainstream. For all intents and purposes, the mob runs the area—collecting protection money from businesses and running goods into and out of the huge port. Over half of the goods that arrive are undeclared, which means the U.S. government wants to know what is moving through the port. There's an entire division in the CIA that deals with organized crime."

Zoe massaged her temples, trying to take it all in. "Why come after you now? After years?" she finally asked.

"Because that's how it is over there. You mess with someone like him and he never forgets. They live by a code—like in the old west. If he finds out who killed his wife and does nothing to take me out, then he's weak. He has to kill me to maintain his power."

"Wait," Zoe said, throwing up a hand. "How do you even know he blames her death on you? He might have found out she was giving you information and killed her himself."

"No. The way she died—there were witnesses. It was a rival crime family. When she was exposed, they realized it was a way to hurt their competitor. But even with that, if he knew Francesca was in contact with me...ultimately, he'd see me as the guilty party."

Zoe shifted in her chair. "Okay, say all that is true. But it doesn't explain why he'd wait to come after you."

Jack downed the last of his tea, then said, "Maybe it's taken him this long to track me down. I did move a few times, and my on-line footprint is small."

Zoe felt as if lights were going on as she connected some things. "That's why you didn't want a Facebook account and why you refused to put any personal info on the GRS website." Zoe had always thought that Jack was a little paranoid because he refused to create any social media accounts.

He shook his head. "No. It was more habit than anything else. You learn to keep everything close, not to share," he said.

Zoe held his gaze. "So I wasn't the only one who pulled away," she said, thinking of several tense arguments when he'd flung that accusation at her. "You just hid it better than me." The tone of their conversation, which had been fairly normal—if you can consider talking about your ex-husband's secret past life a normal conversation, Zoe thought—suddenly swerved into something deeper. "All those times you said I was shutting you out," she narrowed her eyes and felt her face flush, "and you had this *whole history*, another life, that you'd kept from me. I may have not been very good at sharing, at opening up, but at least I tried." The air seemed to simmer around them.

Jack's mouth was set in a firm line. He nodded slowly. "I have to give you that—you tried."

It was the last thing she'd expected him to say, and she was surprised to see a look of sadness in his gaze, which threw her off.

Zoe quickly glanced away from Jack, reminding herself he was a spy—a *spy*. He was trained in deceiving people. Was that sorrowful expression on his face real or manufactured? She crossed her arms and braced them on the table. "Water under the bridge," she said, dismissing the topic. "I still think it's odd that he would come after you now."

Jack raised his hands and shrugged. "Maybe he just found out. Maybe it was those leaks to the media—remember that huge document dump of government files and e-mails? Maybe my name was in there. Or maybe someone else talked. I don't know. It's not important. What I have to do is figure out how to get to Naples."

Zoe sat up straight. "Go there? Why?"

"Because that's where Roy Martin lives. He's the case officer I replaced. Francesca was originally his asset. He went on to be the station chief. He knows the whole history. He can vouch for me, get this straightened out."

"Why not call him?"

"I tried. Just a few minutes ago. My Italian is rusty, but passable. I was able to talk to his cleaning lady. Roy is out of town, but he'll be back tomorrow. Now we just need to find some cash to buy an airline ticket. I can't talk about this on the phone. It has to be face-to-face."

"*An* airline ticket?" Zoe asked.

"There's no need for you to go."

"You think I should stay here in Vegas?" Zoe said, her voice rising.

Jack looked around to see if she'd drawn anyone's attention. Zoe didn't care. "You think I should stay in the same city where a man tried to run me down and then shot at me? A man who knows my face and is probably out there right now looking for me? I'm sure he's conscious by now, and he's probably figured out how to get those cords off."

Jack placed a hand on her arm. "Easy. We'll get you a hotel room. Somewhere safe and I'll come back for you when this is all straightened out."

"Really, Jack? That's your solution? I hole up in a room and wait for you to come back? I don't think so. I'm not letting you out of my sight. I don't know if that story you told me is true. It could be a pack of lies," she said, and his expression closed down. Good, she thought. Much better to have him sullen and withdrawn than looking at her in a regretful way that pulled at her heart just a little bit.

"It may come down to simple economics," he countered, his voice soft and controlled. We can't use plastic to charge an airline ticket because the police will be checking for transactions. I can pawn my watch," he said, twisting his wrist so that the face of his expensive black watch with about as many dials and readouts on it as an airplane dash caught the light. "But I doubt that it will cover two last-minute tickets to Rome."

"Don't you mean Naples?"

"Rome will be cheaper. I'll get a car and drive to Naples. It's only about two and a half hours."

Zoe lounged back in her chair. "How about we make a deal. If I come up with the cash, I go." There was no way he was going to Italy without her. She wasn't about to sit around in a dingy hotel room—and she was sure it wouldn't be at the Luxor or the MGM Grand—probably somewhere far away from The Strip.

And they were talking Italy. *Italy*. It was a destination she'd read about for years in the guidebooks she'd copy-edited. She knew all about the different sections of Rome, the best transportation options to get around the country, how to avoid lines at the Colosseum, where to find the best gelato…okay, so maybe those details weren't critical to their goals here, but the point was she knew plenty about Italy, and she'd always wanted to see it. Jack was not getting on that plane without her.

Jack looked wary. "How are you going to come up with the cash?"

"Don't worry about that," Zoe said as she twisted a strand of hair around her finger. "Do we have a deal?"

"You're thinking of pawning your wedding ring," Jack said flatly, and Zoe shot him a surprised glance.

"Nope," she said, splaying her hands, displaying her bare fingers.

"I know you've got it with you," he said. "It's on that long gold necklace." Zoe wanted to look away and casually deny it, but she couldn't break eye contact. She felt her cheeks heat up again as she thought of the ring hanging heavily on its chain suspended between her breasts. "You always wear it," he said quietly.

Zoe forced herself to keep her hands still instead of touching the necklace or the ring as she was itching to do. She licked her lips and tilted her chin. "It's not the ring."

"No? I'm almost scared to ask what you're thinking of doing in Las Vegas. There are a frightful amount of options in Sin City."

"Nothing illegal." He opened his mouth to make a smart remark, she was sure, so she talked over him, "or immoral. Do we have a deal?"

"Fine. Deal." He extended his hand, and she quickly shook it, ignoring the weird frisson that hit her when their hands touched. She jerked her hand away and opened the messenger bag, which was getting quite heavy. It now contained all the papers purloined from Connor's apartment. She dug around in the bag, then pulled out the envelope she'd brought with her from Dallas.

She opened the flap and tilted it toward him.

Jack hunched forward and peered inside the envelope. After a second, he said, "That's my money."

Zoe glanced around the restaurant at his loud tone. "Finders keepers," she said, folding the flap closed. "Just be glad I'm going to use it to buy you an airline ticket, too."

Jack shook his head, a snort-like laugh erupting after a second. "How did you find it?"

"I broke your lamp."

"I see."

"I also searched your room. I found the passports. They're in here, too."

"Good. That will save us some time—" Jack broke off as a guy moved through the tables and took a seat next to them. With his backpack, faded T-shirt, cargo shorts, and flip-flops, he looked like a student. He busily staked his claim to the table, depositing his backpack on a chair and opening his laptop.

"Of all the tables," Zoe mouthed to Jack, "why did he have to pick that one?"

Zoe could see Jack giving the guy a thorough examination. Zoe didn't see anything threatening about him, and Jack must have felt the same way because he turned his attention back to Zoe and spoke in a low voice. "We'll pick up a few things here and lay low until tomorrow morning. The international flights won't leave until then. What? What is it?" he asked.

An image on the computer screen had caught her attention and she stared at it, a frightened look on her face. "There's a picture of us on his Internet browser," Zoe said.

# CHAPTER FIFTEEN

*Las Vegas, Friday, 7:02 p.m.*

"WHAT?" JACK ASKED, HIS FACE perplexed. He tried to see the screen, but it was angled so that only Zoe could see it.

"It's one of those web browsers with rotating photos that go with the stories," she whispered, leaning to the side as she struggled to see the text. She squinted. "The headline is *Missing Millions and Murder*," she said, sucking in her breath. The photo vanished, replaced by the next story, and Zoe realized she was breaking out in a cold sweat. "It's gone."

"Are you sure it was us?"

Zoe nodded. "It was taken in front of The Venetian, right after Stubby Guy tried to run us down. It's fuzzy, but it's a tight shot of our faces."

"Ham and cheese on rye," called someone from the deli counter. The student grabbed his empty soda cup and went to pick up his sandwich.

"I'll delay him. You see what you can find out," Jack said as he stood and followed the student to the fountain drink dispenser.

Zoe glanced around quickly, but the restaurant was still quiet with only the three of them as customers. She slid into the seat and fumbled with the computer's track pad. Jack walked by the student, who'd just finished filling his drink cup. Their shoulders collided and Mountain Dew cascaded through the air, then rained down, soaking both of their shirts. As Jack apologized, he maneuvered the student so that his back was to Zoe.

The page finally loaded, and Zoe scrolled down the text, scanning as fast as she could. It was a short article, only three paragraphs, but it was some tight writing, Zoe thought grimly. The reporter had managed to hit the highpoints of Connor's death and the FBI investigation, but clearly the focus of the article was the missing money.

She hit play on the embedded video clip. Background noise of passerby chitchat and car engines sounded from the computer speakers. Fingers shaking, she quickly lowered the volume as she glanced around. No one had noticed. Jack and the student were still mopping up. The video was jerky and not centered on them at first, but then there was a screech of tires, and the camera swiveled to find the source of the noise. "There we are," muttered Zoe, shaking her head, half fascinated, half horrified to see the car accelerating toward them.

Zoe watched herself glance over her shoulder, then freeze. Jack reacted, pulled her out of the way, seconds before the car hit the pylon. They were out of the picture for a few seconds as the camera focused on the crumpled front end of the car, but as they stood and hurried away, the camera caught them and followed their movement.

The photo at the top of the article was a still shot from the last seconds of the video. Jack had a look of intense concentration on his face, while she looked like she'd seen the shower scene in *Psycho* for the first time. The name on the byline jumped out at her as she hit the back button and slid back into her own chair. Jenny Singletarry, the reporter who'd known about the search warrant. Now she'd found a video of them in Vegas? And how did she know about the money?

Jack returned, his shirt soaked to his chest, revealing a nicely cut physique above the bulk of what looked like a pillow. Zoe jerked her gaze up to his face. "According to the article, we're on the lam, a modern day Bonnie and Clyde."

*Las Vegas, Friday, 8:22 p.m.*

"JUST DO IT, JACK." ZOE closed her eyes.

"Okay, here we go."

Zoe could hear the *snick-snick* of the scissors opening and closing several times. She cracked an eyelid open and saw her reflection in the mirror. Jack stood behind her shoulders, which were wrapped in a thin white hotel towel, a chunk of Zoe's hair held in one hand and the scissors in the other. They flickered, reflecting the dim light above the bathroom mirror. Irena's passport was propped up on the little tray below the mirror. Shoulder-length dark brown hair framed a face that didn't look so different from Zoe's, which was good since Zoe was going to be Irena during the flight.

Thank goodness Irena had a fairly average face—no hooked nose or heavily hooded eyes. Her lips were neither paper thin or swollen like a Hollywood starlet. Just normal sized. Her face was rounder than Zoe's and her eyebrows were thinner and more arched, but these last two things were easily fixed, Jack had said. Of course, he wasn't the one who would be plucking his eyebrows, Zoe had thought. What Irena didn't have was red hair.

"Jack, just do it. Get it over with," Zoe said impatiently. Her hair had to go. She knew it. It was too long, too bright, and too distinctive. It was the one area where she felt a tiny bit of vanity. Zoe didn't care much for make-up. Mascara and a bit of lip-gloss were about all she bothered with. And clothes—she couldn't care less about designer labels or fashion trends. She didn't give much thought to coordinating outfits or which shoes she'd wear.

But she had always thought her hair was special—probably because as far back as she could remember, it had been the one thing that always drew comments from strangers and friends alike. She'd always had long hair, at least below her shoulder blades; she'd only had the ends trimmed occasionally. Wearing it long saved money was what she told herself, but she felt her eyes welling up and knew it was more that just economy. It was part of her identity.

"Pity to cut it off," Jack said. He raked his fingers through her hair along the nape of her neck and paused with one curl cork-screwed around his finger. "I always liked your long hair."

"You never told me that," Zoe said, blinking and watching him in the reflection. She was not going to cry. Not over her *hair*, of all things. She'd been shot at today for God's sake. A little haircut was nothing, she told herself as she swallowed the thickness in her throat.

"Just one of many things it seems," he said under his breath. He squared his shoulders and snipped. Zoe jerked a little as she felt the tension on her scalp release when he cut the strand he was holding. He glanced in the mirror, zeroed in on her reddening eyes, and added casually, "Perhaps I'll make some of it into jewelry like those morbid Victorians."

She gave him a watery smile. "Keep going," she said, nodding her head.

"Alright," he continued, "I think a brooch is out of the question, but perhaps a bracelet. There's enough length for that, or one of those man chokers. Like that country music guy who's always singing about the ocean."

She laughed out loud. "I meant keep cutting," she said. He nodded and went to work with the scissors.

*McCarran International Airport, Las Vegas*
*Saturday, 11:39 a.m.*

"DON'T AVOID EYE CONTACT," JACK said as they inched forward in the security line.

"Right," Zoe murmured, because that was the only word she was going to attempt with two wads of cotton stuffed in her cheeks to make her face look fuller. She was already nervous and the cotton seemed to be absorbing what little moisture there was in her mouth. If the woman checking passports at the head of the line asked her a question, Zoe hoped she'd be able to croak out a response.

She crept forward another foot, Irena's new passport clutched in her sweaty hand. Would a slightly damp passport give her away? Jack actually looked bored. How he managed it, she didn't know.

"Don't fidget," Jack said, and Zoe realized she was running her other hand over the nape of her neck, which felt oddly drafty without the thick curtain of her hair hanging down her back. Her hair brushed her shoulders and was "Maple Brown Number Six." She'd tried to style it like the photo of Irena, curling the ends under as best she could without a curling iron. She must have come close because when she emerged from the bathroom at the hotel, Jack had looked shocked and surprised for a second then he'd got a grip on his emotions and nodded sharply. "You'll do," he'd said. They had decided that her hazel eyes would have to be close enough to "Irena's" green eyes to pass security.

Zoe felt her hand inch self-consciously to her neckline

again and firmly crossed her arms over her waist. She wished she had a baseball cap like Jack. It was a new one, plain navy blue, which covered his new shorter haircut. He trimmed it himself while she rinsed the dye out of her hair. After their joint makeover session last night, Jack had left "for supplies," as he called it.

Zoe had fallen asleep on one of the rickety double beds. They had stayed in a dodgy hotel that didn't ask questions about why they paid in cash. Zoe had worried that the desk clerk would remember them because they were staying more than a few hours. "This is the kind of place where *not* remembering the guest is the main reason people stay here," Jack had said. Her long night of driving and the intense ups and downs of the day caught up with her, and she'd slept so hard she hadn't heard Jack return or slip into the other double bed.

She'd awoken to find a rolling suitcase situated at the end of the bed beside Jack's backpack. There was a stack of clothes on top of the suitcase and a pair of boots on the floor. Who knew Jack remembered her shoe size? She was thrilled to have a new white fitted T-shirt to change into, but the shapeless black cardigan made her look like a lump. "That's the idea," Jack had said as he pulled a gray T-shirt over his head that morning. Jack had discarded the pillow he'd used to pad his figure yesterday.

There was a jacket for her and a black crew neck sweater in the rolling bag for him. Zoe had held up a double-breasted black jacket and raised her eyebrows. "What are we cat burglars? You have more breaking and entering planned?"

"We haven't done any breaking and entering, remember?" Jack countered. "We want to blend in. Europeans usually wear dark colors, and it will be much cooler there than it is here. You'll need that jacket."

She pushed the no-prescription black rectangular-framed glasses back up the bridge of her nose. This morning she'd thought she was a good match for Irena's passport photo. That was this morning. Right now, she felt like she had the word "imposter" printed on a sign hanging around her neck.

"Ma'am?" a voice called, and Zoe scurried forward to the podium where the woman glanced at their faces, then ran a special flashlight over their passports. She gave Zoe's face an extra glance. "Do I know you?"

Zoe shook her head quickly and mumbled a no.

"You take any classes at UNLV?" she persisted.

Zoe gave another headshake and forced herself not to shoot a panicked look at Jack. "I've just got one of those faces," she managed to say, despite her dry mouth.

The woman handed everything back to Jack with a yawn. "Thank God we dyed your hair," he said in an undertone as they moved forward. Zoe felt hot and sweaty, and her heart was racing. She wondered if this was what a nervous breakdown felt like. The airport was packed, and they had to wait again before going through the scanners. She felt exposed when she put the cardigan in the bin along with her new boots.

The official waved her through the metal detector. Jack was behind her, and once their belongings emerged on the rolling belt, he swept everything up and they walked a few steps away to redress. "Why the rolling suitcase?" she asked as she worked her foot into her boot. They'd had hardly any clothes to put in it.

Jack didn't look up from threading his belt through the loops of his jeans. "Traveling without luggage, especially to an international destination would be unusual." Jack slid his watch onto his wrist, and she had a mental flash of all those times he'd picked up his watch from the nightstand as he rolled out of bed in the morning. The situation suddenly seemed awkward and too intimate. Jack had shaved this morning, so he'd match "Brian's" passport photo. The stubble had given him a

different look, made him seem more scruffy and approach-
able, but with his face shaved clean, he looked more like he
had when they were married. She couldn't help but think of
the last time they'd been in the Las Vegas airport. They'd left
together, a married couple, in a heady haze of affection and
excitement. Zoe shoved her arms into the cardigan, glad to
have the extra layer back on and focused on settling her messenger bag on her shoulder. "This way to the gate," she said
and felt Jack fall into step beside her.

One of the cotton pads was creeping up the side of her
cheek away from her jaw. She worked it back down and asked,
"So, no one said anything when you bought the tickets with
cash?"

Jack slung one strap of his backpack over his shoulder as
he said, "I told the ticket agent we'd had a good night at the
tables. She didn't seem to think it was all that unusual. This is
Vegas. I'm sure they've seen stranger things."

If they had really been jetting off to Europe on an impulse,
it would have been a wonderful trip. No delays, no weather,
no complications. After the Vegas airport, which felt like a
mall on Christmas Eve, the international departure terminal
at Dulles was eerily deserted. Zoe kept expecting a security
guard to come through and tell them it was closing time even
though it was only four in the afternoon. Again, their passports passed scrutiny, and no one gave them a second glance.
"It's all so easy, I'm frightened half out of my mind—not just
for us," Zoe whispered as they settled into their seats for the
flight to Rome. "Think about national security. If we can just
waltz through the system, what does that mean?"

Jack leveled a look at her and said, "It means that the documents the federal government created for my cover are top
notch. Let's just concentrate on getting ourselves out of this
mess, then you can worry about the terrorists." He folded his
arms, and within minutes was asleep—with his seat in the full,

up-right position. Zoe frowned and tried to get comfortable. He'd done the same thing on the first flight. She didn't see how he could sleep. She'd spent the early part of the flight alternately reading through Connor's spreadsheets and his journal and tensing every time the flight attendant walked by.

She examined the photos Connor had mailed to her, but again, found nothing distinctive about them. Was the photo of the Madonna important? Was it a famous painting? A valuable painting? The cobblestones and ancient architecture in the other pictures didn't exactly narrow it down to one location. Several photos included people. A blond woman appeared twice, but Zoe couldn't distinguish her features. A dark cocker spaniel also appeared in several of the photos. Could that mean something? Zoe shook her head and put the photos aside and took the tray of food from the flight attendant.

After eating a turkey sandwich so small that it seemed it would only satisfy a toddler, or perhaps an elf, the cabin lights dimmed, and she settled down to try and sleep, but numbers and names from the spreadsheets and the journal kept running through her mind. She sat up and went back to the papers. There was one spreadsheet with columns of numbers that she studied until her eyes were practically crossing.

The row headings were combinations of numbers and letters, like VB2FQ9, which initially looked like some sort of airline or hotel reservation code, but because the spreadsheets were filled with them, she had to assume they were something else. Connor went out of town a lot, but not that much. And there were no dates or places associated with them. Just column after column of numbers.

"You're a bundle of contradictions, you know that?" Jack said, shifting so that he was mostly on his side, facing her, his pillow bunched between his ear and his shoulder.

"You're supposed to be asleep," Zoe said. "What do you mean?"

"You're so impulsive and such a free spirit, yet you do all this detail work," he said tapping the spreadsheets. "Creating spreadsheets like this, copy-editing manuscripts, stuff like that."

"I'm a complicated woman."

Jack snorted.

"Besides, you're one to talk," Zoe said. "You're so straight-forward, a man with a hidden past, who loves rules and schedules, yet you can use whatever happens to be lying around—like flowerpots—to disarm men with guns."

"Er—right. I'm going back to sleep now."

With a half smile, Zoe went back to the spreadsheets, but after thirty minutes of trying to wrap her mind around the possibilities, she gave up.

Zoe reclined her seat and tried to blank her mind, but the only thing that fell asleep was her left foot. She sat up straight and rolled her head around to work the crick out of her neck. She wasn't the only one who wasn't sleeping. Jack had the window seat and she had the aisle. The seat between them was empty. The man directly across the aisle from her was playing solitaire on his e-reader, which reminded her of the cards she'd found in Jack's car. She tilted her head and looked at Jack.

His head was moving in a slow arc, millimeter by millimeter, down the headrest until he hit the tipping point and his head fell forward. He jerked upright, then burrowed lower in the seat, and drifted off again.

Zoe moved to the middle seat. "Jack," she said in a voice loud enough to be heard over the engines, but not loud enough to carry to the rows around them, "are you awake?"

He made a noise somewhere between a grunt and a groan. Perfect. He might be just groggy enough that she'd get the truth out of him. "Why did you leave playing cards on the seat of your car before you disappeared?"

He yawned and murmured, "A warning. For you."

"But how did you know I'd find them or even know what they meant?"

With his eyes closed, he rotated his head toward Zoe. "The car would eventually get towed. I knew you'd get the car and whatever was inside. You're my beneficiary."

"So you just happened to have a pack of cards from the Venetian, and you knew certain cards had special meanings?"

He rubbed his eyes before opening them. "I had a girlfriend in high school who was into all that mystic stuff…numerology, astrology, reading cards. She did a reading for me once, and the eight of Spades came up. It was about a week before my dad died in the car wreck."

"Oh, Jack. I'm sorry," Zoe said.

He shook his head slightly, waving off her sympathy. "It's been a long time. Anyway," he sighed as he said, "the eight of Spades stuck with me. And the cards were in my car because I picked Connor up at the airport a few weeks ago after one of his trips to Vegas. He tossed them in the console when he got in the car. Said they were a souvenir for me."

"So what if I never figured out the cards? I didn't know they had meanings."

"I wasn't trying to leave you a trail of breadcrumbs. I didn't even know at that point I was going to Vegas. The cards were there and it was the only way I could think of communicating with you without giving myself away. I couldn't very well leave you a note or send you a text. I knew it wouldn't be long before the police figured out that I wasn't dead, and then everything…and everyone I knew would be under scrutiny."

"Considerate of you, to think of me," Zoe said mildly.

Jack sighed, crossed his arms, and leaned back in his seat. "I did the best I could in the situation."

The engines hummed in the silence between them, then Zoe asked, "What did you do when you woke up in the office?"

He cocked his head toward her. "After I figured out—what did you call him?—Stumpy Guy—was going to kill me whether or not the kid with him objected?"

"Stubby Guy. Yes, after that."

"I waited until they were yelling at each other and I didn't see how the argument could get more heated, then I lunged for Stubby. There was a struggle. Fortunately, for me, the kid was so shocked when I moved, that it gave me a slight advantage." Jack looked away for a moment, then said, "I left them there in the office. I knew what they'd come to do and my main goal was to get out of there. I knew Connor was dead. I'd seen the bank transfer, and with their conversation, I figured everything was part of the set up to make me look guilty. I drove to Connor's house, looked around, found the Vegas address, then I bought a burner phone, drove out to Highway 375, set the stage, made the 911 call, then hiked over to the shopping center for a ride."

"A ride," Zoe said, studying his face. "Somehow I doubt a kind stranger gave you a lift to Vegas."

"Nope. I kept some emergency money in the car. I bought that black hatchback we left at the airport from a pizza delivery guy. He said he'd catch a ride home with a friend. The police will track him down, eventually. Probably pretty quickly now that we're having our fifteen minutes of fame." Seeing her face, he said, "Don't worry. We've got a good lead on them."

"It's not that—well, that's always at the back of my mind—I can't believe you bought a car while you were on the run. I thought you'd gone all Jason Bourne and stolen it."

"Why go to more trouble than you have to?" Jack said. "Besides, I only steal cars on weekends. Now you need to get some sleep. We have a lot of ground to cover when we land, and I can't have you asleep on your feet." He crossed his arms and was breathing deeply in seconds.

# CHAPTER SIXTEEN

*Pozzuoli, Italy, Sunday, 1:17 p.m.*

ZOE FOLDED THE MAP AND looked out of the passenger window. She'd spent most of the drive from the
airport fighting to convince the GPS unit that Roy Martin's
address did exist, but there was no arguing with technology.
The GPS steadfastly refused even to admit that Roy's town
existed. She'd given up and switched to the map the woman
at the rental counter had given them, which only helped
them get out of Rome and onto the toll road that ran south.

Not that they'd seen much of Rome. The airport was miles
away from the city, and Zoe was disappointed that the drive
only gave her glimpses of modern apartment blocks, miles of
highways, and an occasional Autogrill, a sort of gas station/
restaurant combo that dotted the freeway and sounded, to her
at least, more German than Italian. There were mountains,
beautiful blue-hued ranges, which marched along the spine
of the peninsula. Some of the highest peaks were still topped
with a white layer of snow. Before they reached Naples, Jack
took an exit that put the mountains at their back. Their route
crossed the relatively flat stretch of land then dipped to the
Mediterranean, a vast expanse of blue that sparkled in the

noontime sunlight until stands of bamboo as well as rows of hotels and walled homes positioned between the road and the sea blocked the view.

Jack hit the steering wheel hard with the heel of his hand. "That's when it happened," he said.

Zoe pulled her gaze away from the window. "What?"

Jack stared down the road as he said, "The gun. It's been in the back of my mind. How did it go from the attic to the office? But with everything happening…I didn't figure it out until now."

"So what happened?"

"You know that pharmacy in the office complex, the next duplex over? It was robbed."

"I didn't hear about that."

"Yeah, well, it happened. Nothing major, but it bothered Sharon. I told her that I had a gun in my attic at home and I'd bring it in, if she'd go to the gun range and take some classes."

"I bet that went over well," Zoe said, her tone indicating the opposite.

"She was scandalized that I even *owned* a gun. She said she'd rather take someone on with her bare hands than fire a gun."

"So you think Sharon took the gun out of the attic?" Zoe said, perplexed. "That would never happen."

"No," Jack said with a bark of laughter. "She'd rather pick up a hot coal than touch a gun. But Connor was there. You can hear everything in that office."

"You think Connor came to our house and—" Zoe broke off abruptly, then swiveled toward Jack. "The day of the storm—when everything happened. I heard someone up stairs, but it wasn't you. I know because I went up there later and there weren't any wet towels. You hadn't showered. And the front door wasn't locked after you left—except it wasn't you. You didn't come home that day. Unless you came home and didn't shower?"

"No, I didn't even run that day."

"Do you think it was Connor?"

"I don't think so," Jack said slowly. "I think whoever took the gun used it to kill Connor. It was probably Stubby Guy. I figure he shot Connor and put it in my drawer to implicate me. My prints would have been on it already." He squinted as he said, "I'm not sure why Stubby Guy and his partner would kill Connor and then leave...but maybe they'd assumed I'd be on my normal schedule. Connor usually didn't take a lunch, and I left for my run and returned at the same time everyday."

"You do usually operate with clock-like precision," Zoe said.

Jack shot her a look with his brows lowered. "That day was different. I went to the post office and skipped my run. Maybe they were supposed to get us both, but when I wasn't there, they shot Connor, planted the gun in my desk, and left, thinking that it would implicate me. They must have seen that I'd returned and had come back to finish the job. I was only in the office for a few minutes before that short guy came inside." His gaze caught on a sign beside the road, and he hit the brakes and made a turn onto a side road at the last moment. "I think this is it."

After a couple of passes up and down the twisty road with no sighting of Roy's road, Jack swung the car into a parking area beside a café. It was a small white stucco building with three tall tables with the Coca-Cola logo in front of its dark doorway. Zoe climbed out of the car to stretch her legs, wrapping her jacket tightly around herself as the cool air hit her, then she followed Jack inside.

A glass counter displayed sandwiches, pizza, and some delectable-looking desserts. A woman with brownish-blond hair and a lumpy face turned from the cappuccino machine to hand a dainty cup and saucer to a man standing near the display case. Jack engaged the woman in some rapid Italian while Zoe selected a Coke Light from a cooler since there wasn't any ginger ale. Jack thanked the woman and paid for the drink with some euros that they'd exchanged at the airport. Jack went to the restroom and Zoe went to the tall tables outside the café and sipped her drink.

The woman came outside and wiped down the table beside Zoe. "Good that you are going to see the signore," she said in halting English.

Zoe got the feeling that the woman wanted to practice her English. Zoe nodded politely.

"He lonely," she continued. "No visitors except," she waved her hand at the cloth in her other hand, "cleaning lady. He needs signora," she said with a definite nod of her head.

"I see," Zoe said, thinking the woman saw herself as ideal for that role. "Arrivederci," the woman said with a flap of the cloth before she went back inside.

Jack emerged from the café, and they clambered back into the car. "She said it's right here," Jack said, as he turned onto a narrow asphalt road lined on each side with tall stucco walls interspersed with gates and steep driveways.

"It looks kind of iffy," Zoe said, studying the high, discolored paint on the walls that lined the tight asphalt street, which was pockmarked with holes and weeds growing through the cracks.

"This isn't the States," Jack said as he bumped from pothole to pothole along the road. "This is a good neighborhood."

"But there's no where to go…if something happened. It's a dead-end," Zoe said. A low-hanging branch dipped over one of the walls and scraped the window beside her. She glanced behind them, but the narrow street, an alley, really, was empty.

"Good instincts," Jack said, "but we're okay here. This is it— second one from the end."

Jack wedged the car into a tiny space, and they followed the white stucco wall to a blue door. Acorn finials topped the wall on each side of the door. Windows from the second story of the house loomed over the gate. Jack pushed the button set into the wall.

"Pronto," said a gruff voice through an intercom.

"Roy. It's Jack."

There was no reply, except for the door buzzing open. They stepped into a minuscule courtyard with a small tree dotted with tangerines and climbed a set of stairs to the front door.

A heavy-set man with a barrel chest and thick, wavy salt-and-pepper hair threw open the door. He removed a cigar from the corner of his mouth and greeted Jack in a deep voice that rumbled around the entry area. "Jack, my boy, good to see you."

They did that manly greeting that was part handshake, part slap on the back. As they broke apart, Jack waved Zoe over the threshold and said, "Roy, this is Zoe."

Roy's sharp blue eyes pinged between Jack and Zoe, questioningly. When Jack didn't add any explanation, Zoe held out her hand and said, "His ex. Nice to meet you."

"Ah," Roy said and clamped his cigar in the corner of his mouth before shaking her hand. "Interesting. Well, come on in. Let's go out back." He closed the door and lead them by a curving staircase, through a white-tiled living room and dining room combination filled with contemporary furniture in shades of tan and brown, and out the back door to a terrace. "Best part of the house," he said, waving them into seats around a patio table situated under another tangerine tree. It was chilly in the shade, and she kept her jacket on.

"You want a coffee? A beer? Cigar?" Roy asked, his hand on the back of his chair.

"None for me," Zoe said, sliding to a seat. Jack shook his head.

"Down to business, eh?" Roy smiled around the cigar. "So how are you?"

"Honestly, not so good," Jack said.

"I heard." Roy's face turned serious.

Jack leaned forward. "What have you heard?"

"That you did in your business partner, took the money, and ran."

"That's news here, too?"

"Nah," Roy flicked the fingers of his right hand as if he were shooing away a bug. "I did some research after you called. Read up on you in the American news sites. I can see why you'd want out of the States." His gaze, which had been focused on the leafy branches overhead, swept back and zeroed in on Jack as he said, "but I don't know why you'd come here."

"Because I didn't kill my business partner or take any money."

"You were framed." Roy said it flatly as if there was nothing unusual about that situation.

"Yes, but I haven't gotten to the best part. I was supposed to die, too."

Roy puffed on his cigar for a moment before saying, "Clean, that way."

Jack nodded. "No one to contradict my story of innocence."

Zoe fought down the beginnings of a yawn. For the first time in how long? Days? She felt almost safe. The tight coil of worry inside her loosened, and she felt herself relax. Part of it was jet lag, but some of it was due to the snug court-yard with its high walls and canopy of green leaves combined with Roy's solid personality and his no-nonsense acceptance of Jack's story. She felt she could almost tilt her head back and go to sleep.

"But you didn't die," Roy said with a mischievous glint in his eye.

"Doing my best not to," Jack said. "I need your help to stay that way. Costa is involved in this."

Zoe blinked at the name, trying to clear the fuzziness from her head. She hadn't heard the name before. He had to be the guy Jack had told her about. It was only in that moment that Zoe realized Jack hadn't mentioned the name to her, probably intentionally. Even when he was revealing secrets, he kept something back. She felt stupid that she'd assumed he'd confided the whole story to her. She should have known better.

Roy's forehead wrinkled. "Can't be. He's gone."

"Gone?" Jack said, "Where would he go?"

Roy shrugged. "Word is, he's living like a German count in a Bavarian castle. I don't necessarily believe that myself," Roy said with a warning tone, "but that's the rumor." A black cat with three white paws and one black paw appeared at the top of the back wall. The cat walked daintily along the wall, leapt lightly to the ground, then positioned itself a few feet from the table, its gray eyes fixed solidly on Roy.

Jack barely glanced at the cat. He looked stunned. "He left Naples?"

"Apparently, he didn't want to end up like Zagaria. You hear about him?" When Jack shook his head, Roy rearranged his bulky frame in the chair as if settling in for a good story. "They caught him a while back, living like a mole in an underground bunker. Done in when they found a pair of expensive socks in the garbage from the house above his bunker. Designer quality—not something that your average Neapolitan wears every day. They raided the place and arrested him. He's in jail. No, I think after Francesca—" He broke off abruptly, cleared his throat, and said, "After Francesca, well, I think Costa realized that we were closing in on him. The Carabinieri were right there with us. He got smart. Cut his losses and high-tailed it out of here."

Zoe had been watching the exchange silently, but it was clear that the news this Costa guy was out of the game was something Jack hadn't expected to hear. He was at a loss for words, so Zoe said, "Just so I understand—I'm new to all this—you're saying Costa wouldn't have been involved in this at all?"

The cat inched closer and meowed.

"Don't see why he would be…I haven't been…connected, you might say, for a few years, but I don't think he'd put himself out there, risk his anonymity, just to…"

"Avenge himself?" Jack supplied, and Roy lifted a shoulder in acquiescence. Jack blew out a breath and sagged back in his chair. "Then, who? Who would do this to me?"

Roy pulled his cigar out of his mouth and leaned forward, putting both elbows on the table. "I read in those articles you're in business for yourself now. Got any enemies? Competitors?"

"No," Jack said, his voice hard. "No one who'd plan a double murder *and* fraud."

Roy held up a hand. "Easy, there. Just asking." His tone had changed. "How long has it been since you've eaten?"

"Hours," Zoe said promptly, cutting Jack off. Zoe knew he was about to decline an offer of food. She was famished and wasn't embarrassed to admit it. She could feel the first twinges of a headache behind her eyes and hoped that food might waylay it.

"Alright, I'll bring us out some food along with Leo's. I've got to feed him," Roy said nodding to the cat, "otherwise, he'll set up outside my bedroom window and yowl all night. I've been adopted," he said ruefully and stood. The cat sprang up and followed Roy into the house.

"It doesn't make sense," Jack muttered. "There's no one else. It has to be Costa."

Instead of answering, Zoe succumbed to another yawn. He was talking to himself anyway. Roy was back momentarily, carrying a large tray with thick slices of mozzarella, tomatoes, large crackers, bread, and a pot of orange jam. He set it down, told them to help themselves, then returned with several sodas and bottled waters. "I'm afraid this is all I've got—bachelor rations," he said.

"This is wonderful," Zoe said, already several bites into the cheese and tomatoes.

"Local products," Roy said and drizzled some olive oil over his plate. "Try some of that jam," he said, hitting the side of the glass jam container. "Made it myself from the tangerines from this tree," he said pointing overhead. Jack gave him a doubtful look, and Roy said, "Retirement does strange things to a man, I'm warning you, Jack."

"So you make marmalade and have a cat?" Jack said, his face carefully blank.

"Damn straight."

They ate in silence, the only noise the wind ruffling the leaves overhead and Leo crunching through his bowl in the kitchen. When they'd finished, Zoe said, "That was wonderful."

"Tasty," Jack agreed. "Especially the jam."

"Thank you. I'll send some home with you if you don't wipe that smirk off your face," Roy said, and then his voice shifted. "Now, about your situation…" he carefully stacked the empty plates on the tray. "I can ask around. See what I can find out."

"I'd appreciate that. I might need you to vouch for me," Jack said.

Roy nodded his head slowly. "Of course."

Zoe felt her eyelids slipping lower. The food had filled her up and she felt lethargic, except for the dull pulse of a headache beginning behind her eyes. The guy's voices seemed to recede into nothingness, then she felt her head bob, and she jerked herself back into a sitting position. The guys didn't notice. It sounded as if they were working their way through a roster of old acquaintances, updating each other on where people were now and what they were doing. Zoe excused herself, asking Roy if she could use his bathroom.

"Sure. Use mine in the bedroom on the right at the top of the stairs. The sink in the one down here is broken," he explained.

Zoe made her way up the curving staircase and through a bedroom with a heavy antique four-poster bed, matching dresser, and nightstand. Several black and white prints of mountains hung on the walls. In the bathroom, she splashed water on her face, which jerked her out of her dozy state.

She patted her face dry with a white towel and still had a moment's surprise when she raised her gaze to the mirror and saw brown hair framing her face. Her eyes looked like she'd pulled an all-nighter and her fair skin seemed paler than it normally did. She looked rather vampireish. She had a love/hate relationship with her skin. She loved her creamy complexion until she put on a swimsuit or a tank top, then she felt like she looked more ghostly than glamorous.

The headache was still there, and she opened the mirrored door to the medicine cabinet, thinking that Roy wouldn't mind if she took a few aspirin. She found some ibuprofen behind a bottle of perfume. A gold chain necklace with a butterfly pendent inset with diamonds was curled into a careful coil beside the perfume. She returned downstairs, thinking that the café owner better make her move because it appeared Roy wasn't quite the lonely guy she thought.

Leo met her at the bottom of the stairs and arched his back. As she paused to run her hand over his fur, Roy's deep voice carried inside from the terrace. He sounded almost angry as he said, "You know that wasn't your fault. There's no way you could have known someone was about to give her up."

"The government thought it was my fault."

"You know what bureaucracy is like, Jack. Someone had to go down. You were it—the lowest man on the totem pole, a perfect scapegoat. But you, of all people, should know that bureaucratic paperwork doesn't mean crap."

"She was my responsibility." Jack's voice was low and unyielding.

Roy's sigh was audible even to Zoe standing several feet away. "Just don't let it ruin your life, Jack. It happened, but it wasn't your fault. Try to get your head around that."

There was a long silence, and Zoe decided she'd probably eavesdropped long enough. She walked outside and Jack stood up immediately. "We should go," he said to Roy, then turned to Zoe. "Roy says the cruise ships come in today, and the hotels will be packed. We've got to get into town and find a hotel before it gets too late."

Roy offered to let them stay with him, but Jack turned him down, saying they were better off if they kept moving. Roy nodded his agreement.

"Thanks for the food and…well, everything," Zoe said.

"You bet," Roy said as the cat curled through his legs.

"Tomorrow?" Jack asked.

Roy nodded. "Piazza dei Martiri."

*Naples, Italy, Monday, 2:22 a.m.*

ZOE ROLLED OVER AND LOOKED at the clock. Two in the morning. She checked her watch. No wonder she felt wide-awake. It was seven in the evening in Dallas. She pushed her pillow around and tried to relax. She could hear Jack's shallow breathing, slow and steady, from the other twin bed. After the meeting with Roy, jet lag had hit her like an anvil. She'd dozed in the car as Jack navigated into Naples. She had been awake enough to haul herself up the two narrow flights of stairs to their hotel room, then she had collapsed onto her twin bed.

Jack had probably followed the recommendations for fighting jet lag listed in the in-flight magazine and stayed awake as long as he could in the new time zone to get his body acclimated. Either that or he'd taken a sleeping pill, but she knew he avoided taking even an aspirin, so she couldn't really see him popping sleeping pills. He probably willed himself to sleep, Zoe thought sourly. He was so freakishly self-disciplined he probably could make himself drop off into REM whenever he wanted.

She tried to sleep, but couldn't. The last few days replayed in an endless loop like a slideshow: the swiftly moving water of Deep Creek, Connor's still body, the wide open sky during the drive to Vegas, the shock of realizing Jack was alive, the panic she'd felt when she saw their photo online. Were they still in the news? She thought of Roy's house and Jack's face—a picture of disappointment at the news this Costa guy was long gone.

What would they do now? She'd been so sleepy then that she couldn't process what the news meant, but now as she stared at the ceiling, she realized they were at a dead end. Not that their plan was all that stellar to begin with. She'd been so worried about getting out of Vegas sans handcuffs that she hadn't really questioned Jack about how Roy could help them.

Remembering Jack's distressed expression when Roy told him about Costa, which he'd quickly managed to hide, she guessed that Jack had expected Roy to contact his buddies at the CIA and explain that Connor's death was related to an old assignment. But it wasn't. And Roy didn't appear to have copious contacts that he could exploit to get them out of their situation.

What would they do now? Go back to the States? Her stomach clinched at the thought. She was sure that the FBI pair hadn't stopped looking for them. And Mr. Stubby Guy, whoever he was, hadn't seemed like the type to just give up and go away either. After about twenty minutes, she slid out of bed, picked up her messenger bag from where she'd dumped it on the floor, and slipped into the bathroom. They'd been on the move since the plane had landed and she'd fallen into bed without so much as washing her face. She took a quick shower, which felt heavenly, then wrapped herself in the cotton waffle-weave robe hanging on the back of the door.

The hotel wasn't a deluxe, five-star hotel with fluffy bathrobes and fresh flowers. It was more low-key, a place in the busy area near the port with about twelve rooms. No room service or concierge, but Zoe didn't care. Their room had crisp sheets, was sparkling clean, and they had plenty of hot water, which checked all the boxes for her.

She put the toilet seat down and perched there, using the small counter surrounding the sink for a desk as she removed everything from her messenger bag. Since it didn't look like Roy would be able to help, their only option was to go back to Connor's death and figure out why he'd been targeted.

She put the spreadsheets they'd salvaged from Connor's apartment, his black journal, and the photos in one pile. Her meager stash of emergency repair makeup went in another. If she'd known how long she would be gone, she certainly would have brought more than mascara, concealer, and lipgloss. Heck, she'd even have thrown in a few changes of clothes or at least underwear she thought, throwing a glance at the underwear she'd washed out before her shower and hung to dry on the bathroom's small radiator.

Sunglasses, breath mints, a few crumpled tissues, a hair clip, and her wallet with her true identity went on the other side of the sink along with the Irena passport. The rolls of money that had been so fat when she first pulled them from their hiding places were looking a little depleted.

She flattened the bills and counted the money. Four hundred seventeen euros. She folded the bills in half length-wise and bit her lower lip. That wasn't much. She hoped Jack had pre-paid for the hotel room with the euros they'd already exchanged.

What were they going to do when they were out of cash? It wasn't as if they could waltz up to an ATM and withdraw cash from their checking accounts back in the US and, even if they could do that, she didn't have that much in her checking account to begin with. Maybe two hundred dollars. On a good day.

She had already cashed the check from Kiki, but she'd used most of it, paying for gas to get to Vegas, then for food, and supplies for their makeover session. Except for fourteen cents and a single petrified stick of gum, that was it—all her resources.

She took a deep breath and pulled the stack of papers they'd lifted from Connor's house toward her. First, she looked through Connor's black journal page by page. She didn't have any spare paper, so she made notes on toilet paper. Fortunately, the hotel had provided toilet paper with less than Charmin-like qualities. It was more like tissue paper. She listed all Connor's travel, arranging it by date and noting city airport codes. LVS had to be Las Vegas. It was always his first stop. He'd spend a few days, sometimes only one day, before leaving for other cities. There were a smattering of places he'd visited, and she recognized most of them, like Atlanta and Chicago. There were a few she could distinguish from the hotel info that was included with each listing.

Thank goodness Connor didn't embrace new technologies. Of course, he probably didn't want to risk keeping his travel reservations on his office computer in case Jack or even Sharon used it for some reason. He could have used the old computer in the apartment in Las Vegas to make his travel reservations or some anonymous Internet café to plan his travel. Didn't matter, Zoe thought as she jotted the last of the airport codes and dates. She recognized or was able to work out almost all of the codes, except for one. Where was VCE?

It was his most frequent destination in the last few months, and there was only one address associated with it, a street called Calle delle Botteghe, which sounded Italian or Spanish to her. She tapped her pen against the toilet paper. They'd have to find an Internet café of their own to look up the city codes and the street name. There were a few names associated with the cities, but none with the VCE notations. There were also a few random lists of mundane household things like milk, cereal, and plastic spoons. She skipped over those, but paused at one of the last lists.

Contacts
Wig/hair dye
Fake tan

Zoe noticed that the first two items on the list were written in blue ink and the slant of the letters were more pronounced that the letters of the last item on the list, which was written in pencil. It looked like he'd written the first two items, then added the last item later. Was he planning some sort of disguise? She shook her head. All their slouching through airport security and worry about the Internet video had her paranoid. She had disguises on the brain. Why would he plan to change his appearance?

There was a set of numbers scrunched on the last line, 13.4.75.1.6.10. Zoe frowned at them. More numbers. She was beginning to hate numbers, and she'd never had an aversion to them before. She hadn't disliked math in school like some of her friends, but all these numbers floating around without a code or key or some way to explain them...well, they were beginning to annoy her. She supposed that if you took out the periods they might be a phone number? Not an amount of money—there were too many periods. Not an address. Maybe an account number? GPS coordinates? Lock combinations? She sighed. There were too many possibilities.

She tore off her toilet paper list, which resembled more of a scroll at this point, and tucked it into the black journal.

She moved to the printouts of spreadsheets. She'd tried to make sense of them on the airplane, but the print was so tiny and she'd been so jumpy that she hadn't made much progress. Instead of reading everything straight through, she tried a new approach and sorted them by date. Although the columns weren't headed with titles, she'd worked out that the first column in each spreadsheet was a date. After about twenty minutes, she felt as if her eyes were beginning to cross. There were some duplicate pages, which kept throwing her off. She sorted those into stacks, blinking and opening her eyes wide, fighting off a returning wave of sleepiness. She checked her watch. Only three a.m. She could still get a couple more hours sleep, but the stack was almost sorted, so she pressed on. If she ever had insomnia, she now knew reading spreadsheets would put her out in a couple of minutes flat. She struggled through the last pages, tossing them in the correct piles and then quietly tiptoed back to bed.

X

BURROWED deep in the covers, it was the aroma of coffee that woke her. She pried one eye open—it still felt like the middle of the night, despite the sun blazing through the parted curtain—and focused on a paper cup on the nightstand. She struggled into a sitting position and consulted her watch. No wonder she felt like it was the middle of the night—it *was* the middle of the night back in the Midwest. She took a cautious sip of the coffee and noticed Jack sitting on the end of the matching twin bed, his head bent over the spreadsheets.

"Hey, you kept those in order, didn't you?" she asked. "I worked hard on that last night."

He shot a look at her over his shoulder. "You always were cranky in the morning," he said in a neutral tone. "Have some more coffee. Yes, I kept everything in order. There's food in the bag, too." He went back to the spreadsheets.

Zoe opened the bag on the nightstand and found a warm chocolate croissant. Light and flaky and rich with dark chocolate, she decided it was the best breakfast she'd ever had. When she emerged from the bathroom, dressed in her freshly hand-washed clothes, Jack was flipping back and forth through the pages at a frantic pace. "What is it?"

He ignored her. Pages fluttered through his fingers until he stopped abruptly, his hands going slack. Zoe caught the stacks before they slid to the ground. "Watch it."

"Two sets. He had two sets, the bastard."

Zoe tapped the edges of the sheets to straighten them. "What?"

"Connor. He had two sets of books." He strode away, then back. "The number and letter codes were abbreviations for our clients."

Zoe slowly sat down across from him on her bed. "Of course. The two sets of dates. I thought he'd printed the same spreadsheet twice."

Jack rubbed his hand down over his face and stopped when it covered his mouth as if to keep his words internalized. Zoe scanned down the two top sheets, comparing columns of numbers. The differences weren't huge, but they were there. "Subtle enough that you wouldn't catch it."

"I couldn't catch it if I never saw the real numbers," Jack said as he stood and paced to the window. "No wonder he was always doing the books on his laptop and the files were never available." He hit the window frame with the open palm of his hand. "I should have seen it. I should have picked up on it. I should have done more than just glance at the accounts."

"I don't see how you could have. Connor handled all the money and the accounts, right?"

"I should have realized something was up when Sharon offered to update the accounts receivable, and Connor brushed her off. He never passed up the opportunity to avoid work."

"You can't beat yourself up about not realizing Connor wasn't honest with you. Most people don't assume their business partner is embezzling money."

"But he did," Jack said, pushing away from the window. "And there's nothing in there that shows where the millions came from. Even his second account didn't have that kind of money in it."

Zoe didn't have an answer for that, so she said, "Did you see this?" She held up her toilet paper list, which unfurled down to her feet.

The frustration and self-recrimination was still there in his expression, but it went down a notch. "No, I thought it was your list to Santa, and I didn't want to peek."

She rolled her eyes, but was glad to see his mood lighten a bit. "The only thing I want from Santa is to not be one of the most interesting people to the FBI. Or to be shot at again," she added. "It was the only paper I had. Do you know if Connor traveled to these places?"

Jack took the list. "Most of these are legit, as far as I know," he said with a flare of an eyebrow. "I think we have contacts and accounts in these cities, but maybe that was all a smoke screen, too."

"What about VCE?"

"That one I don't know, but we can find out."

# CHAPTER SEVENTEEN

*Naples, Monday, 10:25 a.m.*

A S ZOE AND JACK EMERGED from the hotel into the narrow cobblestoned street, the desk clerk, who was washing down the front steps called, "Ciao." Jack replied, then took her hand and led her down the steeply declining street. Zoe had been so tired when they'd arrived that she hadn't taken in much about their surroundings.

Buildings painted pale lemon, light tan, even salmon pink towered five, six, sometimes seven stories high on each side of the street, creating a dim, canyon-like feel. Laundry dangled from balconies, and wires crisscrossed the tiny band of blue sky above. Peeling advertisement flyers pasted to the walls warred with graffiti and street signs for attention. Car horns, the buzz of mopeds, and the steady drone of some sort of drill filled the air.

"This goes to the Via Chiaia, a pedestrian shopping street," Jack said as a small car approached. Her knowledge of Italy centered on tourist highlights of the major cities, mostly Rome, Florence, and Venice along with information on the easiest ways to get around the country. While the guidebooks she worked on had sections about Naples and other cities, they were brief. Jack had lived here. This was his territory, and she was glad to let him take the lead.

They shrunk toward a pink building, and Zoe found herself nose to nose with—inexplicably—an image of Yoda on an advertising poster plastered to the wall as the car edged passed them. A second later, a moped whipped around the corner and buzzed by them. The driver of the moped held a kid of about three braced between his arms. Under the pink helmet, the kid had a pacifier in her mouth.

They resumed walking, and a few blocks later, Jack said, "Here we are." He pushed open the door to a shop with the words "Internet Point" above it. Zoe blinked, adjusting to the dimness of the room then headed for an open computer, climbing up on a tall barstool positioned under a high counter. Jack paid at another counter, then joined her. She quickly logged on and brought up a search engine, selected English as the language, then typed in the airport code.

"Marco Polo Airport in Venice," Jack read, his voice baffled.

Zoe sat back, her chin in her hand. "You didn't know he went there?"

"No. No clue at all. My standard answer lately it seems," he said bitterly.

"What do you think he was doing?"

"I don't know. Venice is a tourist town. We didn't have business prospects there."

"This isn't the first time Venice has come up. The glass paperweights are from there."

"But we ordered those online. There was no need to go there. It must have been personal."

"Let's see if this street is in Venice." She typed in Calle delle Botteghe along with the word "Venice" and hit enter. Zoe clicked on one of the results, and a map popped up with the street pinpointed near the sinuous curve of the Grand Canal. "Street of Shops," Zoe read the translation then pointed to a hotel icon near the pinpoint. "I bet that's where he stayed, Hotel Art Deco. I remember that name from his journal."

Zoe's fingers did a gentle tap dance on the keys, but she didn't push any buttons. "It's got to be important. Should we go there?"

"Not until I hear from Roy."

Zoe swiveled on the barstool, and her knees bumped against Jack's thighs. He shifted back an inch. "Sorry," Zoe said and forcefully ignored the thoughts shooting through her mind about how weird it was that she was hyper aware that her legs were so close to his. She'd lived in the same house with this man and never once thought about his thighs during the last year.

Mentally, she told herself to focus. "Jack," she said, looking up into his face, "I don't know if Roy is going to be able to help us. He didn't seem very…confident."

"I know," Jack said, "but he might surprise us. He's done it before. We'll meet him tonight and then decide what to do next."

Zoe nodded, then glanced at the computer out of the corner of her eye. "Should I?"

Jack frowned. "What?"

"You know…Google us?"

"God, no. We've got enough to worry about as it is."

"But it's better to know."

"Fine, just don't type in our names." Zoe bit her lip, then spun back to the computer and typed.

"Who's that?" Jack asked, peering over her shoulder.

"Oh, so you do want to see after all?"

"You're a pain, did you know that?" Jack said, but Zoe could tell from his voice that he was smiling.

"It's a reporter. She's the one who told me about the search warrant."

Zoe expected some links to the newspaper to come up

with Jenny Singletarry's name, but to her surprise, there were many more links to a blog called *The Informationalist*. It was a blend of hard news, commentary, celebrity news, and Dallas event listings. The video of them in Las Vegas topped the news column.

A quick scan of the Italian media sites confirmed Jenny Singletarry's summary at the end of the article, which stated that investigators had no new leads, and the couple was still at large.

"At large," Zoe said as they emerged on to the pedestrian shopping street filled with window displays of high-end designer goods. "It makes us sound like criminals."

"They think we are." Jack led them under a crumbling barrel-vault arch with angels and horses adorning the stucco, down through a short street lined with low-branched trees, and around another corner back into a street packed with taxis. "Where are we going?"

"There's someone I need to talk to." They entered the parking garage where they'd left the car. Keeping up with Jack, avoiding pedestrians, and not being run down by speeding mopeds had brought her attention back to the city. "It's too much to take in," Zoe said as she climbed into the tiny car. "Too much to see."

"That's Naples for you. Barely controlled chaos. About three million people squashed into this city." Jack merged into traffic, and Zoe sucked in her breath as they bounced along the rough pavers.

"That wasn't even an opening," she said as the car shot through a gap between two cars.

"Plenty of room," Jack said as he touched the horn and a car that had been drifting into their lane shifted away. "At least, in Naples it is."

Another car slid in front of them and Zoe said, "There wasn't an inch to spare!"

"Yep." Jack shifted gears and deftly maneuvered the car in front of a bus. "Like a live-action Mario Cart game, isn't it?" Several mopeds whined by them, lacing in and out of the gaps. Zoe did a double take and saw a dog on the foot platform of one of the mopeds. Ears flapping and tongue lolling, the mutt's head was tucked between the front of the scooter and the driver's leg.

Jack yielded briefly at a red light before zipping through the intersection along with the rest of the cars in the street. The buildings and their coatings of graffiti blurred as their speed picked up. "No one really pays attention to red lights here. Or lane lines." He laid on the horn again as another car veered toward them as they circled a roundabout.

"The Smart Travel guidebooks warn tourists about the traffic in Naples, but this is …crazy," Zoe said, instinctively flinching to the side as a tour bus closed in on her side of the car as it attempted to merge into the traffic circle. Brake lights flared and all the cars came to a dead stop. "Look at that bus," Zoe said. "The driver is practically in the seat with me."

"He won't hit us," Jack said calmly, watching for a gap in the cars that had begun to inch along. "They hardly ever actually hit you. Scrape you, yes. Hit you, no. Come on, you should love it here—all this chaotic activity, this impulsive, passionate motion."

"I can't believe I'm saying this, but I miss Dallas traffic," Zoe said and fought off the urge to stamp on the non-existent brake pedal as another teeny car breezed blithely into the miniscule gap between their front bumper and the next car.

"Good thing it's not rush hour, then," Jack said and spun the wheel, turning onto a less crowded street. People on the sidewalk, signs in Italian, piles of trash around garbage bins, and street vendors selling purses and gold jewelry flashed by. They followed the twisty maze of bumpy streets until the tires gripped smooth asphalt and Jack said, "There, we're on the freeway. You can open your eyes now."

"I didn't close my eyes. Well, not much. I think I need to provide some detailed feedback for the next Italy edition," Zoe said. "It focuses on the quaint and beautiful. You know, crumbling butter-colored villas, ancient ruins, scenic vineyards."

"That's Tuscany," Jack said with a smile. "Naples is a little more…gritty."

There wasn't as much traffic on the freeway, and Zoe looked out at the city, which spread from the sea to the side of a mountain rising in the distance, its gentle slope swirling out like the folds of a vintage 1950s woman's skirt. As they sped toward it, Zoe studied the top of the mountain, which looked as if it had been sliced off at an angle. "Mt. Vesuvius," she breathed.

"I thought you'd want to see it."

Jack periodically checked the mirrors, but didn't seem to see anything that worried him. He took an exit slowly, maneuvered through more tiny streets, until they came to a parking area near a grouping of shops and a small train station. "Come on. Nico should be around here somewhere," Jack said as he slammed the car door.

"Who's Nico?"

"An old friend."

They strolled by vendors selling fruit, orange juice, lemon juice, pizza, and Panini sandwiches from tented kiosks. Tourists in bright jackets and sensible shoes with cameras slung around their necks thronged around an ugly modern building labeled Scavi de Pompeii. "You brought me to Pompeii," she breathed, grabbing his arm.

"If you go to Naples, you've got to see Pompeii," Jack said.

She smiled at him and, for a second, she flashed back to that crazy night with the dark sky as a backdrop to the flashing lights of Vegas. It all came back to her in a rush, the press of his hand on the small of her back as they moved through the crowds, the wind stinging her face as they rocketed through the air, the cascade of water dancing in synch with music at the fountains.

"It was a good drive. It let me make sure no one was following us. And it got us out of Naples. I'd rather not stay in one spot too long." His matter-of-fact tone was like a spray of cold water on Zoe's cozy memories.

He handed her some euros. "You get our tickets. I'll meet you by the gate." His gaze was fixed over Zoe's shoulder. He crossed the courtyard area to the group of men selling guidebooks. He approached a young guy with short, dark hair combed up into a spike that ran down the center of his head. He wore a tight royal blue jacket over a white shirt with jeans, which managed to both sag at his waist, but fit skin-tight around his legs like the legs on her tightest pair of skinny jeans. He had mirrored sunglasses and flashed a white grin when he spotted Jack.

Zoe got the tickets, refusing to think about money. She was at Pompeii, and she wasn't going to pass up a chance to see it.

Jack rejoined Zoe, and they moved quickly through the gates, then passed the guides hawking their individual tour services. "You found him? Nico?" Zoe asked.

"Yes. He'll be along shortly," Jack said, unfolding the map that came with the tickets. He waved toward the tall stone archway, the entrance to Pompeii. "Have at it."

*Dallas, Monday, 11:45 a.m.*

MORT LOOKED UP FROM THE file and rubbed his eyes. Sato dropped a bag onto the conference table, then flopped into the chair. "Man, I don't know why you're reading that thing again."

Mort grunted and turned a page.

Sato shrugged out of his suit coat, tossed it over the back of another chair, then removed a foot-long sandwich from the bag, placed it beside his can of Sprite, then slid the other sandwich across the table toward Mort. "Tuna. No cheese."

"Thanks. Didn't go to the mall for lunch?"

"No."

Mort sniffed. No flowery scent wreathed his partner. "How's Althea?"

"Don't know." Sato unwrapped his sandwich. "Haven't seen her in a couple of days." His phone vibrated, and Mort saw the readout on the screen—Chloe, the crime scene technician. Mort smiled as Sato grabbed the phone, then lolled back in the chair to have a conversation that wasn't related to the case at all.

Mort made a mental note to buy Jenny some Twizzlers. She was right about Sato moving on to a new girlfriend. She'd called that one. Mort chewed on his sandwich. He still couldn't believe Jenny had pulled that Vegas lead out of thin air. It almost made up for tipping off a witness who'd fled.

Sato hung-up with a satisfied smile on his face. "So, find anything new?" he asked.

"Not really." Mort picked up a piece of paper. "I don't see how two people can be so elusive. There's nothing. No credit card charges, no bank withdrawals. How are they surviving? Who's hiding them? They can't have disappeared into thin air." Sato shrugged, and Mort let out a gusty sigh before going on. "Got the info on what Andrews and the redhead did in Vegas on their last trip." After Jenny came up with the Vegas lead, he'd put out the order to run down everything on their prior trip. "Late night dinner at the Bellagio, visits to a few clubs, then—get this—they rode roller coasters on The Strip."

"Coasters?" Sato said, "Not exactly a typical date night."

"Right. But nothing about these two is typical, is it? Anyway, credit cards show an early morning breakfast at an IHOP a few blocks off The Strip, then a trip up the Eiffel Tower later that morning." Sato nodded his head, approvingly. A trip up the Eiffel Tower was more like it. "Then a stop at a jewelry counter for a 1.23 carat square princess-cut diamond ring, and on to the wedding chapel. No charges after that."

Sato laughed. "I bet not."

"That's it, except for room service and a charge at an airport restaurant." Mort tapped the thick file on Connor Freeman. "Got in a few more things on Freeman last night, too."

"More fraud?"

Mort nodded as he ate a bite of his sandwich. "Utah this time. Had a con going up there involving seniors and new siding. Went through neighborhoods posing as a city inspector and told people they weren't in compliance with a new city code. Threated a fine if they didn't get it fixed within a month. His partner came around a few days later, set up repair jobs, took deposits, then skipped town with the money."

Sato stood and used a thick marker to add the scam to the list on the whiteboard at the side of the room as Mort called out the dates and specifics. Their investigation had focused on Jack Andrews in the beginning because it was the logical place to start, but as the information began to roll in, they found that Connor Freeman had many more brushes with the law. Sato capped the pen, then stood there tapping it against the palm of his hand. "So what have we got?"

He stepped away from the whiteboard. "Connor Freeman grew up in Vegas with his single mom, stayed there, even after she moved on. Had a couple of breaking-and-entering charges on his record. We've got several complaints against him in Vegas, a few in surrounding states. And on the other side, Andrews looks like a boy scout. Not even a parking ticket on his record."

"Let's stay on Freeman. All the jobs were low profile cons," Mort said.

"Nothing of this magnitude," Sato agreed, swirling the pen in the direction of the stacks of paper that had accumulated on the conference room table, all related to their current case.

Mort leaned back in his chair. "Local, short term, and not very imaginative. In other words, small time. How did he go from small time cons to such an elaborate job?"

"And why the change in territory? Why Dallas?" Sato asked. "Maybe he met someone who hooked him up?" Sato speculated.

"With enough cash to fund GRS as a start-up and set him up in here in the huge house?" Mort looked doubtful.

"Yeah, unlikely," Sato agreed. "Maybe Freeman had been planning this con all along? Saving up from the small cons to fund his big one, the one that would be big enough to fund his retirement," Sato said, making quotes in the air when he said the word retirement.

"You ever known a thrifty con man?" Mort asked.

Sato shook his head. "Then what? How did they get together?"

Mort selected a file from the stack and flipped it open. "Their secretary states Jack Andrews had the idea for a green tech recycling business that would outsource the recyclables from large companies in an environmentally-conscious way. He went to Vegas for a trade show, met Connor Freeman, who agreed to back the company as long as he became a partner."

Sato had returned to the table and was eating his sandwich. He opened a bag of Sun Chips. "So maybe Jack Andrews was the patsy?" Sato said the words slowly, trying out the idea.

"It's feasible," Mort said. "He caught on to the scam and took Freeman out, then took the money?"

"Possible. Any word on the money trail?"

"Nope. The tech guys are working on tracking it—everything is electronic now—but they haven't got anything yet," Mort said, waving off the bag of chips Sato had tilted toward him.

A woman opened the conference room door and leaned in, "Mort, the Frisco Police have a man in custody who says he knows something about the Freeman case."

X

SAMMY DOVITZ HAD TURNED EIGHTEEN four months ago and sat alone in the small room on the other side of the two-way glass, hands clasped calmly despite the handcuffs on his wrists, but his left heel jittered below the table. If Mort had seen him on the street, he wouldn't have pegged him as a thief. He was a clean-cut kid with short blond-brown hair, big dark eyes, and slightly uneven teeth. A chain link pattern was tattooed slightly above his collarbone and he wore a diamond stud in one earlobe.

"Caught him leaving a house near the Sweetbriar Mall with two laptops. He had jewelry, two hunting rifles, and other electronics in his car." The officer handed a file to Sato, who passed it on to Mort. "Picked him up a few months ago, same situation, he got probation, on account of his age—first offense—but I don't think it'll be so easy for him this time, and it seems there's a certain person in prison he's anxious to avoid. He's hoping to cut a deal."

"Let's see what he has to say," Sato said and pushed through the door. The officer held the door open for Mort to follow.

"Thanks, but I'm good here," he said, waving the officer off.

The door closed, and Mort skimmed the file then turned up the audio, catching Sato in mid-sentence. "...that's it. I can't promise you anything. I have to hear what you have to say."

Sammy stared at Sato for a long moment, and then seemed

to come to a decision. "Okay, last week on Monday my friend Rick calls me. He's got someone who needs help with a job. Something easy. 'Cake,' he says." Mort watched the kid's face change. His air of forced unconcern broke and he laughed. "*Worst job ever* is more like it."

"So you took the job," Sato prompted.

Sammy's shoulder moved up a few millimeters. "I say sure, put me in touch, but this guy, he doesn't want to talk on the phone. I'm supposed to meet him at the Mobil station on Hickory by the Denny's at six in the morning on Tuesday." He reached up to rub his neck, but the handcuffs caught his hand and he stopped mid-motion. Sato didn't interrupt, which Mort thought was a good thing. "So I show up. There's an old, short guy waiting out by the air pump. He gives me an address, says there's a handgun in the attic crawlspace above the upstairs master bath. Get it and bring it to him at the next address he'll give me."

"Where was the first address?"

"Vinewood. Two story on Red Fern Way. I can show you," he said.

"Later," Sato said, motioning for him to continue. Mort could see Sammy's whole leg bouncing, tremors from the movement running all the way up the kid's collar. "So I did it. There was a—" he checked his language with a quick glance at Sato, "a woman home. No one told me there'd be someone home. She must have been one of those home office people because all she did was sit in her kitchen and type. I kept thinking she'd leave, but she didn't. Rick kept calling me. Telling me to get it done, that the old dude was gonna freak if I didn't get that gun. So I broke in, got the gun, and got outta there."

"The woman didn't know you were there? She didn't hear you?"

Sammy looked offended. "Course not." He opened his

mouth to say something, then quickly shut it. Mort grinned, sure that the kid was going to say he was good, a professional.

"So you got the gun," Sato said, "Then what?"

"I go to the next address, some office complex. Rick isn't there, but the old dude is. I hand off the gun. I'm ready to leave—only the guy won't pay me. Says he's got to do something first. Tells me to wait in the parking lot in his car and tell him if a guy in a blue Accord drives up. So I do it." He threw one hand up. The cuff yanked on his wrist. "I wasn't leaving without payment. So he goes into the office and comes out a couple of minutes later."

"Anyone show up?"

"Not that I could tell. It started raining, and I could barely see through the windshield. Anyway, as soon as he gets back in the car, a blue Honda parks beside us and the old guy tenses up and watches the driver. A tall guy—young, too. Around twenty-five or so with dark hair." Sammy swallowed. "The old guy got a look on his face…it was weird, man, the way he watched him. Creeped me out. So I tell him I want my money, but he says one more thing—help him knock out the guy who just went in the office. He had some story about how there was a ton of cash in the safe, but it was a special lock, and only that guy who went inside had it. Just knock him out and he'd split the cash with me."

Sammy paused, shook his head a fraction. "Anyway, I believed him. I thought he was going to stiff me on the job and the thought of more money—well, I did it. He went in the front, and I went in the back window. When I got in there, they were struggling. I hit the man with the dark hair on the back of the head with the fire extinguisher. Knocked him out cold." He stopped, leaned over the table, his hands curling into fists. "That's when I saw the other man."

# CHAPTER EIGHTEEN

*Dallas, Monday, 2:17 p.m.*

"WHO DID YOU SEE?" SATO asked.

"The man with a bullet hole in his head." Sammy reared back, his hands cutting through the air as far as the cuffs allowed, palms down, fingers splayed. "That was it for me. I was done. I don't do that."

"What?" Sato asked.

"Kill people. That's what the old dude was setting up. He was gonna prop the dark-headed guy up in his office chair while he was out, then shoot him, set it up to look like a suicide."

"You know this how?"

"Because he told me. He wanted me to help him move the dark-headed guy. I said no. I was outta there, but he said I was already involved. Better to make it clean, finish the job, that way it wouldn't come back on me. I told him I didn't care. I was gone. When I made a move for the door, the dark-headed guy on the floor...kinda, well, exploded. He moved fast. He knocked the gun out of the old dude's hand and hit me in the face," he said, lifting his chin, showing a purple bruise on the underside. "I went down. I don't know how long I was out—a couple of minutes, maybe?—but when I came to, the guy with the dark hair who'd been on the floor was gone, and the old dude was laid out on the floor beside me. I left before he woke up."

Sato sat back, his arms crossed over his chest. "That's quite a story."

"It's true," Sammy said. "Every word."

"Oh, we'll check it out. Every word." Sato flipped back a few pages in his notebook. "Okay. Let's clarify a few things. This Rick got a last name?"

"Sure. Smith."

"Really?"

"Yeah. At least that's what he calls himself. Works out of a warehouse over in Fort Worth."

"Okay. We'll come back to that," Sato said. "Describe the old dude. You said he was short…"

"Yeah, he didn't come up to my chin. Maybe five-three. He had thin brown hair. It was cut short. He was medium size—not skinny, but not massive, either. Bit of a belly. Black eyes."

"What was he wearing?"

"Ah…black. Black windbreaker kind of thing, but heavy. Black pants."

"Age?"

The corners of Sammy's mouth turned down. "I don't know. Fifty? Sixty?"

"Anything else about him that stands out? Scars, tattoos, that sort of thing?"

"Nah, nothing like that. He had some kind of accent. I don't know what kind. He didn't say anymore than he had to."

"Alright," Sato said, leaning back in his chair. "We've got a short, old guy. Maybe fifty, maybe sixty in dark clothes with an accent." Sato sighed, shook his head. "I don't know, that's not much to go on. You told me a really interesting story, but there's not much there we can use."

"You want to know who he was working with?"

"How would you know that?"

"He left his cell phone in his car when he went inside the office the first time. I got all his recent calls saved in my phone. I ain't no dummy. I gotta look out for myself, man, 'cause no one else is looking out for me."

*Pompeii, Monday, 4:30 p.m.*

"SO AMAZING," ZOE SAID, STOPPING in her tracks to admire a fresco with a rich gold background. They were inside one of Pompeii's more luxurious homes, walking along an arcade surrounding an open courtyard area at the center of the home. In the fresco, a figure of a young man in a toga was seated on a chair reading. "It's so realistic. Look at how they captured the contours of the face and arms and the sagging cloth. Hard to believe this was painted hundreds of years before the Renaissance. That's Menander, a poet. The house is named for him," Zoe said.

"Of course, I'm sure his exposed chest has nothing to do with your admiration," Jack said.

"No more than yours of the Venus we saw in the other house. Oh look, more baths," she said with delight.

"More mosaics," Jack said and followed her into the doorway of the room with impossibly small tiles covering the floor.

"I love the mosaics," Zoe said.

"I know. I can tell," Jack said, adjusting the strap of his backpack on his shoulders.

"You have to admit they're amazing, too. Maybe even more amazing than the frescos. They have the same depth and look so realistic, but they're made with tiny tiles. It's amaz—"

"Amazing," Jack finished for her.

"Do you have a better word?" Zoe asked as they left the house and returned to the elevated sidewalk that ran along each side of the street paved in rounded cobblestones.

"Yes. Food."

"That does sound good."

"There's a restaurant back near the Forum." As they retraced their steps, Zoe realized how tired she was. They'd walked all over the city. It was much larger than she'd expected. Street after street with crumbling rock walls of what had once been homes and street-front businesses extended around them on the careful grid of the typical Roman city plan. They had seen the beautifully proportioned semi-circular theater, the temples, the city's Forum, and the impressive amphitheater, which grass and moss seemed to be reclaiming. But the parts Zoe liked best were the examples of everyday life that she saw as they trooped through the streets.

They passed what had once been a bakery with huge hourglass shaped millstones and a half-circle opening of a brick oven that looked like if you fired it up, you could cook a pizza right then. Another turn and they passed what would have been a restaurant with counters right on the sidewalk with hollowed out pits to keep large cauldrons of food warm. "The Roman version of McDonald's," Jack quipped.

"I wish it was open," Zoe said.

Zoe had expected for there to be the equivalent of museum guards posted on every corner, keeping a watchful eye on the tourists. It was an open-air museum, after all. But there was nothing like that. She saw a few video cameras, but they mostly had free reign and were able to wander in and out of houses, stores, even clamber up crumbling staircases to non-existent second stories.

A few areas were gated off, like the one they were approaching, the area with some of the casts of human bodies. Protected by iron gates, the figures sat mixed in with other finds in an open-air storage facility. Intermingled with fountains, slabs of marble, and endless rows of pots, were the plaster figures that the first archeologists made as they excavated. Some figures were lying flat; others were twisted and crouched, obviously trying to escape the ash and fumes that had covered the city. Zoe thought the saddest one was a figure sitting on the ground, knees in the air, hands covering its face.

"Wretched, isn't it?" Jack said.

"Exactly what I was thinking," Zoe said. "It's easy to get lost in the history here—the beautiful art, the ability to walk around a first century city—and forget that thousands of people died here…in hours," Zoe said, glancing into the distance where Mt. Vesuvius was clearly visible, dark against the blue sky.

Zoe felt a presence behind them. Too close. Jack pivoted on his heel, his arms tensed, then stopped. "Nico."

It was the guy Jack had bought the guidebook from earlier, looming close to Zoe. "Who's this?" Nico asked smoothly in English. He'd lost the jacket and looked Zoe over in a way that made her wish she were wearing another layer or two.

"A friend," Jack said, tightly.

"Does this friend have a name?" Nico asked, gazing at Zoe intently.

"I'm Zoe," she said, extending her hand. Nico clasped it and raised it to his lips. "I hope you will be my…friend, too," he said as he deposited a lingering, sloppy kiss on the back of her hand. Jack rolled his eyes.

Zoe worked her hand free of his clamp-like grip, studying Nico's face. He couldn't be much more than seventeen or eighteen. Just to make his day, Zoe said, "How charming." Nico's grin widened, and he shifted, placing his arm around Zoe's shoulders. "You must help me with my English. I need practice."

"Your English is excellent," Zoe said, and Nico stood a little straighter.

"It is the special words, the…how do you say…idioms I need help with. Like 'head over heels.' What does that mean?"

Jack wedged himself between them, breaking them apart. "Here's an idiom for you: cut to the chase."

"This one I know," Nico said excitedly, as Jack moved them away from the knots of people looking at the casts and into an open area between the Forum and the Temple of Apollo, where a lone remaining statue of Apollo stood, arm extended. All that remained of the temple were the brick-fronted steps leading up to a raised platform with a few columns rising in the air, which were surrounded by tourists, alternately consulting maps and taking pictures. "It means to get to the important thing."

"Yes," Jack said approvingly. "And the main reason you're here…"

"To meet your beautiful friend," Nico said, with a lingering glance at Zoe. She couldn't suppress a smile as Nico caught sight of Jack's face and quickly added, "and to tell you about Costa. What you've heard is true…he is gone. Vanished. Into the skinny air."

"Into thin air," Jack corrected, slightly deflated at the news.

"Into *thin* air," Nico repeated. "People say he is in South America, Brazil, even India."

"Are you sure he's not still involved with things here in Naples?"

"No, not here," Nico said, and there was none of the teasing, playfulness in his tone that had been so evident before. "If he was here, I would know. Even if he wasn't here, but was controlling things, I would know."

Jack camouflaged his sigh. Nico missed it, but Zoe was aware of it. Jack slipped Nico some folded bills, and Nico managed to kiss Zoe's hand again before Jack waved him off and he melted into the crowds. He didn't go in the direction of the entrance-slash-exit, Zoe noticed, but she figured with a site as large as Pompeii and someone as wily as Nico, there were probably lots of ways to get in and out without going through the main gates.

"Is that true," Zoe asked as they walked slowly toward the restaurant. "Would he know if Costa were still here or still in control of things?"

"Undoubtedly. He's such a good asset because he plays the clown so well. His family is one of the best-connected in Naples. He'd know."

"So, then Roy was right."

"It appears so," Jack said as they stepped inside the restaurant with crusty sandwiches and pizza slices dripping with mozzarella cheese on display. With the distraction of Nico gone, Zoe's hunger came roaring back. While they were waiting in line, Zoe asked. "Nico—he was one of yours?"

"Did I recruit him? Yes. One of my first."

"I think you did good." Their turn came and Zoe pointed out which pizza slice she wanted then left Jack to pay, saying, "I think I'll wash my well-kissed hand."

※

THE return drive through Naples was again a trip Zoe thought better suited to bumper cars or a dirt track speedway. They parked in a different parking garage, and Zoe dug her nails out of the dash, then they walked to the Piazza dei Martiri, which seemed to be the Napoli equivalent of Fifth Avenue with designer stores ringing the piazza. Zoe spotted the names Ferragamo and Gucci as they found a table at a restaurant with several rows of tables outside. The restaurant had a view of the column at the center of the piazza, which was topped with a statue of a winged angel in a flowing gown. Their espresso arrived in miniature cups along with a plate of pastries. "Try these," Jack said pointing to a pastry curved like a tiny conch shell with golden ridges. It was flaky on the outside, but creamy on the inside with a twinge of cinnamon.

"That's so good," Zoe said. "What is it?"

"Sfogliatella. Ricotta cheese with cinnamon."

"I love it…and it's not even chocolate." They polished off the last of the delicate morsels in silence. Zoe sipped the strong coffee. The sun was almost down, and the lights from the stores glowed in the twilight.

She took another sip and watched Jack scan the piazza, eyeing the strolling pedestrians, the speeding scooters, and the people seated at the small tables around them, who all seemed to be either leaning forward over the table, gesturing theatrically as they talked or busy smoking cigarettes. "So you lived here over a year…and you never mentioned it," Zoe said, her head tilted to one side.

He rotated his small coffee cup. "I learned it's easier not to say anything at all. You mention something, even a throwaway comment, and it draws attention. People want to know more. It was easier to never mention it in the first place."

"I can't imagine doing that—editing everything I said. I'd be terrible—" she broke off. "There's Roy." He was striding quickly across the piazza, directly toward them. He didn't make eye contact.

He circled the column, which was enclosed with a raised grassy area ringed with low hedges that surrounded four massive lion sculptures placed around the base of the column like the directional points of a compass. Roy wore a long dark overcoat and Zoe lost him for a second in the crowds. Jack had been right. Everyone, except Nico it seemed, dressed in black, gray, or brown. She picked him up again as he paused near the statue of a snarling lion. He dipped his head, cupped his hand to his face, lit a cigarette and walked on, never glancing at their table.

Jack checked his watch. "That's not good, is it?" Zoe said, watching Roy's dark shoulders meld with the crowd going up the short street to the waterfront.

"No. Not good at all. It means we're blown."

# CHAPTER NINETEEN

*Naples, Monday, 7:31 p.m.*

Z OE STOOD AND MOVED SWIFTLY through the tables. She didn't look back. She knew Jack would be right behind her. "Parking garage?" Zoe asked as he fell into step with her. They circled around the far side of the piazza, moving in a different direction from Roy. "Did you leave anything at the hotel?" Jack asked. He'd brought his backpack with him and it was on his shoulder now. "The rolling bag is there, but there's nothing in it except clothes."

"No...I have my messenger bag," Zoe said automatically, as she opened the flap and shifted its contents. "I have every—" She stopped and locked on his gaze. "The spreadsheets. We left them on the foot of your bed."

Without a word, they took off at a speed only a notch below running. Everyone seemed to be either on a leisurely stroll, arms linked with a companion, as they walked their dogs or window-shopped. They shifted and dodged until Jack grabbed her arm and pulled her into a narrow street. "Short cut," he said and Zoe could tell they were moving up a street parallel to the one where their hotel was located—at least she thought that was the way they were moving because of the steep grade.

Jack zigged to the left down a short street and around a mass of mopeds, all parked at odd angles in a small triangular area where three streets met. She caught up with him. "Where will we go after the hotel?"

Jack opened his mouth, then stopped and shook his head. "Not sure. Let's get out of here clean first."

"Here it is," Zoe said, recognizing the street from the dusty pink building on the corner with a peeling Yoda poster. They turned and halted. A blue and white car with the word Polizia on the side filled the street, leaving no room for a car to pass in the other direction. Among the people mingling around the hotel entrance, Zoe spotted several blue-uniformed men with white hats. She recognized one of the civilians, the young man with curly black hair and liquid dark eyes who'd been on duty as the desk clerk when they'd left this morning. He caught sight of her, and Zoe stared at him unable to look away. "No, no, no," she whispered as she reached out blindly and touched Jack's arm. The clerk raised his arm, pointed their direction. White hats spun toward them.

Zoe turned and fled back the way they'd come. She heard Jack's breathing behind her, but she didn't spare a second to look as they took the turn to the steep street that would take them down to the Via Chiaia and the pedestrian crowds there. They hit the corner and Zoe lengthened her stride, glad for the flat ground and even paving stones. She concentrated on weaving through the crowds, sliding left and right.

Ahead of them, a terrier on a leash leapt daintily out of a small doorway within a doorway, his leash stretching out across the pedestrian walkway at knee level as his owner lingered inside the midget-sized cut-away doorway in the imposing sixteen-foot double doors of the building.

Zoe veered left around the dog, who perked up his ears at her pounding footsteps. Jack hurdled the leash. Several white hats bobbed in his wake. The dog bounded after Jack, his barks echoing up the narrow space between the tall buildings. With a quick glance behind her, Zoe saw the dog reach the end of its leash with an abrupt yank. It immediately reversed course and made for the pursuing policemen, yapping away. Two of them got tangled in the leash and went down hard, the dog skipping away, then circling back to bark and lick. The wails of distinctly European emergency sirens filled the air.

Two policemen still pounded behind them, shouting words Zoe didn't understand. It was fully dark now, but she could see the end of the pedestrian area ahead where the street opened up into an intersection with traffic swishing by, headlights cutting through the night.

Zoe and Jack shot out of the pedestrian street, sending a waiter, who had been walking along the street holding a covered circular tray with several drinks, spinning like a top. They burst into an intersection with traffic circling the roundabout, which enclosed a fountain at the center of the intersection. Zoe saw pulsating blue lights atop several approaching cars straight ahead. Jack's hand closed around her wrist and pulled her to the left. "This way."

They ran, angling their shoulders, pushing through the crowds. Suddenly, Jack ducked off the main street and they were in a small market area with vendors hawking jackets and jewelry under plastic awnings. The shouts weren't that far away as they slipped into another narrow alley, then zigged and zagged through the labyrinth-like maze of streets.

They followed one street until it curved abruptly into a dead end with several apartment buildings and a pile of trash overflowing several dumpsters that were as tall as Zoe.

"Damn," Jack said, turning back. "We're going to have to stay with the larger streets. I don't know my way around well enough to get through these small roads."

Zoe didn't want to go backward, but she really didn't want

to hide in the garbage pile, either. They retraced their steps as best they could through the snaking streets. With every corner, Zoe braced herself, expecting to find the Polizia, but they only came across moped drivers with death wishes and people who seemed to be interested in getting to the local café for a pre-dinner drink.

Zoe heard the sound of traffic and saw bright lights, signaling they were close to a major street. They emerged onto the same busy street they'd been on a few moments ago, the Via Toledo, Zoe saw, locating an Italian street sign, a stucco plaque on one of the buildings with the street name carved into it.

A siren grew louder as a blue car with flashing blue lights crept down the street. The officer in the window scanned faces on the street. Zoe instinctively turned away, saw a table at one of the sidewalk cafés was open, and dropped into the chair, pulling Jack down into the chair beside her. She felt too exposed, too vulnerable, standing up. At least here they were hidden behind layers of other diners at the café.

"Good idea to stop running," Jack said, placing his backpack under the table at his feet. He hunched over the table, one hand propped on his cheek, shielding his face from the street. Zoe found the hair clip in her messenger bag and secured her hair in a loose knot on her head, then shoved her bag under the table. "It seemed better than walking along the main road," she said choppily, her breath coming out in rough gasps. She pulled off her jacket and stuffed it in the messenger bag, ducking down as the waiter came and Jack ordered two coffees. Short of buying new clothes, she'd done all she could to change her appearance.

"Caffeine is the last thing I need right now," Zoe said. Her fingers were visibly trembling. She splayed them on the cool metal of the table. Two uniformed police officers trotted by, their gaze sifting through the pedestrians strolling along the street. Zoe watched Jack, not wanting to look their way. He shot a quick glance over his shoulder, and then said, "They're gone," before taking a sip of his coffee that had arrived.

Zoe brought the cup to her lips, but couldn't manage a drink. Another siren approached as she set the cup in its saucer. "Carabinieri," Zoe breathed, taking in the dark blue car.

"They probably have nothing to do with us. Probably going to dinner," Jack said. "They're notorious for that here—using their sirens just to get through traffic when there's no emergency at all."

Two more dark cars marked Carabinieri pulled to a stop at the curb. Four men in their distinctive dark blue uniforms with red stripes down the outside of the pant leg, emerged and fanned out, two men on each side of the street.

"Or maybe it does have something to do with us," Zoe said.

Jack kept his eyes on his small coffee cup as one of the Carabinieri, hands clasped together behind his back, strolled along the front row of café tables. Zoe developed an interest in her fingernails. She noticed in a disassociated way that she could really use a manicure. Jack leaned over, gripped her hand tightly and said, "Wait here. I'll be right back."

He slipped away before she could protest or gather her messenger bag and follow him. Out of the corner of her eye, she watched the dark pants with the red stripe move methodically through the crowd. She took a sip of her coffee, and then set it down quickly. Her heart rate was already equal to a hummingbird's—there was no way she needed to up it anymore. A second Carabinieri officer joined the first one. They settled into the middle of the small enclave of shops and restaurants, watching the constantly moving crowds. Every time their gaze ranged around to the café tables, she tensed, ready to sprint. *Where was Jack?* She couldn't believe he'd gone off and left her. *When would he be back?* A thought struck her and she almost growled. *He better come back. If he'd pulled another disappearing act…*

She was busy cataloguing the various tortures she'd put him through when he sat down across from her. He slapped some change on the table. "Let's go," he said.

"Where were you?"

He looked up, perplexed at the fierceness of her tone. "I went to buy bus tickets," he said, nodding his head at the Tabacchi, a small shop that sold cigarettes, bus tickets, and phone cards.

Zoe set him an exasperated look. "Why didn't you say so? I didn't think you were coming back."

"You thought I'd left you?"

"It has happened before."

"Touché," Jack said. "Sorry that I didn't explain, but time is critical here."

"Okay," Zoe said. "I get it. Just don't do it again."

"Fine. There's our bus," Jack said. "Let's walk calmly to it."

It turns out they could have jogged across the sidewalk area and shoved their way into the bus—all the Neapolitans did. They sauntered so casually by the Carabinieri that they almost didn't get inside the bus. Zoe managed to slip under a man's elbow and Jack muscled his way in behind her. The doors closed and Zoe looked down at her feet as the bus lurched away from the curb under the watchful gaze of the Carabinieri.

※

THEY got off the bus at the train station, along with almost every other bus rider. They moved down a long row of buses to a glass-fronted building with a McDonald's sign blazing in one corner. Once inside, they made for the ticket counters. "I wish we could use a credit card," Zoe said biting her lip as she looked at the automatic ticket dispensing machines without lines. Their line was moving at approximately one millimeter every ten minutes. "At this rate we won't get out of here until tomorrow morning," she said, shoving her hands into her pockets so that Jack wouldn't see her trembling fingers.

"Nothing we can do about it," he said calmly, so calmly that Zoe wanted to punch him. How did he do it? Sprint through a city with the police chasing him one minute, then the next minute, he stood calmly, looking unconcerned, bored even?

"So what do you think happened back there with Roy and at the hotel?" Zoe asked in a low voice.

"I don't know about Roy. Maybe he heard something through one of his friends. At least he gave us some warning or we'd be sitting in an Italian jail cell right now asking to talk to the Consulate. Not a place I want to be."

"Me either," Zoe said and shifted her feet half a baby-step forward. "So that only leaves...."

"Nico," Jack said with an unhappy sigh. "I shouldn't have contacted him. It was risky."

"Well, can't change it now. Now we just have to get out of here." Zoe rocked on her heels, still antsy but trying to fight it. "Look, a new line," she said and took off to the window that had just opened. She slid into place and looked into the bored attendant's face.

"Si?" he said.

She looked over her shoulder at Jack, who was ambling across to the new line, probably trying not to attract attention by moving too quickly. Where were they going? She'd been so glad to get to the train station she hadn't thought past getting out of Naples.

She took a deep breath, hoping that they had enough euros. "Venezia," she said.

# CHAPTER TWENTY

*Italy, Monday, 11:47 p.m.*

ZOE AWOKE WITH A START, jerking up on her elbow and looking around. Murky darkness. Rhythmic Movement. Right. Train, she realized, taking in the thin light coming in around the curtains across the panels and door that opened into the corridor that ran the length of the train. She rotated her neck, which seemed to have a permanently contracted muscle from sleeping in a half-sitting, half-slumped position. Despite the dimness, she could see that the opposite seat was empty. The woman who'd begun the journey with them in Naples must have gotten off at one of the stops. There had been a confusing train change at some station in the middle of the night. Zoe couldn't even remember where it was. She and Jack had stumbled from one train to another, and she'd pretty much collapsed into unconsciousness, relieved there hadn't been a party of Carabinieri on the platform.

A hasty check for their bags showed Jack was using them as a pillow. He'd reclined on the seat beside her, head toward the outside window, legs sprawled out, taking up most of the room. He shifted, reached out and pulled her head onto his chest. She stiffened, then relaxed. It was so much more comfortable than trying to sleep sitting up. She shifted her chin up and down, burrowing into a more comfortable position. Ten seconds and she was out.

She wasn't sure how much time had gone by when she blinked her eyes open. It was still dark. She didn't move for fear of waking Jack. His chest moved with his even breathing under her cheek. She probably could have stood up and sung a complete rendition of the Copacabana and his eyelids wouldn't have even fluttered, but she should stay still, she reasoned. It had nothing to do with how incredibly safe she felt. She snorted, thinking that was about the most absurd thought she could have.

They weren't safe. The police on two continents were pursuing them, not to mention the FBI. They'd been shot at, and they still hadn't figured out a way to make it stop or even discovered who was behind it. She was about as far from safe as she could be.

"What's funny?" Jack asked without moving.

"Nothing. You're sleeping. You didn't hear anything."

He murmured an agreement. She couldn't drift off to sleep, but stayed curled up on his chest, watching the occasional lights outside the train flick by, throwing brief strips of illumination through the chinks in the curtains.

A long time later, Jack said, "I think you'd be smart to go to the police when we get to Venice. We could come up with a little act at the train station where there are plenty of witnesses. Make it look like I kidnapped you." His voice wasn't groggy, and he spoke in a conversational tone. "Don't say anything yet. I appreciate that you've hung with me and helped me try to sort this out, but this doesn't involve you."

She heaved a sigh into the fibers of his sweater. "Do we have to do this again?"

"It's the best thing—"

"So we are having this conversation again," she said, speaking over his words. Without moving from her position curled on his chest, she said, "Right. Okay, let's take it from the top. Even if I go to the police with some story about how you coerced me into going with you from Las Vegas to Europe—and anyone who knows me would know I'd never fight anyone who wanted to take me to Europe—but, let's say I go with that story. One, I'd be in Italian custody. Not a place I want to be," Zoe said. "Two, once they found out who I was and who you were, I don't think they'd let me go easily."

"This is quite the gloomy analysis," Jack cut in.

"Now, best case scenario. The Italian officials take me in, ask a few cursory questions, and somehow I'm able to get back to the States. I don't know how I would do that—I guess I could use a credit card for an airline ticket, but I don't think my balance could handle that. But forget that tiny detail because, otherwise, I'm stuck in Italy living off scraps of pizza crusts the tourists throw away. Let's say I get back to the States. I go home. The first visitor I'll have will be the FBI. Those two guys aren't going to let up. They want to know where the money went and then—even worse—there's Connor's murder. They think I had something to do with that as well. So, to sum up, I can stay here with you and see if we can figure out why all this is happening and who's behind it, or I can possibly, maybe, if I'm lucky, return home and become a suspect in a fraud and a murder investigation."

"Always looking on the bright side, aren't you?" Jack said. "When you put it that way, my plan sounds terrible."

"Because it is," Zoe said, feeling his chest move as he chuckled.

There was a pause, then he said, his voice serious, "I appreciate that you're boxed in as far as options go, but remember, my track record isn't that great. Sticking with me may not increase your odds. I screwed up, and Francesca got killed."

"How is her death your fault?" Zoe asked. "How were you

supposed to know she was in danger? Did she suspect?"

"She was worried, nothing specific or verifiable. She thought she was followed to our last meeting. I should have brought her in right then."

"Really? What if she was wrong? Then she would really have been 'blown.' That's the right word, isn't it? If that had happened, you would have lost ...what did you call her? An asset?"

Jack rubbed his hand over his mouth, and then reluctantly said, "No I wasn't supposed to bring her in with only her intuition that something was wrong. I followed protocol, but that doesn't matter in the end. She's dead. Then, I went all in with GRS. I put everything into the business because I didn't want to mess things up again. Now I'm a failure twice over. Three times, actually, if we're counting personal and professional things, since my marriage failed, too. So, you see, staying with me might not be your smartest move."

Zoe pushed herself up and looked into his face. "You can't control everything. Even Roy said Francesca's death wasn't your fault. Yes, I overheard what he said to you. Someone talked. You couldn't control that. And GRS...well, you certainly didn't murder Connor or dupe your investors."

She leaned back to get a better look at his face in the low light. "You didn't murder him, did you?"

His bark of laughter filled the small compartment. "Thanks for the vote of confidence. For the record, no, I did not."

"I didn't think you did—really—no, really," Zoe said.

"That's comforting. Remind me to call you as a character witness at my trial."

Zoe rolled her eyes. "Really. When everything first happened, I defended you. The Jack I knew would never do something like that, but then...I realized there was a lot I didn't know about you. When I found the money and the passports, it was obvious you weren't exactly a self-employed businessman who was once a federal worker. Deep down, I didn't think you'd hurt Connor, but with all the strange revelations about your past—well, I had to ask," she said.

She felt the motion of the train change and sat up to reach over Jack and sweep the curtain away from the window. A flat, dark expanse stretched out under the black sky, but it wasn't land as she'd thought at first glance. Tiny sparkles of light flickered on the undulating surface. It was water.

"We're here," she said.

*Venice, Tuesday, 6:32 a.m.*

THEY STEPPED OUT OF THE train station into the milky light of sunrise and walked down a set of stairs to an open piazza-like area paved in cobblestones and lit with Victorian lights, each with three lights positioned like a trident. "So what are we going to do so that we don't end up eating discarded pizza crusts?" Jack asked. "Although, I do like the crust, one of my favorite parts. Wouldn't be so bad," he added philosophically.

It was overcast and drizzling and much colder than Zoe expected. She hugged her jacket closer and said, "The Street of Shops, I suppose."

"Too bad it's such a dreary day."

"Are you kidding? It's beautiful. We're in *Venice*."

The Grand Canal, murky and green-tinged, flowed in front of them. She hurried over to the edge of the open terraced area where the water slapped against the foundation. A sleek boat cut through the canal, waves fanning out behind it in a V-shape. An imposing church with columns, an ornate pediment, and a dome tinted mint-green dominated the far side of the canal. Tightly-packed buildings stretched out on each side of it in shades of cream, white, tan, red, and even lime, each with unique architecture: Moorish windows, arched colonnades, and curving wrought-iron balconies. At the waterline, boats bobbed among the tall poles, some just weathered wood, others painted and in bright curving stripes, marking the various docking points.

"We're in Venice," she breathed. "I can't believe it. We are in Venice."

"You look a little dazed." He pulled her back a step from the edge.

"Do you know how many guidebooks I've edited about Venice? Four! Two general Italy guidebooks, one Northern Italy, and one specifically on Venice. And I'm here. We have to see San Marco and the Basillica and the Doge's Palace—you'll like that. It was a prison, not just a palace...There's the vaporetto stop," Zoe said, noticing the people streaming out of the train station to a small metal building with gangplanks attached to large boats. "Let's go," she said, striding off.

"I think I've created a monster," Jack murmured under his breath as he hurried to catch up with her.

After boarding the vaporetto, a Venice version of a city bus, they cruised the Grand Canal, Zoe nearly hanging over the railing to take in the sights. She saw a boat labeled Servicio Postal, which she took to mean a mail boat. An ambulance boat floated by at a sedate pace, then there were several barge-type boats, some loaded with cardboard boxes, others with crates overflowing with produce. The sleek black gondolas were scarce at this early hour—because of the lack of rolling suitcases and cameras among the people moving around the city, Zoe guessed most of them were commuting to work.

The views of the palazzos fronting the Grand Canal were spectacular, even in their crumbling state. All that salt water seemed to do a number on the stucco surfaces and most of the buildings looked a bit ragged around the edges with flaking patches. There was an abundance of graffiti, too. Not on the scale she'd seen in Naples where no building seemed to escape the ugly scribblings, but it was evident in Venice, too. While Zoe soaked up the atmosphere of elegant decay, Jack searched the map they'd picked up at the tourist office in the train station.

As they disembarked at the San Marco stop, a blue and white Polizia Municipale boat whipped by, abruptly reminding her of reality. She was in Venice, but she was far from a tourist. They passed the colonnaded walkway of the Doge's Palace, a curious mixture of ornate archways, intricate cutouts, and restrained geometric brick patterns. Jack headed for the two towering granite columns, the one on the right topped with a winged lion and the other with a statue of a man. Behind the columns, the small piazzetta opened into the larger piazza of San Marco with its solid, square bell tower dominating the skyline.

"What's the significance of the statues, do you think?" Jack asked, his head tilting to take in the figures at the top of the columns.

"The one on the right is the Lion of St. Mark, a symbol of the city. The one on the left was the city's saint until some merchants confiscated the bones of St. Mark in Alexandria. That guy got bumped." Jack switched his gaze to her and she shrugged. "There was a sidebar about them in one of the guidebooks."

"At least he still has the top spot on the column," Jack said and resumed walking.

Zoe caught his arm and steered him to the side. "Bad luck to walk between them," she explained. "It was the site of executions and other…grisly stuff."

"Superstitious?" Jack asked.

"I figure we don't need any more bad luck coming our way. Where to?" Zoe asked when they came to the bell tower, her gaze sweeping from the horses atop the lavish entrance of St. Mark's Basilica to the cafés positioned at the opposite end of the piazza, their chairs stacked neatly away at this early hour.

"No sightseeing?"

"No," Zoe said with a sigh. "We have work to do. Besides," she grinned as she said, "everything is closed right now."

They delved into the winding streets behind the piazza and walked until they found an open café where the juice was fresh squeezed, and the small brightly colored fruit tarts mixed with flaky pastries filling the display case looked like some sort of incredible, beautiful modern art. Despite the stunning perfection the food presented, Zoe had no compunctions about gobbling it up.

"How are we doing on money?" Zoe asked, dusting away pastry flakes. She'd noticed when Jack paid for the food that his stash of euros was pretty thin.

"We're getting low—about sixty. I can probably find somewhere to pawn my watch, if we need to," he said.

Zoe fingered the chain around her neck. Below her neckline, the ring hung heavy against her chest. "There's my ring, too," Zoe said. When the divorce was final, she tried to return it to him, but he wouldn't take it.

Jack's gaze slipped to the chain at her neck, drifted lower for a second, then lazily moved back up to her face. "Let's not go to extremes yet."

She suddenly felt too warm. "So did you find the Street of Dreams—er, I mean, Shops?" Zoe asked.

"It's on the map. Shouldn't be too hard to find."

# CHAPTER TWENTY-ONE

*Venice, Tuesday, 8:37 a.m.*

"THIS PLACE LOOKS FAMILIAR," ZOE said forty-five minutes later as she glanced around the campo, a small cobblestoned square lined with shops, cafés, and stately buildings with Moorish windows. "I think I remember that green awning at the restaurant next to the gondolas."

Jack consulted the map again. "We must have taken the second street, instead of the third." He sounded a bit frustrated.

"Don't worry about it," Zoe said. "Venice is notorious for being a difficult city to navigate. We should probably just ask."

"We don't want to draw any attention to ourselves."

"Then we should buy a camera and some clothes in bright colors." The layer of clouds had burned off as the sun rose and with every minute that passed, there seemed to be exponentially more tourists wandering the city. "It really is a tourist city. It seems like almost everyone here either is a tourist or works in a tourist-related job," she said as they left the campo, or small piazza, and walked over a small arched bridge to a skinny street lined with shops. "Do you think there's some pattern to the stores? It seems to be mask, glass, leather, and paper, repeated over and over again," Zoe said, glancing into the window crammed with gaudy carnival masks in every possible shade.

"No idea," Jack said, his attention focused on the map. "Take a right here," he said, "then *left*. That's what we did wrong last time." He nodded down the tunnel-like street and said, "The Street of Shops." They meandered down the street, matching their pace to the browsing tourists.

Zoe stopped in front of an alcove set into the stucco wall. "It's the Madonna," she said, excitedly. "From Connor's pictures." Inside the pointed arch, the flat-featured mother and child looked serenely at one another. A note, a candle, and a few dried flowers rested on the ledge of the small shrine.

"Are you sure?" Jack asked.

"Yes. It's the same pose and the same background—dark blue with stars. Connor was definitely here."

They continued down the street, and even at their slow pace, they almost missed the small sign, a plaque set into the wall beside a doorway. "Wait," Zoe said, catching Jack's sleeve. "There it is, Murano Glassworks," she said coming to a stop in front of a window with several glass vases and exquisite glass sculptures on display. The interior of the shop was dark.

"Open at ten," Jack said, reading the card behind the iron bars covering the glass door.

They paced back the way they'd come and Jack pointed to a small sign for the Hotel Art Deco.

Jack stuck his head in the empty reception area. There was a wooden desk with baroque engravings atop a worn red Oriental rug, two small bentwood chairs in front of the desk, and a row of cubbyholes on the wall behind it. "No computer. Either they only keep paper records or they use a laptop that isn't here," Jack said. "I guess we'll have to ask." His tone conveyed that he'd rather be snooping through computer records.

He made a move to go inside, but Zoe said, "Let's get a picture of Connor. He may not have used his name. We can ask if anyone remembers him. I bet we can find an Internet café."

They returned to the street. "Sounds good. There's only about ten rooms, so hopefully someone will remember him."

After more walking, they found an open Internet café and used some of their dwindling euros to buy an hour's worth of Internet. Zoe went directly to the sites of the Dallas newspapers. She swallowed and shot a glance at Jack. They were front-page news. "I'd hoped that the story would have faded," Zoe said. Jack just shook his head as he said, "There's one with a picture of Connor. Print that and I'll pick it up at the front."

Biting her lower lip, Zoe skimmed through the article, then let out a whoosh of breath. "Nothing new," she informed Jack when he returned. Then read aloud, "The pair was last seen in Las Vegas. Local and federal law enforcement officials are coordinating their investigation and urge anyone with information to contact them." She turned to Jack. "Then what happened at our hotel in Naples? They knew we were there."

"Maybe they're not releasing that detail," Jack said. Zoe switched to Italian news, opened a window on a translation program and began searching news from Naples. Jack, who had been hovering over her shoulder, sighed and pulled up a chair. "What? We have time," Zoe said. "The store doesn't open for another half hour and we paid for the whole hour of Internet access." She paged through several lines of results, then clicked on a story about an incident at a hotel in the Via Chiaia area. The translation wasn't flawless, but she got the gist of the article. She twisted toward Jack. "Someone called the police and reported a bomb at the hotel in Room 12."

Jack gave the article a considering look. "That could be what the police released to the media."

"You mean that may not be what happened? Why would they lie? Why would they do that?"

"Maybe that's what they were asked to do. We've been a lot

more relaxed this morning because we think they don't know where we are. Maybe that's what they want us to think. We let our guard down, they'll catch us unaware."

Zoe glanced at the window, almost expecting to see uniformed men closing in on them. But there was no one there except a short, sixtyish Italian woman puffing away on a cigarette as she walked her Corgi and a delivery guy pushing a cart full of boxes.

"Or maybe it was a coincidence. Maybe we got caught up in some crank call," Jack said.

"I don't believe that," Zoe said.

"Me either."

"Okay, one more site," she said as she went to Jenny Singletarry's blog. She'd broken the story about the sighting of them in Vegas. Maybe she had something else. The page loaded with a picture of Connor smiling roguishly, his eyes twinkling under his blond hair. The title of the article was "Con Man."

Zoe read aloud, "Connor Freeman appeared to be a partner in a small business start-up that had beaten the odds in the sometimes brutal green industry sector, but his murder reveals that he was more con man than anything else, and his business was more a house of cards than a solid investment. A man with a shady past, he'd spent most of his life in Las Vegas, running small time scams…" Zoe quickly ran through the list of known scams Connor had pulled to the next section.

"Questions remain as to why Freeman moved his scams to Dallas and whether or not his business partner was also his partner in the GRS con, which bilked money from companies and investors, promising green recycling options, but then disposed of the products in the cheapest—and least green—way possible. Bogus press releases and chatter on trading message boards pushed the stock price up until it collapsed. Investors, who are left with huge losses after the stock bottomed out, are fearful that they will never see the return on investment they were promised."

Zoe swiveled toward Jack. "Could that be true? That GRS was a front? That's what she's saying, right?"

Jack closed his eyes for a few seconds. "I don't see how it's possible. I checked everything. I approved everything. I talked with our clients, the presidents of those companies. And our contacts overseas…I spoke to them, too."

"She has a long list of sources," Zoe said, reluctantly. The fine print, complete with lots of links was almost as long as the story. "And, Connor did have two sets of books," Zoe said, slowly. "I don't suppose it's crazy to think he could set things up to make it look like you had clients when you didn't."

Jack ran his hand down over his mouth as he shook his head. "Most of them were very hard to get in touch with. I'd call them; they'd call back and leave a message. I wrote it off… time zones, they were busy people. It was all fake," he said quietly. "A mirage."

"Not all of it," Zoe said, pointing to a paragraph. "It says there were some legitimate contracts and some recycling was done as promised last year, but then everything else…"

"Our explosive growth, our amazing rise, that was phony." Jack blew out a breath and shook his head. "It was engineered to make it seem like we were a good investment. Connor was always all about the stock. He wasn't too interested in what we actually did, just the stock price."

Jack said something under his breath, and Zoe gripped his arm. "You're not the first one to be conned and, apparently, he was really good at conning people. I never suspected he did this. I knew he was a jerk. I had him pegged on that one, but the rest…I had no idea. He'd fooled a lot of people. I'm beginning to see why someone wanted to kill him."

Jack didn't reply. His face was tight and angry as he scrolled through the article again. Zoe knew he was mentally beating himself up over the mistakes he'd made. She decided to leave him alone. Instead, she concentrated on sorting out her thoughts. Things had been moving so fast that she'd barely had time to process everything that had happened. This was the first chance she'd had to catch her breath and think.

"So, first, we assumed Connor's death was somehow related to your old job and the incident with Francesca, but Costa is deep in hiding somewhere. Retired and living the good life, probably taking senior bus trips and doing water aerobics at the local Y, at least according to two people who have connections and would know if he was involved. So we scratch him off the list and move on. You don't have any other possible personal enemies—right?"

Jack gave a little half laugh. "God, I hope not."

"Good. Okay, then back to Connor. Maybe all this is centered on Connor, and you just got caught up in it. Maybe one of the companies...."

"Unfortunately, it appears that we only had about three true clients according to this," Jack said throwing his hand at the computer in disgust.

"Did any of the people who ran the companies seem like the type who'd...do something drastic if they found out about the fraud?"

"No, these are legitimate businesspeople we're talking about. They're into profit and loss, stock ratios, stuff like that. And lawyers," he added. "They'd sue us before they'd try to kill us."

Zoe leaned back in her chair, arms crossed, and looked thoughtfully at the ceiling. "Then one of the investors?"

Jack focused on the table. "I don't think so, mostly because of the timing." He angled the keyboard toward him and brought up a financial website. He typed in the code for GRS stock and looked at the last few weeks. "No, everything looked great, spectacular even, right up until the day Connor was murdered. Our stock was rising steadily, goosed on by fake press releases," Jack said, running his hand over his mouth.

"According to the article on that blog, Connor spent quite a bit of time on financial message boards talking the stock up, too."

"Right, but the stock price didn't begin to fall until after Connor died. It looks like it's bottomed out," he paused and swallowed as if it were painful for him to even say the rest of the sentence, "at seventeen cents. Even if an investor suspected something, the stock didn't go down until after Connor died. No, I don't think it was a disgruntled investor."

"And killing Connor and framing you wouldn't solve the problem of their lost investment," Zoe said.

"That's the other portion of this equation—the money. Where is it?"

Zoe spread her hands. "I don't know the first thing about tracking missing money."

Jack said, "I'm sure the FBI is tracking that. If there's a way to find out where it went, they'll uncover it."

"So that leaves us with...no money and no suspects?" Zoe said, a feeling of gloom sweeping over her.

"About right."

"There has to be a reason for all this. It wasn't random," Zoe said, straightening her back, determination returning. "We still don't know what Connor was doing here in Venice. Let's run that down and see what we find out. Maybe that will answer our questions."

"It's all we have left."

# CHAPTER TWENTY-TWO

"I'LL BE FINE," ZOE SAID, placing her hand firmly on Jack's shoulder as he rose to follow. She pushed him back down into the chair at the café table. "Only one of us should go. Two people will stand out more, and it's better if she only sees one of us. That way, if the police question her later...if they track down where we went, she'll only have seen me."

"If you're not back in five minutes, I'm coming in."

"Fine. Just don't be early."

Zoe squared her shoulders and tried not to look anxious as she crossed the campo to the hotel on The Street of Shops. She gripped the photo in her hand and stepped into the tiny room that served as the hotel lobby. A woman in her twenties with a beaky nose and frizzy golden hair in a halo around her head sat behind the desk.

"Buon giorno. English?" Zoe asked.

Zoe thought the young woman's sharp nod didn't bode well for potential information gathering. Zoe held out the picture of Connor, but the woman kept her clasped hands together on the desk. She seemed to be all business.

"Have you seen this man? He's gone. Just up and left," Zoe said. It was true. Connor was gone. He wasn't ever coming back.

The woman looked at the picture for a long moment, her lips clamped together. Zoe had to get something from this woman, she thought, quickly looking over the desk. There was now a laptop among the papers and, if she knew Jack, his next suggestion would be to get a look at the laptop. Zoe didn't want to do that—look what had happened last time they'd tried to look at someone's computer. Surely, she could convince this woman to help her? The blond had unclasped her hands and was now tapping a pen against a stack of papers impatiently.

"I'm sorry to take up your time, but if you could help me out, I'd really appreciate it." Still no change in her facial expression. Zoe was seriously beginning to wonder if the woman spoke English at all. "He was supposed to be somewhere else, but I found his travel plans, and he's been here—a lot." She stumbled on, thinking of everything that had happened in the last few days, she let the horror of finding a dead body, the questioning by the police and the feds, the thought that Jack was dead, the fear that had raced through her when Stubby Guy shot at her...she let her emotions surface and felt her throat go scratchy and her vision blur slightly. She sniffed, trying to get herself back under control. She couldn't completely lose it here in front of this cold stranger.

"You should sit," the woman said as she yanked opened a sticky drawer, pulled several tissues out, and handed them to Zoe.

As Zoe leaned forward to sit down, the ring she wore on the chain slipped over the neckline of her shirt and swung free. Zoe took the tissue and wiped her eyes while the woman stared at the ring for a moment. Then she abruptly held out her hand for the picture. Zoe handed it over.

"Because I hate cheating bastards, I will help you," she said. She gave the picture a quick glance. "Yes. He was here. Several times. Signor Johnson. He comes, stays in Room Eight, always alone. He does not meet anyone here or bring back anyone," she said, and Zoe was surprised to see a trace of compassion in her face. "That is all I know."

It wasn't much, but it was confirmation that he'd stayed there. "Room Eight? Do you think I could see it?" Zoe asked, wondering if that was pressing her luck, but the woman glanced at the cubbyholes behind her and gave a very Gallic shrug. She pulled the key out of the slot, and Zoe quickly followed her to a narrow staircase. "Is broken," she said, gesturing at the elevator that looked big enough for either one skinny pre-adolescent or two emaciated runway models.

As they stepped onto the third floor, the top floor, she said, "He was a strange one, always in his room. I asked him if he saw the basilica or the palace, and he said, 'no time.' Why come to Venice to sit in a room?" She shook her head at the incomprehensible Americano.

She unlocked the door and stepped back. Zoe entered, glanced around, and thought that asking to see the room had been a stupid idea. There was nothing to see. Connor hadn't been here in weeks—what was the last date? Two or three weeks ago? The room had been cleaned and probably occupied by several other tourists during that time. The room had dark exposed beams on the ceiling, a carved armoire, and a delicate Venetian glass chandelier, all beautifully kept and perfectly clean. There wasn't even a tissue in the trashcan in the white-tiled bath.

"It's charming," Zoe said as she moved to the room's window. The floor was high enough to give an excellent view of the faded orange roofs interspersed with domes and bell towers. Her gaze dropped lower, and she realized she was also high enough to see over the burgundy awning at the hotel's doorway. In fact, she had an excellent view down the Street of Shops and could see the front door of Murano Glassworks. Zoe stepped away from the window. "He asked for this room, especially?"

"Si, always," she said.

✗

JACK WAS WALKING TOWARD THE hotel when Zoe emerged from the doorway. She quickly paced over to him, threaded her arm through his. "Connor stayed there," she said, her voice excited. "He specifically asked for Room Eight." She paused when they were far enough down the street to get a good view of the whole street. She studied the hotel's façade for a moment, then said, "It's the only room with a clear view of Murano Glassworks. The other rooms are either too low or the view is blocked by the hotel's awning or the sign for the trattoria," she said glancing up at the sign for the Trattoria da Lucia.

"You got into the room?" Jack asked, surprised.

"Yes, the desk clerk doesn't like cheating bastards, which is what I let her think Connor was." Zoe tilted her head. "Actually, he was a cheating bastard, just not in the area she thought. Anyway, the woman said he always asked for that specific room, and he never met anyone at the hotel or brought anyone back. He didn't go out to sightsee. He spent most of the time in his room."

"Watching Murano Glassworks, you think?"

"What else could he be doing?"

They both looked toward the store, which now had the door propped open. A man emerged and walked in the opposite direction. Jack tensed as Zoe said, "Hey, that was Stubby Guy."

"Your turn to wait at the café," Jack said, handing her some euros from his pocket.

"But—"

"One person attracts less attention," Jack said, already moving away across the cobblestones.

"I hate it when my own reasoning comes back to bite me," Zoe said under her breath. Jack disappeared around the corner. Zoe's glance pinged between the café on the campo and the glass shop. It really was no contest. She wasn't thirsty. She wanted to shop, specifically at Murano Glassworks. She knew Jack would not be happy, but she gave a mental shrug and headed for the shop. She'd just take a quick look around.

A bell over the door jingled as she stepped inside. The thin sunlight lit up the door and display window, but once she'd moved a few steps into the shop, it was much dimmer and cooler. The shop was fairly small, about ten square feet. The richness of the decoration made Zoe think it must have been part of a larger palazzo that had been divided into shops. The lower portions of the walls were paneled in a rich, dark wood. The floor was a terrazzo mosaic in shades of pink, cream, white, and gold with a compass rose at the center. A pink all-glass chandelier with gold leaf accents hung suspended from the coved ceiling. The chandelier had been converted to electricity. Modern light bulbs glowed from plastic candle-shaped holders. Exquisite glass displays ranged around the room: bowls in pale pastels, vases in brilliant bursts of primary colors, even figurines in the shapes of horses, flowers, and fish. A counter at the back of the room showed off jewelry in bright colors. A very modern cash register and credit card machine sat atop the counter at the back of the room. Beyond the counter, a door stood open, revealing a large dark-paneled corridor.

The shop was empty, so Zoe strolled carefully among the glass. She tucked her messenger bag close and stepped cautiously, afraid that if she bumped something and broke it, she'd never be able to pay for it. A price tag peeped out from behind a translucent pale blue bowl with a fluted edge. One hundred-twenty-nine euro. She didn't need to do the currency conversion to know that she couldn't afford to break anything.

Zoe edged her way through the tables and shelves for a few minutes, but no one arrived to mind the store. She'd assumed they had a closed circuit camera somewhere and were monitoring the room, but maybe not. She browsed carefully through the displays. Why would Connor care about this shop and all this glass? She hadn't seen anything like the decorative glass in his apartment or his house in Dallas. He didn't seem the type to collect *objet d'art* either. She stopped at the back of the store at a small table covered with the round paperweights filled with millefiori.

These paperweights were exactly like the ones Connor had insisted GRS give to clients. She picked one up. The rounded glass magnified the intricate designs captured inside. She turned it over. A green felt pad covered the bottom, but unlike the GRS promotional paperweights, this one didn't have the GRS logo and contact information on it. She put it back, eyeing the white boxes on the table, which contained more paperweights.

She'd also seen them in Eddie's store in Vegas as well as Connor's apartment. A cardboard box half filled with the white paperweight boxes was shoved partially under the table. It looked as if someone had been unpacking the box and been interrupted. Some of the square white boxes that filled the interior were piled on the floor. Each white box, the perfect size to hold one paperweight snuggly was topped with a black stamp of the winged lion.

Stacks of the small boxes lined the back of the table, stock to move to the front of the table as the paperweights sold, Zoe assumed. She scanned across the pristine imprints of the winged lions, each figure crisp and sharp, except for one. It was in the cardboard box at her feet. The smudged outline stood out sharply among the other perfect imprints.

Connor had a box of these paperweights at his apartment. She remembered looking at it as she explored his place and thinking it odd that he'd had some delivered there. GRS didn't have any clients in Vegas—they only had three clients, period. Why would he need a whole box of these paperweights? It really wasn't much to go on, but there was nothing else that even remotely connected to Connor here—at least, not that she could see.

She reached down and picked up the white box with the smudged winged-lion imprint. The lid held tight, but she pried it off and saw it contained a paperweight, this one in shades of red and blue with little flecks of white and gold worked into the design. She pulled it out and turned it over, feeling a wrinkle in the green felt.

"Buon giorno." The voice came from behind Zoe's shoulder and she jerked with surprise, almost dropping the paperweight. She caught it, tucking it into her chest and turned to the woman. The woman's attention was fixed on the paperweight Zoe held close. She murmured something to Zoe in Italian, an apology, Zoe assumed, but she wasn't concentrating on the woman's words because she was so fixated on her face.

It was Francesca.

# CHAPTER TWENTY-THREE

FOR A SECOND, ZOE THOUGHT she must have gotten it wrong—that the woman had to be Francesca's sister, or even possibly her daughter, but as the woman busily took the paperweight, replaced it in the box, and put it on the counter by the cash register, all the while chattering away in Italian, Zoe looked closely at her face.

If Zoe hadn't stared at the passport picture for so long as she got ready for the international flight she probably wouldn't have been able to tell, but it was Francesca. The woman was too old to be Francesca's daughter because of the fine spray of lines at the corner of her eyes. Her hair was champagne blond, cut short and spiky around her face, not a dark brown. Her eyes were brown, not green. But the shape of her face was the same, and she had the same delicate lips and arched brows as the passport photo. Her skin was a shade darker, but it had an orange tone to it that made Zoe think, "fake tan," instead of "time in the sun."

Her thoughts caught on those words—fake tan. She remembered Connor's list, the photos he'd mailed, the paperweights. Thoughts skittered through her mind, the primary one being, *get out of here now.*

The woman was smiling at her expectantly, and Zoe realized she had asked her a question.

"No Italian," Zoe said with a shrug. She turned away quickly, pretending to browse. She would ease back to the door and get out of there, she decided, but then she saw the table of paperweights. Somehow they figured into this mess she was caught up in. They kept turning up. It couldn't be coincidence. Blindly, she picked one up and checked the price. Twenty euros. She had that in her pocket. She swallowed and turned back to the woman who was now behind the counter and indicated she wanted to pay for the paperweight.

As the woman rang up the sale, Zoe studied her. She wore a form-fitting cowl-neck jersey dress cinched in at the waist with a wide leather belt and high-heeled boots. A heavy gold necklace encircled her throat. A ring shaped like a butterfly set with diamonds flashed as she rang up the sale. Whatever had happened to Francesca, she wasn't scraping by. Quite the opposite, in fact. She looked like a woman who had a standing appointment at the spa for pedicures and massages.

The cash register chimed, Zoe placed her money in the glass dish on the counter, and the woman boxed the paperweight in a small white box. The box with the smudged imprint was sitting on the counter only inches away. It was right beside the cash register among several pens, a phone, a handset, and a pump bottle of antibacterial hand gel. The woman slipped the white box into a plastic bag and handed it to Zoe over the counter.

As Zoe reached for the plastic bag, she let her messenger bag swing forward and bump the phone, pens, and paper. They spilled off the counter. "Oops, sorry," Zoe said, her heart thumping hard in her chest.

"Is okay," the woman said, squatting down to pick everything up. "No problem."

With trembling fingers, Zoe quickly switched the white box in her bag for the one with the smudged imprint. Zoe was already backing away from the counter, tightly gripping the plastic bag as the woman stood and replaced the items on the counter. "Sorry," Zoe said again. *Almost to the door*, she thought as she navigated the little tables and shelves.

"Ciao," the woman called as she pumped some hand gel and rubbed her hands together. Zoe stepped out the door into the sunlight, the little bells over the door clattering frantically from the force that she'd used to open the door.

She heaved a sigh of relief as she made her way to the campo, her heartbeat still pounding. A few deep breaths and she felt better, calmer, as she sat in the shade of a huge umbrella at the back of the rows of outdoor tables. Jack wasn't around. She wondered how long to wait for him here. What if Stubby Guy went a long way? What if he went off the island? Would Jack follow him? And how would he let her know what was going on? She knew he wouldn't risk calling her. They hadn't use a cell phone at all. Hers was still dismantled, but she didn't want to put it together. She was too paranoid. She didn't know how long she could wait here for Jack, but she intended to hang out as long as she could.

She sipped the fizzy water the waiter had brought her and opened the box with the paperweight. She traced the edge of the wrinkled felt with her thumb. There was something under the felt, something square and hard. She worked her fingernail under the edge, pried away the glue, and created an opening.

A square memory card fell into her palm. Great. They needed a card reader, not to mention a computer, to find out what was on it. Her glance swept the campo, but it was lined with tall palazzos and the usual stores catering to tourists. If she wanted a pizza, gelato, or a carnival mask, no problem. But Venice was a little a short on electronic gadget stores, at least in this part of the city.

A familiar figure strode across her line of vision. Stubby

Guy crossed the campo in a diagonal, making for the café. Zoe slumped down and glanced around for a menu to hide behind, but she only had napkins. She pretended to blow her nose, then grabbed the sunglasses from her messenger bag and shoved them on. When he was within a few paces, he veered to her left into the Street of Shops. Zoe glanced back and saw Jack emerge from the same street where Stubby Guy had entered the campo.

Jack slipped into the seat beside her. "Shopping?" he asked, glancing at the bag from Murano Glassworks. "At a time like this?"

"More like research," Zoe said holding out the memory card. "Stubby Guy went into Murano Glassworks," she said tilting her head in the direction of the shop. "Where did he go when you followed him?"

"He had a coffee at a café."

"Oh. That's kind of…mundane."

"Isn't it? Normal, almost. It didn't look like he was carrying a gun either."

"That's comforting, I guess."

Jack examined the box and memory card in between glances at the door of the glass shop. "I thought you'd be wait-ing here, biting your nails, and worrying about me. I should have known you wouldn't sit here and twiddle your thumbs. You do have a rather proactive personality."

"Well, it was worth it. I got that," Zoe said tapping the memory card in his hand. She showed him the distinctive smudged imprint on the box, then described the similar one she'd seen in Connor's apartment. "The saleswoman didn't want me to hold this box, but I distracted her and switched the boxes."

Jack turned the memory card over in his hand. "So you think the paperweights were…what? Cover for smuggling?" He waved the memory card. "To get whatever is on this, to

Connor. You think he was their distributor?"

"It's got to be something like that. I mean, who puts memory cards under the felt padding of paperweights? The box with the smudged winged-lion imprint would be easy to find, but if someone opened it and examined the contents, they would think it was a printing error. And," Zoe said, rushing her words together, "because of the smudge, it would look perfectly logical if Connor kept those boxes back and didn't give them away. They weren't top quality. Spoilage, I think it's called."

"And selling information—whatever is on that card—would fit. It sounds like something Connor would be involved in." Jack handed the memory card back to Zoe. "Better put that in a safe place. Got anywhere in that big messenger bag of yours where you can hide it?"

"Sure." As she dropped it into her plastic makeup bag and slid the zipper closed, she asked, "Do you think we can find a card reader somewhere around here?"

"I'm sure there's one somewhere in this city. Maybe in a pharmacy, but we should stick around here for now and watch Stubby Guy."

"Yeah, about the shop," Zoe said, fiddling with the water bottle the waiter had left on their table, "I found out something else..." she trailed off, not quite sure how to explain about Francesca. She had to do it. She had to tell him. She paused and had a second's misgiving. *What if she was wrong? What if it really wasn't Francesca?*

She stared out at the scene on the campo for a second. Tourists wandered, gaping and snapping pictures. A few kids kicked a soccer ball at the far end of the campo, their shouts carrying across the stone and brick of the old buildings to the café. Italians, noticeable because of their dark, dressier clothes, and more purposeful stride, crossed the campo without gawking at the architecture, but they still had a leisurely attitude that indicated they weren't rushing. It all looked so normal. It seemed absurd to even think that the woman in the shop was Francesca. But she was.

Zoe pulled her sunglasses off. She folded the earpieces and gently set the glasses on the table. "I know this is going to sound crazy, but the woman in the shop—it was Francesca."

Jack narrowed his eyes and stared at her like she'd spoken in a foreign language. "It can't be. She's dead." The door to the glass shop opened, and Jack focused on it, but it was only a dark haired woman leaving the shop. Jack looked slightly disappointed as if he was hoping to see Stubby Guy so he could take off after him again.

Zoe pressed her lips together. "Jack, I'm serious. I wouldn't say anything unless I was sure. That woman in there, the one who sold me this," she tapped the white box, "it was Francesca. I know it."

Jack stopped scanning the campo and returned his attention to her. Zoe felt a bit like she'd stepped into the glare of a spotlight. She licked her lips. "She's changed her appearance. Her hair is short and blond, her eyes are brown, and she's got a deep tan—fake, I'd say by the orange tone to it—but," he opened his mouth to speak and she held up her hand, "but," she repeated, "the shape of her face is right. Her lips and eyebrows…it's her. I stared at that passport photo for a long time, Jack. I know it's her. She's dyed her hair and has colored contacts, but the bone structure is the same. It's her."

"Zoe…she's probably just someone who looks like her," Jack said in a you-poor-thing-all-this-stress-has-sent-you-around-the-bend voice. Next thing Zoe knew he'd be pressing a sleeping pill on her to knock her out like some delicate character in an old movie.

"No," she said, tapping the table forcibly. "I'm right. You might not want to believe it, but I'm right. Do you think I'd even bring this up unless I was sure? I know she's a painful subject for you. I wouldn't say a word unless I was sure." Zoe leaned across the table and gripped his arm. "And Connor thought she was Francesca, too." Zoe said, excitement quickening her words.

She twisted around, pulled her messenger bag into her lap. "I thought this campo looked familiar. It was in the photos Connor mailed to me," Zoe said as she spread them on the table. "They're of this campo and the Street of Shops." The colored awnings and the architecture of the buildings matched the blurry photos.

Zoe picked up one. "And the blond woman...you can't really tell who it is, but I think it's Francesca. Connor was trying to document that she was alive, but his phone was too crappy to take high quality pictures."

Jack didn't look convinced, so Zoe added, "And there's the list in his journal. Remember the one that I thought was for some sort of costume or disguise? Hair dye or wig, contacts, and fake tan," she said as she pulled the journal out and flipped to the page. "It was a disguise all right, but not for him. It's Francesca's disguise."

Jack took the journal from her, his movements impatient. She watched him scan down the list, then he stilled as he caught sight of the numbers on the last line. His whole demeanor had changed.

"Thirteen, four, seventy-five and one, six, ten," he said softly, not really speaking to her.

"What is that? Do you know what it means?" Zoe asked. She'd studied those numbers and couldn't come up with anything. "I thought they might be a lock combination or an account number. Do you recognize them?"

"I do now," he said, his voice low as he glanced from the journal to the photos. "April 13, 1975, Francesca's birthday, and June 1, 2010, the day she died." He quickly splayed the journal open and flicked through the pages. "It's written in the European format: day, month, year." As he reached the end of the journal, he said, "How would Connor know about her? And how would he connect all this to find her?" Jack dropped the journal, then propped his elbows on the table and rested his forehead in his hands. Zoe picked up the journal.

"Well, from what we've learned about Connor in the last few days, we know that Connor was always looking for an angle, right? Somehow he must have found out about your old job. Did you ever mention it to him?"

Jack slowly lifted his head. "A week ago I could have said, no. Never. But after everything that's happened…I don't know. I don't think so. I was always very careful about what I said."

"I'll say. I had no clue and I was married to you."

They sat quietly for a few minutes. The only sounds were the animated discussion going on at another table between two Italians and the radio from inside the café playing American eighties pop tunes. Currently, The Police were singing about *Every Breath You Take*.

"Did you have anything, old paperwork or anything, at the office that he might have seen? Anything on your computer?" He shook his head. "Any old friends…contacts?"

"No, nothing—"

They looked at each other and spoke at the same time. "Eddie." Zoe's tone was more accusing. Jack's voice held a questioning note.

"Did she know about Francesca? The whole story? Her death and everything?" Zoe asked.

"Yes," Jack said with a sick look on his face.

"She must have told Connor what happened. He was in contact with her, right?"

"No, I ordered the paperweights—" He stopped and closed his eyes for a second. "I introduced them, at a business expo in Vegas. Connor and I were there, and we ran into Eddie. She had a table with upscale promotion products. That's where

Connor first saw the paperweights." He shook his head as if he were arguing with himself. "But Connor didn't order the paperweights. I did. And we only needed one order. We didn't have enough clients to need a second box."

"But Connor had a box in his apartment…" Zoe trailed off as she made the next connection. "Which came from Murano Glassworks through Eddie to Connor," Jack said, heavily. "So they had some sort of smuggling thing on the side. Eddie must have told him outright about Francesca. Neat little triangle," Jack said, severely. "Too bad I was at the center of it and had no idea."

"But that doesn't make sense," Zoe said slowly, working it out. "It doesn't fit with his notes about the disguise…why would he write that down if he knew the woman in the shop was Francesca? And why all the trips here? Why all the time watching the shop?"

Zoe shook her head, "No, I think he figured it out. I bet Eddie told him what happened, how the assignment went bad and how Francesca died, but then something happened that drew his attention to the woman in the shop. Maybe Eddie let something else slip that made him suspicious that Francesca wasn't really dead. Or maybe he overheard something. Whatever happened, he started digging around on his own to see what he could find about Francesca. He had her date of birth and death. He was researching her," Zoe said, tapping the journal. "And he was watching the woman in the shop, taking notes and pictures. He must have sent me those photos as a backup. I was connected to him, but not in an obvious way. It wouldn't be like sending a copy to his e-mail or his home. I can really see him doing it, Jack. He wouldn't let an opportunity to make some money go by. Maybe he was going to use it to blackmail you…or her. She'd be the better target," Zoe said.

"And he ends up with a bullet in the head," Jack said somberly.

"That would explain why they wanted to kill you, too. If they suspected Connor had told you about her. If you knew Francesca was alive…"

Jack nodded. "Besides being a tidy way to explain Connor's murder, it would make sure I didn't threaten her."

Zoe was still thinking about Francesca and her staged death. "How would she do it?" Zoe asked, frowning. "It must have been risky. How would you fake your own death and start a new life somewhere else?"

"I never did see her body," Jack said. "They pulled her body—a body—out of one of the lakes near Naples. She was identified with dental records. As far as why?" Jack shrugged, doing a good imitation of the hotel clerk's Gallic shrug. "Her husband was…a hard man. Her life wasn't easy. He would never have considered divorce."

Jack zeroed in on movement at the glass shop. "Got to go," Jack said and squeezed her hand as he stood, his gaze fixed on the street where Stubby Guy was walking away from the glass store in the opposite direction of the campo.

"You're going to tail him again?"

"This is the best break we've had. The more information we have on both of them, the better off we'll be. Stay here," he said, then slipped though the tables.

"Stay here," Zoe muttered to herself, irritated. He sounded like a dog trainer. What was next? Fetch? She swiped the box off the table and slipped it into the plastic bag. She wasn't going to stay put. She couldn't stay at the same seat for hours on end. That wasn't blending in. She knew Italians lingered over their food, but she'd only had a bottle of water. Better to stroll the campo, window shop, and then settle down at the other café across the square. She could keep an eye out for Jack from there.

She sidestepped through the tables and went to gaze into

the window of a shop with a display of leather-bound note-books and hand-made Venetian paper. She squinted in the light and reached for her sunglasses, but realized she had left them on the table. Zoe turned to go retrieve them, but a woman bumped into her, throwing her off balance.

The woman exclaimed, "Buon giorno," and clasped her shoulders, pulling her in for the traditional Italian greeting of a kiss on each cheek. Zoe tried to pull away, but the woman held her arms in a tight grip just above the elbows.

"Finally. I thought he would never leave," the woman said as she linked her arm through Zoe's, cinching them tightly together. She spoke in perfect English, the syllables drawn out with the leisurely pace of a Southern accent. It took Zoe a second to work it out. It was a wig, she realized. Looking out at her from under the sleek black bob, it was Eddie's brown eyes fringed with her impossibly long lashes.

# CHAPTER TWENTY-FOUR

EDDIE GESTURED WITH HER POINTY chin at the campo. "Don't get any ideas about yelling to anyone," she said, and Zoe felt something poke her in the ribs under the arm that Eddie had plastered to her side. "Yes, that is a knife," Eddie said conversationally.

"So many complications with guns—noisy, bulky, so difficult to travel with," Eddie continued. "Knives, on the other hand," Eddie put some pressure on the knife and Zoe felt a hot needle-like prick skewer into her side as Eddie said, "are quiet and quick. If you make a sound, I'll stab you. In through your ribs, puncture your lung, and then a twist up to your heart in seconds. I'll be gone, and you'll be past saving before anyone even realizes what happened," Eddie said. "Understand?"

Zoe managed to nod, her pulse thumping. The knife tip was still in her side. With each step, little jabs of pain radiated out from it. *Eddie. Here with a knife.* Zoe tried to work her mind around that fact, but her brain didn't seem to be working very well. The street looked fuzzy. Zoe felt light-headed.

"Don't worry," Eddie said as she turned them in the direction of the glass shop. "It's just a small puncture. A bit like a shot, don't you think? It's only so you know I'm serious."

Zoe swallowed hard and forced herself to concentrate on breathing evenly in and out a few times. Her vision cleared, and she scanned the faces of the people they passed as they walked, but each person was in their own world and didn't make eye contact. "Don't be nervous," Eddie said, strolling along at a slow pace. "I'm not going to kill you—unless you do something stupid like yell. I'd *like* to kill you because you've been such a headache. Unfortunately, I don't have a lot of time."

Eddie's annoyed, almost petulant tone cut through Zoe's fear, leveling it off. The jolt of fright still had her pulse pounding, but the sheer panic she'd felt receded. "Pressing appointment? Another friend to betray?" Zoe asked as they turned onto the Street of Shops, and Eddie steered them toward the door to Murano Glassworks. Eddie looked at her scornfully but didn't reply.

Zoe tensed, thinking she would twist away when Eddie reached out to open the door, but a customer exited seconds before they reached the door, and Eddie deftly swept them through the open door and locked it behind them before Zoe could attempt to break away.

Once again, the shop was empty. The bells tinkled overhead, their cheery sound an odd contrast to the mix of fright and anger buzzing through Zoe. "How does Francesca manage to stay in business, if she's never in the shop? Oh that's right, glass isn't really her business...or yours either." Zoe gave a tentative tug, trying to pull away, and Eddie gouged the knife in a bit deeper, sending a pulse of pain through her side. Zoe sucked in a breath. Okay, she wasn't going to make a break for it here, not with these thick walls, and Eddie looked like she actually hoped that Zoe would try and run away so she could go for her full-throttle with the knife.

Eddie ignored her and marched them between the glass displays. Zoe's hip tagged a shelf and a glass bowl fell, shattering behind them, but Eddie plowed on around the counter and through a door to a hallway.

"Don't feel like talking any more?" Zoe licked her lips, which had gone dry and tried to get her breathing back to a normal pace. "You were so talkative before."

"Shut up," Eddie said, and Zoe could tell she was speaking through gritted teeth. The hallway was gloomy and even though her eyes hadn't fully adjusted, Zoe could make out more dark wood paneling, intricate stucco decorations of angels in flight over two heavy doorways, and another more massive Venetian glass chandelier. Eddie shoved her toward the back corner of the hall, away from the ornate doorways, and it was only as she got closer that Zoe realized there was a door fitted into the paneling. It wasn't latched because Eddie shoved it with her shoulder, and it creaked open, releasing a musty, damp scent.

Eddie loosened her grip on Zoe's arm and transferred the knife to her back as they marched down a short set of stone steps set against a brick wall into a room that must have once been an interior dock for goods arriving at the palazzo. A strip of opaque water filled the center of the room. A small flat-bottomed boat with low sides bobbed gently in the water. At one end, sunlight glinted off the water undulating below two high wooden doors that were bolted closed over the entrance to the canal. The bright light was such a contrast to the darkness of the rest of the room that it hurt Zoe's eyes, leaving a bright imprint when she looked away. The stairs didn't have a handrail, and Zoe found herself leaning toward the rough brick of the wall that snagged her sleeve as they descended.

The air was cooler and thick with moisture. Dim, uncovered light bulbs hung from a high ceiling over a stone floor that ran on each side of the swath of water. Mirroring sets of steps on each side of the floor disappeared down into the water. The water slapped gently against the bottom steps, which were covered with a vibrant green moss that surged languidly back and forth with the movement of the water. At the far end of the stone flooring, cardboard boxes were stacked several deep on wooden pallets. A battered metal desk, which seemed to be turning slowly orange with rust, was set against one wall near the stairs. A mess of papers, folders, tape, small boxes, and a bottle of hand gel were scattered across the desktop under a lamp. An old-fashioned wooden desk chair was slowly rotating in front of the desk, as if someone had stood up from it only seconds ago.

Eddie whipped the chair around and shoved Zoe into it. "If I'd had my way, you wouldn't have left Vegas," she said, spitting her words out with such intensity that the wig tilted forward on her head. She jerked it off and tossed it on the desk, then ran her fingers through her pixie cut. "You or Jack. It was the perfect opportunity—" Her fine, blond hair stood on end around her head, which combined with her furious expression, gave her a crazed look.

"Now, Eddie, do not work yourself up." The Italian-ac-cented voice came from the area with the boxes. Zoe didn't want to look away from Eddie. She heard the sharp click of shoes on the stone, then a set of high-heeled boots came into view at the corner of her vision. Zoe swiveled in the chair a millimeter. Francesca held a large cardboard box in one hand and a roll of tape in the other.

"This will be better, you will see. There will be no trace, no blood…" she said, her gaze straying to Zoe as she spoke.

Zoe swallowed. It was her blood they were talking about. Francesca was eyeing her in an assessing way as if she wasn't a person, but merely a composite of various parts—blood, hair, flesh—all things to be contained and removed without leav-ing a trace of her presence.

"Too late for that," Zoe said, touching her side. Her fingertips came away red. A drop of blood slid off the tip of one finger and plopped onto the arm of the chair.

"No, no, no!" Francesca dropped the box on the floor. Her hand shot out, and she grabbed Zoe's wrist, cranking it backward away from the chair. Her grip was tighter than Eddie's had been. Francesca shot an exasperated look at Eddie and sent a stream of Italian her way, gesturing animatedly with her other hand that held the tape. She switched to English. "Now I will have to get rid of the chair. Get me a towel." Francesca flung the tape onto the desk with a disgusted expression, then waved at Eddie to get moving.

A faint smile curled up the corners of Eddie's mouth. "Told you she was trouble." She disappeared up the stairs. Zoe eyed Francesca while they waited. Francesca didn't make eye contact or loosen her grip. Zoe's fingertips began to tingle. She rotated her wrist. Francesca squeezed and cut her a warning glance. "Do not make this difficult. You will regret it."

Zoe believed her. Francesca spoke quietly, but a fierce determination underlined her words. It almost made Zoe wish it were Eddie—knife and all—who was holding her arm. Eddie was so furious that she was about to lose it. A few more goading comments might have done it. No chance of that with Francesca. Even in the middle of her yelling fit, she had been rigidly controlled, aware of exactly where Zoe was and everything around her.

Eddie trotted down the steps and tossed a towel in Francesca's direction. She caught it, wiped the blood off the chair, wiped Zoe's fingers as if she were a child who'd been caught making mud pies then pressed it to the small dark circle of blood at Zoe's side. Francesca folded Zoe's arm at the elbow and pressed it into the folded towel to hold it in place. Zoe flinched as the pressure hit the wound. Francesca didn't blink.

She stepped back, studying the floor around the chair and the stairs in a methodical way and, apparently finding them clear of any blood, nodded her head in satisfaction. She vigorously pumped the hand gel into her palm, then massaged it into her hands. She returned to Zoe and took the plastic bag with the paperweight that she was still clutching from her hand. Then she worked the messenger bag off Zoe's shoulder carefully—obviously not out of concern for Zoe. She was only making sure she didn't have more blood to clean up later.

Francesca opened the plastic bag, then held it out to Eddie, who was returning from the far corner of the room, a rolling suitcase bumping along noisily behind her. The knife was gone, Zoe saw. Probably stowed away in some pocket or pouch in her suitcase.

"There," Francesca said shortly. "The rest is in the box upstairs on the floor."

Eddie ripped the bag from her hand, checked inside as if she didn't believe Francesca, then glowered at Zoe. "You sure you don't need any help?" she asked to Francesca's back. Francesca was bent over the desk where she'd dumped the messenger bag.

"No. Go." She swished her hand through the contents. Zoe watched Francesca's fingers glance off of the makeup bag where she'd put the memory card. Thank goodness it wasn't a transparent plastic bag. She forced herself not to stare at it. Although, if she thought there was a chance she could offer it to them in exchange for walking away, she would have done it in an instant, but she knew they weren't going to let her leave. Besides, whatever scam they had going, she knew Francesca's real identity. Any doubts about what Zoe knew would be gone the minute Francesca opened the passport.

"I will take care of it." Francesca's long fingers sorted quickly through her meager items—she avoided touching the wadded tissue, pushed the hairclip and breath mints to the side, and plucked out the wallet and passport.

Zoe wondered how long it would be before Jack returned

to the café. Would he realize she was missing right away, or would he assume she'd gone for a walk or to snoop around on her own as she'd done last time? Hopefully, he'd assume she'd gone back to the glass shop, but even if he went to the shop himself, it was locked. The chances of him finding his way to this back room were small—miniscule even—especially since he didn't even know she was here.

Her plan had been to meander around the campo and window-shop. He might assume that was what she was doing. She couldn't count on Jack to find her. She didn't even know when he would get back to the campo. He might not even know she was missing for hours. And then what would he do? He couldn't very well go to the police and report her missing. Zoe felt a tightness in her chest as the frightening weight of being on her own sunk in. She had to figure something out... even if it was jumping in that vile water and swimming away. She knew how to swim. Could she make it to the water and swim out under the door before they reacted?

"You're sure?" Eddie asked, reluctantly.

"Yes. Go or you will miss your flight." Francesca pulled a cell phone from her pocket. She made a call, said a few words in Italian, then hung up.

"This can't be like last time," Eddie said, her gaze steady on Zoe. "No mistakes."

Francesca spun toward her. "I have not made any mistakes. You were the careless one, the one who babbled. It wasn't enough that you wormed your way into my new life. You had to jeopardize everything." She walked forward as she spoke, and Zoe tensed. They were focused on each other. Unfortunately, they were directly in front of the stairs. The only other way out was the water. She'd heard stories about the canals—how the disgustingly dense, brackish water was full of bacteria and who knew what else. It would be her last resort, she decided and glanced back at the women.

Eddie's shrill tone cut into her thoughts. "You needed me," she shot back. "Don't pretend like you didn't. You needed a contact in the States. Two years ago, you were happy when I figured out who you were and what you were doing." Eddie yanked up her suitcase and climbed the stairs, talking over her shoulder. Zoe tensed, turning the chair slightly so that she faced the water more directly. "Don't blame me for Connor," Eddie continued.

Zoe moved her feet, positioning them so she could leap from the chair. Eddie said, "He would have figured it out on his own. He was half-way there anyway. I only filled in the last blank. He knew you weren't who you said you were, just like I'd figured it out before him. It was your precious *Stefano* who botched killing him." Zoe felt her tense calf muscles quiver. "You're quite a pair, you know. For someone who is trying to stay hidden, you're not doing so well. Terrible, in fact."

A quick glance at Francesca froze Zoe into place. Francesca had pulled a small black handgun from her pocket. She pointed the barrel squarely at Zoe's chest.

"This is it for me. I'm done after this shipment," Eddie said from above them. Her words hardly registered with Zoe. She was too focused on the gun and Francesca's unwavering gaze that seemed to pin her to the chair. Eddie's voice had gone peevish, as if she couldn't stand not to be the center of attention. "You're too much of a risk," Eddie said, then pushed through the door and slammed it behind her.

Francesca rolled her eyes and strode back to the desk where she picked up the passport with her free hand. "She does not mean it," she said, leaning toward Zoe, like she was taking her into her confidence. She tossed her head in the direction of Eddie's dramatic exit. "That one, all voice and bluster, but it means nothing. Next week, it will be," she waved the passport through the air as if she were erasing writing on a board, "as if nothing happened."

"Well, I for one, am glad to see the last of her," Zoe ventured in an effort to connect with Francesca, which seemed to work because Francesca chuckled.

"Do not worry about her," Francesca said, "She is gone. Hand-carrying an important package back to the States. She will not bother you anymore." She opened the passport. Her eyebrows shot up, her gaze flew to Zoe. "So you do know everything. It is sad. I like you. You have spirit, but—" she shrugged in a what-can-you-do manner, "I cannot let you live. You must see that. Jack either."

For a second, Zoe thought of bargaining with her, begging even, but that steely gaze stopped her. Francesca wasn't going to relent or change her mind. Zoe's pulse accelerated. Could she jump up, push her over? Grab the gun? Sprint up the stairs? It was almost as if Francesca sensed her thoughts because she paced a few steps away from Zoe. She flicked open the passport and looked at the picture, a hint of sadness flickered across her face. "I wish it had not been Jack," she said with a small shake of the head. "He took it too hard."

"He thought you were dead," Zoe said. "What should he have done? Forget about it?"

"Yes. He should have. He cares too much, that one. Too involved." She rubbed her thumb over the picture as she stared at it.

Zoe shifted her feet, moving the chair an inch toward the water. If she could get close enough, she might be able to hit the water before Francesca could aim and fire the gun. "How did you do it?" Best to keep her talking, thinking about the past. The huge box Francesca had dropped was between her and the water. If she could edge the chair slightly backward she'd be able to make straight for the water.

Francesca looked at her consideringly for a moment, then seemed to come to a decision. "It was not hard. I told Jack I thought someone suspected I was an informant. The next meeting I had…a friend follow me. Jack saw it and began to prepare," she said, lifting the passport.

Zoe waited until she focused on the passport then shifted her toes and moved the chair again. "Once he believed I was in danger, it was easy. I did not go to the next meeting and did not reply to his attempts to contact me. He assumed I'd been caught. I was on a train to Milan."

"You make it sound so easy. What about your husband?"

"I was not stupid. I picked a time he was out of town," she said scornfully. "I had been saving for years—all the money Jack and Roy paid me, I saved it all. So considerate that they paid in cash. I had been planning it for years."

"What about the body? It was identified as you."

She laughed as she tossed the passport back to the desk. "You have not been in Italy very long, if you do not know that anything can be bought. A little money to the right people and," she waved her fingers, "all the forms were filled out with my name. Witnesses swore they saw me die. The body was beyond recognition. All that mattered was the paperwork."

"But who was she?"

Francesca said sharply. "I do not know." She seemed to make an effort to calm herself. "It does not matter," she said with forced briskness. "She was nobody. Nobody missed her." Her gaze drifted up to the ceiling and the dim bulbs. "I never speak of it…although, I dream of her sometimes. More and more, lately." She nodded as she strode a few steps closer to Zoe. "It is good that I speak of it to you. Now, maybe I will sleep better."

"How could you sleep better?" Zoe asked, incredulous. Forgetting about her stealthy chair shifting, she said, "You're planning to kill me and Jack. It's guilt keeping you awake! Don't you see that? If you kill me and Jack, it will only make it worse."

It was like a shutter descended over her face. "It must be

done. I will not lose everything."

Faintly, bells jangled. "That will be Stefano," Francesca said, a look of pleasant satisfaction settling on her face. "With Jack. I knew he would come once we had you. Always playing the knight."

The small circle of the gun barrel dipped slightly as Francesca looked up the stairs to the door. Zoe lunged, shoving the box at Francesca as she ran. There was a clatter of metal on stone. Zoe didn't look back.

A crash and shouting sounded behind her, but she was only vaguely aware of it. *Too far. I'm too far.* Something solid collided with her leg, tangled with her foot, and brought her down.

# CHAPTER TWENTY-FIVE

STUNNED, ZOE LAY WITHOUT MOVING, as she tried to get her breath back. She'd landed face down, her knees and elbows taking the brunt of the fall. The steps with their coating of moss were only inches from her nose. So close.

She crawled forward, but strong hands gripped her ankles and yanked her away from the edge. Her chin bumped on the cold tiles, and her vision blurred for a moment. She kicked out, a pain seared through her side where the knife had pricked her, as she struggled to get her hands under her body, so she could lever herself up.

Hands on her shoulders roughly dragged her upright into a sitting position on the floor, then clamped her wrists together. Zoe's vision blurred at the quick change from lying down to sitting up. A ripping sound cut through the air. Two men were encircling her wrists with stiff, sticky packing tape, attaching her wrists to the arm of the rolling chair. Foggily, Zoe realized it must have been the chair that brought her down.

Part of her mind wondered why Francesca hadn't just shot her. Maybe she was a bad shot or it could be her issue with blood. Maybe she didn't want to have to clean it up. Shooting someone would be messy, and she definitely seemed paranoid about blood.

Zoe blinked at the men laboring over her with the tape. There was something wrong with the image. They were moving in tandem. She blinked a few times and they merged into one man. Stubby Guy.

He sent her a cold look with his dark eyes as he spoke over his shoulder to Francesca in Italian. Zoe was glad she didn't know what he was saying, but she suspected it was that Francesca should have shot her. Zoe looked beyond him to Francesca, who was standing with the gun pointed at Jack. He was lying motionless at the bottom of the stairs. A mixture of relief and fear hit her as she looked at him.

Stubby Guy gave the tape a final twist, then crossed to Jack, gripped his heels, and dragged him toward her, his head bobbing on the stones. Stubby Guy—Stefano—Zoe remembered, released Jack's feet, and they thumped to the ground. His head lolled toward Zoe.

Jack got the same treatment with the tape. Stefano wrapped Jack's wrists and bound them to the other arm of the chair. Jack's upper body was beside her, his legs extended on the opposite side of the chair. She could see his chest moving a fraction. Stubby Guy strode over to Francesca for a low-voiced consultation.

Zoe rested her forehead on her knee. Pained flickered in her kneecap when her head made contact, but at this point it only slightly registered. So this was it. They were going to kill them, then dump them, probably at sea. Zoe wasn't much of a religious person, but she figured if there ever was a time to pray, this was it. She had no idea of what to say or how to go about praying. *Help me*, was about all she could come up with before her thoughts flashed to her family and friends, her mother, Aunt Amanda, Helen, even Kiki. They'd all worry about her, wondering what had happened to her. And they'd go on worrying. They would probably never know what had happened.

The chances of their bodies being found were miniscule. And if they were found, would they be able to properly identify them? Helen would be devastated. And Mom, Zoe thought. Poor, messed up, Mom. She would thrive on the attention in the beginning. Zoe had no doubt that when the news reached her about her disappearance, Donna would milk the situation for all it was worth. She'd be the distraught mother with the missing daughter, a tragic situation. But what about later when it became obvious that Zoe wasn't going to be found? Would Donna completely lose it? She was self-centered, but she did love Zoe in her own misguided, crazy way. Zoe had separated herself from Donna's toxic lifestyle—the constant cameras and attention seeking, the neediness—Zoe had decided it was better to keep her distance. Phone calls on holidays were about the extent of their contact. Well, if you didn't count every time Donna called and pitched a new show idea at Zoe. But even though she couldn't be around her mom all the time, Zoe didn't want this to be it.

There was a thickness in her throat. In a matter of hours, maybe less, they would be dead.

A whisper floated to Zoe, barely audible above the slap of water. "Hey, it's not that bad. No, don't look up. Keep your head down."

Zoe shifted her chin and looked under her arm. Jack smiled at her, a lopsided, upside down grin. "You okay?"

"Not really."

"Yeah. I'm not happy with our situation either." He spoke low, barely moving his mouth.

"You were right—that's Francesca. I got a good look at her before Stubby Guy pushed me down the stairs."

Zoe risked a quick glance at Francesca and Stefano, who were talking in raised voices now. Francesca was pacing back and forth, dumping the contents of Zoe's messenger bag into the large cardboard box. Stefano was trailing along behind her, waggling the gun at Zoe and Jack, trying to talk over Francesca. She shook her head, tossed the blood-spotted towel into the box, and then picked up another flattened box. She opened it and folded the flaps down.

"They're going to put us in the boxes, weigh us down, and dump us at sea," Jack said. "The debate is whether to kill us before we go in the box or knock us out and let the sea do the work."

Jack continued in a low voice, "I hate to say it, but it is clever, using the boxes. They won't be seen transporting bodies, just the boxes, which must be a normal activity for them."

Zoe said, "It's either that, or it's because Francesca can't stand the thought of us sprawled on her floor, contaminating the place. She seems to have a germ phobia and an obsession with keeping things clean. She doesn't want to get blood on anything." A rending sound cut through the air as Francesca yanked the tape across the flaps of the box.

"Less worry for them that way about our death being traced back to them," Jack said.

Francesca muttered a curse, tossed the empty tape dispenser on the floor, and slammed through the desk drawers quickly, searching their contents.

Zoe shifted, blinked and tried to get a grip on her emotions as she said, "Eddie was here, too. She found me in the campo and brought me here, but I think she's gone now."

"Let me guess. She used a knife?" At Zoe's nod, Jack let out a sigh audible only to Zoe. "She's got a thing for blades," he said. Zoe twisted, and Jack saw the dark circle of blood, now sticky and beginning to harden, on her shirt. His face went hard.

"Don't worry about her. It was enough to scare me and get me moving, but I think it's stopped bleeding now. It's not deep. It annoyed Francesca, too. Anyway, that's the least of our worries. Eddie is taking some special shipment back to the

States. It's what we thought. They've got some sort of smuggling set-up between her and Eddie. Connor was involved, and he got suspicious about Francesca. I guess Francesca sent Stub—er, Stefano to take care of it—meaning you and Connor—but you got away."

"And I ran straight to Eddie, who told Stefano exactly where I'd be—first at The Strip where he tried to arrange that car-on-pedestrian accident, then at Connor's apartment," Jack said, disgust with Eddie evident on his face even in his whispered words.

In her peripheral vision, Zoe saw Francesca march up the stairs. Stefano followed her, looking over his shoulder at them. Jack had his face turned away and hadn't moved from his prone position. Zoe kept her head tucked to her knees. The door closed and Jack sprung up. They dragged the chair to the desk.

"They've gone for more tape," Zoe said as she crawled along, her kneecaps screaming with each impact.

Jack used the toe of his shoe to open the lowest desk drawer near him, then angled his foot so that he could shove everything around inside. "Nothing but paper," he said moving quickly to the other two drawers.

Zoe angled herself up as high as she could, surveying the desktop. "No scissors or letter opener, but there's a few big paperclips." Zoe used her nose to drag several across the desktop, then twisted the chair so that her hands were directly under them. She nudged the paperclips with her nose. Several slipped through her fingers and pinged onto the floor.

Jack was wiggling his foot, working off his shoe. "Hold still," Zoe said, sharply. "I can't believe we're doing this...all our hopes hanging on paperclips," she muttered as she shoved another paperclip over the edge. Her fingers felt thick and clumsy, but she managed to pinch it between her thumb and first finger as it fell.

"Excellent," Jack said. He went back to moving his socked foot around, scraping it over the bumpy floor.

Zoe concentrated on not dropping the paperclip and tried to pry one section of it back. Her fingers felt like sausages. When she managed to get one piece at a right angle, she stabbed at the thick layers of tape awkwardly. This was going to take a while.

"Ah," Jack said as he used his foot to drag a forgotten pen from under the desk. Jack gripped it with his toes and brought it to his hands, performing a move that wouldn't have looked out of place in a yoga class. He twisted his foot back into his shoe, then went to work with the pen, trying to work it into an angle where he could puncture the tape.

The room was silent except for the lap of water on stone and the tiny popping sound of each puncture. Zoe could feel sweat gathering on her forehead as she concentrated. Press, puncture. Move a millimeter lower. Repeat. Endlessly.

She'd perforated a zigzagging line of holes about an inch long, but Stefano had been extra generous with the tape, winding it around and crisscrossing her wrists several times in wide arcs, so there were several more inches to go. Zoe wasn't sure how much time had gone by when she heard something. She raised her head. Voices. Definitely voices.

Jack nodded his head, motioning behind them. Zoe understood instantly. Surprise was about the only thing they had on their side. They scooted backward like two crabs scuttling over the sea floor. Jack resumed his prone position, the pen hidden in his hand. Zoe hunched over the paperclip, punching away with renewed vigor, her hands trembling from the effort.

Footsteps echoed closer, and then receded again. After a moment of silence, Jack scrambled upright and went back to work on his tape.

They punched for a few seconds. Zoe shot a glance at Jack.

Every few seconds, he tucked the pen into the corner of his mouth then twisted his hands back and forth. She could see the raw skin where the tape had given away—a tiny strip. It was working. She twisted her hands. About an inch of the tape gave, ripping away a thin layer of skin on the back of her hands. She caught her breath. "God, that hurts."

"Be glad it's not on our mouths. That's the worst."

"That's looking on the bright side," Zoe said. She paused a moment, then resumed her sewing machine-like trek through the tape.

With his head bent in concentration, Jack said, "We could sing a few show tunes. You know, help pass the time."

"Let's not. I've heard you sing."

"It's atrocious, I know, but it would be distracting," Jack said, pen in his teeth as he wrenched his hands back and forth, his shoulder muscles contorting with the effort.

The bells tinkled, footsteps tromped across the floor, and Jack dropped to his back.

"Darling, where are you?" called a male voice.

Zoe's gaze shot to Jack's face. He was staring at her, and she knew they were both thinking the same thing. They knew that voice. It was deep and rolling. Footsteps moved closer, then away. "Roy?" Zoe whispered. "What is he doing here?"

Jack resumed work on the tape with ferocity.

"Why would he…" her words trailed off as the image of the butterfly necklace coiled in a neat spiral came back to her. It was like an image finally loaded on the computer and everything jumped into focus, sharp and clean. "Roy helped her. He's in on it, too," Zoe said, horrified. "We went directly to him. Told him exactly where we were in Naples. *He's* the one who sent the police to our hotel, not Nico."

Jack spared her a quick look out of the corner of his eye. He looked grim, like he didn't want to believe it, but he didn't argue with her.

Zoe felt the same way. She shoved the paperclip through a particularly thick layer of tape while shaking her head. "I should have figured it out. I saw her jewelry and knew there was something about it...I didn't put it together until now."

Jack refocused on his tape. "Go on."

"She's wearing a ring with a special design—it looks custom to me. I'm no expert, but I've never seen anything like it. It's a butterfly with diamonds set in the wings. There was one exactly like it, except on a necklace in the upstairs bathroom at Roy's house. There was a bottle of perfume, too."

Jack worked on the tape silently for a few minutes. "Roy went out of his way to mention being a bachelor." Jack's voice was rough with anger. "He really played it up—all that about not having much food in the house. He was setting us up. No one was in a better position than Roy to help Francesca when she wanted to disappear. Roy finished out his assignment, then he retired in Naples."

"So, they're cautious," Zoe said. "They must have decided to go their separate ways for a few years. She moved to Venice, he stayed in Naples." She stared at him, her eyes widening. "The cleaning lady," Zoe said and explained what the woman at the café had told her. "I bet Francesca goes to visit him disguised as a cleaning lady so no one recognizes her, and she doesn't raise any eyebrows in the neighborhood. He comes to see her in Venice, too, obviously," Zoe said nodding toward the door where they'd heard his voice.

She broke off at the sound of voices mingled with sharp footsteps. Jack dropped back to the floor seconds before the door swung open. Francesca led the way down the steps, a fresh roll of tape in her hand. Stefano trotted along behind her, his pace brisk. Zoe palmed the paperclip. She didn't see the gun, but she was sure it wasn't far away. Probably in his jacket pocket. Instead of the gun, Stefano held something long and narrow and metal in his hand. It was heavy; Zoe could see that by the way he held it. He shifted and she realized it was a set of industrial-sized tongs. He gripped the pinching end together in one hand, the other heavier end, rested in the palm of his other hand.

He paused a moment at the foot of the stairs, exchanging a glance with Francesca. The tape screeched in her hand. She gave him an impatient what–are–you–waiting–for nod. Stefano quickly crossed the floor to Jack. Zoe thought, *Oh, God. This is it. Francesca won the argument. Instead of killing us here, they're going to knock us out, then tip us into the water.* Zoe shoved with her feet, trying to move away, but Jack lay prone, weighing the chair down like an anchor. Stefano went for Jack.

He raised his arm. The tongs whooshed down.

Zoe screamed. Jack flinched away at the last second, jerking the chair and Zoe around.

The tongs slammed into the stone with a scratchy sound. Stefano's arm vibrated with the impact, but he didn't pause. He spun to Jack, and his arm whipped down again. Jack shifted, shoving the chair between him and the tongs. Wood cracked as the metal slammed into the chair.

Stefano, his face suffused with red, raised the tongs again. Jack was angled around, trying to keep his body behind the chair. Zoe, her heart racing, had matched his moves and skittered around on the opposite side of the chair trying to use it as a shield, but with both their hands still taped to the arms of the chair, they were exposed. Jack sent her a quick glance, and Zoe knew what he was thinking. She gave a nod.

Stefano raised the tongs over his head. Zoe and Jack shoved together, sending the chair into Stefano. He half-shouted, half-yelped as it smashed into his shins and a caster crunched over his toes, causing him to pitch forward. The tongs clattered to the floor. They yanked the chair backward, and Stefano thudded onto the stone, landing awkwardly on his elbow with a crunching sound that would normally have turned Zoe's stomach, but at the moment, she was actually quite glad to hear it.

Stefano lay motionless for a moment, then groaned and rolled onto his back, his arm draped unmoving along his side.

"Stop!" Francesca shouted. "Do not move," she commanded in a voice trembling with anger.

Zoe halted and realized she was breathing hard and shivering. Francesca stood with her arms extended, elbows locked, and the gun gripped between her hands. She'd didn't have the casual air that Stefano had when he held the gun. The dark circle of the barrel wavered back and forth between Zoe and Jack, her knuckles already showing white because of the hard grip on the gun. She and Stefano exchanged a few words. Except for his arm, he seemed to be all right. He slowly sat up as Francesca took several steps to the side so Stefano would not interfere with her line of sight to Zoe and Jack.

Cradling his arm, Stefano moved to his knees and stood, grimacing with each movement. Zoe felt as if the scale had tipped slightly in their favor. With Stefano limited, they stood a better chance of getting away. Stefano's blows had damaged the arm of the chair. She could feel the looseness of it. Francesca's attention strayed to Stefano, so Zoe pulled her wrists toward her body and felt the wood give away where the arm connected to the chair. Unfortunately, it also made a splintering sound. A *loud* splintering sound.

The tear she'd created earlier in the tape with the paperclip widened, and she rotated her hands and wrists, catching her breath as she wrenched her hands free. The wooden piece of the chair arm clattered to the floor as she flexed her fingers a few times. The air felt cold on the back of her hands where the tape had been.

"Stop!" Francesca screeched. "I told you, *do not move*."

Zoe froze.

"You are not good at following instructions, no?" Francesca

said, a slight tremor running through her arm and down the gun's barrel. She was not as cool and collected as she had been earlier, but there was determination and methodical lilt to her words as she said, "It does not matter what you do. I do not want to kill you here, but I will. I will do it if I have to."

Fear spiked through Zoe. Francesca was serious and intent. She was going to do it. The door at the top of the stairs creaked open. Roy stepped through the door, closing it gently behind him. Zoe closed her eyes briefly, feeling the scales tip back out of their favor again. They were outnumbered again. "Don't do it, darling," Roy said, a look of almost pity on his face.

Francesca took a step back and swiveled the gun toward Roy.

# CHAPTER TWENTY-SIX

"YOU MUST LEAVE," FRANCESCA SAID. She checked the position of Zoe and Jack, then refocused on Roy. He took a few steps down the stairs.

"No, no, no, no!" Francesca said rapidly. "You must leave. This does not concern you." She released one hand and waved him off. "Go home. Go away."

Roy moved down another few steps "Of course it concerns me. Everything you do concerns me. That is why I keep an eye on you and your...activities." Zoe picked up on an undercurrent in his words as Roy looked between Francesca and Stefano. A faint blush suffused Francesca's cheeks, and Stefano seemed to puff up like a wild animal on a nature show, defending his territory.

"You didn't realize I knew about all this? Your side business, shall we say?" Roy said quietly, circling his hand to indicate Zoe and Jack. "I know. I've known for a long time and looked the other way, but I can't anymore. Not about this," Roy said and looked directly at Jack for the first time since arriving in the room. There was regret in his expression. Roy moved down a few more steps.

Francesca tilted her chin up. "It must be done," she said. "There is no other way."

"There is. There is always another way. We can leave, right

now. Go somewhere new. Together. No one will be able to find us."

She shook her head sharply. "I do not want to start over. Not again."

"Murder, Francesca?" he asked, moving down another step. "That is not what we planned. The other woman—the one in Naples—she was already dead. There was nothing we could do, but here…this is different."

"It has to be this way because you did not take care of things. You said you would keep an eye on him." She gestured at Jack. "You said you would make sure he didn't become a threat, but you didn't do that. Do you think he will just go away?" she asked, tossing her head. Her hands were still clinched around the gun, but she'd pulled her arms in a little. She had to be getting tired. "No, this is the *only* way to make sure I am safe. This is the only way. I will not run again. I have worked too hard to start over."

"I was afraid you'd say that," Roy said, an expression of resignation settling on him. There was a moment of silence, and then almost as if they'd synchronized it, Roy and Jack moved at the same time. Roy surged toward Francesca. Jack jumped up, tugging on his wrists. The wooden chair arm cracked away from the chair. He grabbed the back of the chair and flung it at Francesca.

A gunshot reverberated through the room, the sound echoing off the stone walls and floor. Zoe ducked, raising her hands over her head. There was an eerie vacuum of sound. Her ears felt as if they were stuffed with cotton. It took a second for her to figure out what had happened. Jack looked okay. It was Roy who was sprawled on the floor.

Stefano and Francesca exchanged a look. He was pleased, almost grinning, and Francesca looked relieved. So it was like that, Zoe thought, a love triangle. She almost felt sorry for Roy. Conned by the woman he loved, cheated on, and then shot. He had deceived her and Jack, and before that, he'd duped Jack and set him up to take the blame for Francesca's "death," so Zoe's sympathy was a bit tempered. Of course, he didn't deserve to be shot. Zoe thought she saw a movement from his body, but when she looked closer, he was motionless.

Roy had been closer to Francesca, and she'd shot him before he could get to her, but now she had the gun trained on Jack. "I will do it," she said, then snapped out a sharp command to Stefano in Italian along with a toss of her head in the direction of the stacks of boxes. He moved to the far end of the room.

"Then do it," Jack said, taking a step toward her, stripping the tape from his wrists, his face set, not showing a flicker of pain as the tape ripped away. "Go ahead. It's not going to make a bit of difference if you kill me here or if you knock me out and toss me in the water later."

"Oh, it does make a difference," Francesca said. Zoe glanced between them and the far end of the room where Stefano was rummaging among the boxes, wincing with each motion that jostled his injured arm. Zoe realized he was working a flattened box free from a pile. Great, she thought, another box. That meant they were sticking to their plan, only they would be dumping three boxes instead of two.

Jack took another step toward Francesca, and she backed up. Zoe stood uncertainly. No one was focused on her. Too bad, there was nowhere to go. Roy blocked the stairs, Stefano was at the other end of the room, and Jack and Francesca were in front of the water.

"Francesca," Jack said, "I hate to break it to you, but, in case you haven't noticed, your little plan has fallen apart."

Zoe had to admire how easy and relaxed his voice sounded. "You didn't plan for Roy, did you? What will you do when they come looking for him? You know there will be a search for Roy. A few days, a week, and then someone will realize he is missing. His movements will be traced. I assume you are used to moving about carefully—incognito, I'm sure. But Roy? He didn't have a need for the same level of stealth. He wouldn't have taken the precautions you would have."

As Jack talked, Zoe inched to the left, positioning herself directly behind Jack so that his body blocked her from Francesca's view. She rotated her torso and scanned the desk, looking for some sort of weapon.

"It may take a while, but the police will work with the American Consulate, which of course will be involved in the investigation of an upstanding expat. They will follow his movements here. To you. Just as the people searching for me will eventually pick up my trail and follow it to the campo and, then eventually, here."

"That is why there must be no trace of you—any of you— here."

Zoe looked around for something to hold—some sort of weapon, even some sort of distraction—but there was nothing within reach except that wretched cardboard box and she couldn't think how it would help her.

The tongs, Zoe thought. Where were they? On the floor? There was a blur of movement at the corner of her eye. She turned, but it was too late. She didn't even have time to process the thought that it was Stefano before his good arm whooshed through the air toward her.

✕

A horrible screeching sound penetrated Zoe's oozy, half-conscious state. It was right above her, almost on top of her. Confusion and fear washed over her. She couldn't see anything. She was curled up, almost in a fetal position. Her head felt heavy as if it were too big for her neck, like she was some sort of oversized bobble-head toy, a bobble-head with a huge, tender bump on the top of her head, she mentally amended as she gently touched her head.

The awful noise stopped then started again, like fingernails on a chalkboard only magnified as it echoed around in her head. She knew that sound. What was it? If she weren't so sleepy, she could figure it out. She gave her head a little shake. Big mistake. Pain rolled through her body topped off with a seasick sensation that made her break out in a cold sweat. She held herself motionless and concentrated on taking deep breaths. The nausea cleared her mind and mentally everything came into sharp focus. That sound. Packing tape. Directly above her head.

She was in that blasted box. She wiggled and felt the sides press in against her. The air was stuffy and hot, and now the smell of cardboard registered as she fought to make herself breathe slowly. *You won't suffocate*, she reminded herself. Cardboard boxes aren't airtight. Are they? Sweat beaded her hairline and her armpits at the thought.

Of course not. She'd played for hours in cardboard boxes as a kid. After their move to Dallas, she'd squirreled away the larger packing boxes and created a hideaway. She'd loved the cozy feeling of pretending it was her own snug house. Granted, that box had been bigger than this one, and it hadn't been taped shut.

She forced another breath in and out as she ran her hands over the interior, feeling the flaps of the box and bits of plastic and fabric under her. The contents of her messenger bag, she realized. Francesca had dumped them in the box. So efficient, getting rid of all trace of her presence along with her body. Zoe heard a sound and frowned, then realized it was a half-sob that had come from her.

She had to get a grip. What was it Jack had said? Something about keeping your head when everyone else was losing theirs. *Okay, keep your bruised, lumpy head, she lectured herself. Don't panic. You're just taped in a box. Surely it can't be that hard to get out of a box. It's just cardboard.*

Where was Jack? Taped into his own box for easy transport as well? She heard sounds that she realized had been going on, but she'd been too freaked out to process. It was as if someone had turned up the volume and the noise suddenly came through, making Zoe feel even queasier than during the initial wave of nausea.

Thumps and thuds. Grunts. Ragged breaths. Blows landing and bodies struggling. A fight.

She crunched herself down and folded one of the interior flaps down, exposing a sticky line of the underside of the tape running overhead along the seam where the two exterior flaps of the box met. On the sides, above the edge of the folded down interior flaps, there were gaps, thin slivers of light interrupted only by the thick press of tape.

She wormed her way around and pressed her face to the slice of light. Two forms, Jack and Stefano, writhed on the floor, locked together, each struggling to gain an advantage over the other. Francesca was pacing around the room, her head tipped over, her gaze raking the floor. She surged forward, dipped out of Zoe's sight, and reemerged with the gun gripped in her hands. She spun toward the men and shouted in Italian.

Zoe's heart seemed to stop, but the men remained locked together, ignoring Francesca's shouts. She circled to the left, the gun trained on them, but they were a bundle of flailing, twisting arms and legs.

Zoe's heart seemed to start beating again, this time double-time. Francesca didn't have a clear shot at Jack. Zoe wasn't sure if Jack was keeping himself glued to Stefano in self-preservation or if they were both so intent on their fight that they had blocked out Francesca's voice. Zoe let out a shaky breath and wiggled her fingers into the sliver of light. She pulled with all her strength. The cardboard crunched down a bit, but no more than a quarter of an inch.

Until that moment, Zoe realized she hadn't truly appreciated the strength of cardboard—or of tape, either, she thought as she tried to pry the flap away from the tape. Her nail broke, and she came away with a pitifully thin strip from the outer layer of cardboard. At this rate she'd work her way out of the box by next Christmas.

Francesca yelled commands. The men's bodies shifted heavily over the floor.

Zoe scrabbled through the items at the base of the box—makeup, breath mints, tissue, billfold, and passports. Nothing useful. Not even a paperclip. The one she'd used to puncture a perforated line in the tape that bound her hands was somewhere on the floor. Pity Francesca hadn't scooped it up and dropped it in the box. If she ever got out of this alive, Zoe vowed she would never go anywhere without a nail file, scissors, and pepper spray, at a minimum.

There was a burst of movement from the men. They tumbled across the floor and knocked into the box, sending it skidding across the floor. Zoe managed to contort herself around and put her eye to the small slit on the other side of the box. All she could see was the strip of water and the wall on the opposite side of the room. She edged as far as she could over to the other side of the box, the side that was farther away from the water.

Another few bumps like that would send her straight into the water, and she'd be trapped inside. How fast would the water break down the cardboard? How fast would the box sink? How fast would it fill with water? Would the water weaken the cardboard quickly enough for her to get out before the box sank too deep? She didn't want to find out. She wanted out now.

She scrabbled at the tiny slit of the opening, pushing, pulling, and trying to work it away from the tape. She attacked the corner where the seam of the box had been glued together, but it was stuck fast. The background noise of Francesca's screams and the mens' struggle went on. They hit the box again as they flailed around. It shuttered as it scooted another inch toward the water.

# CHAPTER TWENTY-SEVEN

ZOE RAN HER HAND OVER her face, which was now covered in sweat from the stuffy air in the box and her own panic. *Don't lose your head*, she whispered to herself because she knew she was very near the point of doing just that. What else had Jack said? *Use what you have.* He'd slammed the potted plant down on Stefano, knocking him out. Unfortunately, she didn't have a handy potted plant or box cutter secreted away. She had nothing. Sweat was literally dripping into her eyes. She ran her hand over her face again, then her neck. Her fingers grazed her necklace.

Her ring. Her diamond ring. She still had that.

She quickly lifted the chain off her neck, careful not to let it catch on the tender lump as she worked it over her head. She twisted the large square-cut diamond with its beautiful sharp edges over the knuckle of her first finger, then bent her finger down to hold it there. She ran the ring along the exposed underside of the tape where the box flaps met overhead. It dragged in a few places, but when her fingers traced the line, she felt little snagged bits of tape. It worked.

She hunkered down and went to work with her improvised box cutter, working through the thick layers of tape.

She'd almost broken through when the sound of the men

fighting surged closer and banged into the box. The impact knocked Zoe backward toward the side by the water, then the box tipped and she flipped over like she was doing a backward roll as the box tumbled. The bits and pieces from her messenger bag swirled around her, then settled on the bottom of the box.

She immediately felt the temperature difference as a coolness settled into the air around her. The tape she'd been hacking away at, which had been above her head, was now under her and despite the definite bobbing sensation she felt as the box floated on the surface of the water, she knew it wouldn't be long before the cardboard soaked through and the box disintegrated. Water seeped between the gashes in the tape and bubbled up through the slivers where the flaps came together. Without really thinking about it, she braced her hands on the side of the box and kicked at the ragged tape seam.

Two kicks did it. The seam gave, water gushed in, and she sucked in a gulp of air as her weight pulled her into the frigid water. She kicked out, toward the light. She surfaced and saw the moss-covered steps. She tried not to think about the water and its curiously oily feel. Her fingers glided over the furry surface of the moss, then slipped away and she sunk lower.

Zoe kicked herself up and tried again, this time aiming for the top step, the one out of the water. She burst through the surface and blinked water away from her eyes, then froze, the water dancing around her shoulders.

Stefano had his good arm around Jack's neck and was squeezing his throat in a chokehold. Francesca barked an Italian command that finally seemed to penetrate Stefano's thoughts. He released Jack and Francesca stepped closer, the gun aimed at Jack's head.

Francesca was going to do it. She was going to shoot him. She was past caring about the blood and any traces of their presence. Zoe tried to scream, but the sound came out as a rough cough instead.

Suddenly, Roy tilted up on one shoulder. Zoe caught a flash of his waxy-colored face, a grimace of pain twisting his mouth. His hand shot out, grabbed Francesca's ankle, then he dropped back. As he fell back, he yanked her foot out from under her. She went down hard, her head slamming against the stone.

No one moved for a second; the only sound was Roy's raspy breathing and the slap of water against the stone steps. Francesca's face was turned toward Zoe, and she could see a thin trickle of blood emerge from Francesca's lips.

Jack levered himself up, plucked the gun from her limp hand. Stefano spun and ran toward Zoe. She cringed back down into the awful water, but he sailed over her head, landing in the water with a splash that sprayed over Zoe and half the stone floor.

Zoe dragged herself up the steps and collapsed on the stone floor. Stefano's noisy splashes sounded behind her as he swam clumsily toward the canal door with his one good arm. Zoe thought about standing up, but decided to stay put because her limbs suddenly felt useless and trembly.

Jack stood over Francesca for a moment, and then he leaned down and pressed his fingers on her neck. He straightened slowly as if every inch of movement hurt. He glanced at Roy, who hadn't moved from where he'd dropped back to the floor. Jack shook his head once. Roy closed his eyes as if he already knew Francesca was gone.

Jack pulled his black sweater over his head maneuvering it around the gun with ease, switching it from hand to hand as he stripped the sweater off his arms. He wadded it up and moved to Roy where he squatted down, then pressed the sweater to the wound on Roy's chest. Roy made a flicking motion with his fingers toward Zoe. Jack stood but didn't move, his gaze still fixed on Roy.

Jack had on a gray T-shirt that he'd worn under the sweater and seemed to be considering taking it off, too, and adding it to the sweater, but Roy said, "Go on. I'm fine." His voice was so faint that his words were a whisper that Zoe caught more by reading his lips than by hearing him.

Jack crossed the room to her, the gun held loosely in one hand. He was scuffed with dirt and grit and blood. There were welts on his arms and across one cheek and a deep red color ringed his throat where Stefano had choked him. He had several gouges on his face and a deeper cut over his eyebrow. She saw all of that in a sort of hazy out-of-focus peripheral way because the only thing she was really focused on were his eyes. There was a fierce, determined glint in them, but there was something else that Zoe couldn't identify as he locked his gaze on her. Zoe didn't think she could have looked away if she wanted to.

But she didn't want to look away.

He tucked the gun into the back of his waistband as he walked, then reached down and pulled her to her feet. *He's going to kiss me*, she realized, and then his lips were on hers and she couldn't form one coherent thought.

It was like the time when she was a kid and touched the exposed wires when her stepdad was remodeling. Except this wasn't a little jolt of electricity. Something sparked when their lips touched and that energy fizzed through every inch of her, all the way down to her wobbly knees.

He lifted his head and Zoe blinked. There were other things going on…important things, she knew, but at the moment, she didn't care about any of them. She didn't remember wrapping her arms around him, but she was gripping his shoulders as tightly as she'd grabbed the stone step when she pulled herself out of the water, which was a good thing because if her legs had been shaky before, she probably needed a wheelchair after that kiss.

His face looked the same as always, tightly controlled, but there was something about his eyes, a softness, a tenderness that surprised her. "Roy called the police," he said, his breath uneven and his words ragged.

"That's all you have to say?" Zoe said, leaning back against his arms, against the solidity of his hands on her back and shoulders. "After a kiss like that?"

"A kiss should never require explanation," he said, then his face turned serious. "I'm afraid to say anything else."

That caught her off guard. Jack, afraid?

"I thought you were unconscious," he said. "When that box went in the water...I thought..." he swallowed.

"But I wasn't," she said lightly, but decided she couldn't let him get off too easily. "Serves you right. Now you know what it's like—thinking someone is dead. Not so great, is it?"

"No, not good at all." He pushed a strand of hair away from the corner of her eye. "They'll be here any minute," Jack said.

"Who?" Zoe asked. If she stretched up on her tiptoes she could kiss him. Despite her quivering legs, she thought she could do it. In fact, she absolutely had to.

"The police. Roy will interpret." Jack closed the narrowing distance between their lips and kissed her hard. He pulled away with a muttered curse. "Here's the gun." He pressed it into her hand. "In case you need it. You shouldn't. Safety is on."

"Where are you going?" She asked, suddenly feeling cold and exposed. She was dripping wet, a fact that hadn't registered at all, but now the air felt chilly. She began to shiver as her wet clothes pressed against her goosebumpy skin.

"To get Stefano," Jack said as he worked one shoe off, then the other. "I'll see you soon," he said, then executed a perfect dive into the water. He surfaced and swam to the canal door, his arms cutting through the water in long, even strokes. He ducked under the door and disappeared with a flick of his foot that kicked up a few drops of water that landed at Zoe's feet.

# CHAPTER TWENTY-EIGHT

*Dallas, Tuesday, 4:45 p.m.*

"AND THAT WAS THE LAST time you saw Jack Andrews?" Sato pushed back from the table, arms crossed over his chest, a look of disbelief on his face.

"Yes." Zoe leaned back against the uncomfortable plastic chair and mirrored Sato by crossing her arms. "No matter how many times you ask me these questions, my answers aren't going to change." She looked around the small room with its gray walls and bare office furnishings, marveling that she'd actually been glad when the Italian police had escorted her to the airport and told her she'd been booked on a flight back to the States. If she'd known Sato would meet her at the airport, she might not have been so relieved. That had been a week ago, and she'd been asked to "clarify" her statement several times.

'I know you don't believe me, but it's true. He went after Stefano and didn't come back."

Her throat prickled, and her vision blurred. She swallowed and blinked a few times. She didn't want to lose control of herself, especially not in front of these two men. The older man was here, too, leaning against the wall on the other side of the room. "Has there been any word from the Italians? Any sign…" she asked.

Sato shook his head. "Nothing."

She bit her lip. *I'll see you soon.* Those had been his last words to her. Apparently, his last words ever. She'd been allowed to read the English translation of the Italian police report. Several witnesses had reported seeing two men in the canal—struggling as they surfaced. They plunged under the water, then reappeared and disappeared below the surface several times. The observers thought one man was trying to save the other, but that the second man had panicked and was fighting his rescuer. Witnesses reported the men went under for a final time for at least two minutes. One body, Stefano's, surfaced. There was no trace of the other body.

She realized Sato was speaking and tried to concentrate on him, pulling her thoughts back from Venice. "You must realize, Ms. Hunter, that we find it an extremely odd circumstance that Mr. Andrews has disappeared in almost exactly the same way he attempted to fake his death after the murder of his business partner. A presumed drowning without a body is very convenient for him."

"What are you saying? That you think he's not dead?" Zoe said, aggressively. The same thought had crossed her mind. She'd thought about it several times, especially on that long flight back to the States, but each time she'd immediately pushed it away.

After Jack dove in the water in pursuit of Stefano, she hadn't expected Jack to return to her side right away, and those first few hours had been a blur of rapid Italian, broken English, and Roy's somewhat garbled translation and explanation. By the time Roy had been strapped to a gurney and transmitted (via ambulance boat) to the hospital, the authorities were looking at Zoe as more victim than villain. When the sun set and Jack hadn't come loping into the roped off crime scene, Zoe felt the first pricks of unease.

He would come back, she told herself. He'd said he would. But after the flutter of activity around the removal of Stefano's body from the canal died down, the Italian authorities became even more tight-lipped with her when she asked about Jack. By the next morning, she'd retreated into a protective shell, emotionally shutting down. If she didn't think about it, she didn't have to deal with it.

The investigator's questions didn't stop, but someone must have eventually come to the conclusion that she really had been accidentally caught up in the mess. After the Italians shipped her home, she had to go through the whole thing again with the American authorities, who consisted mostly of Sato and his older, quieter partner.

She'd existed in a numb state, keeping anything remotely emotional at a distance, but Sato's prodding had cracked her façade. She was as surprised as Sato that it was anger that oozed out of her carefully constructed shell instead of grief. Sato didn't respond to her anger. He lifted a shoulder. "You must admit it's a possibility. That he has tried it again."

"How could that even be a possibility? There were witnesses. It happened in a canal in Venice with people draped over the scenic arched bridges. How could he simply disappear?"

"Your husband was a highly trained operative."

"Ex-husband," Zoe said sharply. "And he wasn't an agent anymore. He hadn't done anything like that in years." She sat up straighter in the chair. "This is the third time you've asked me to come down here in five days. Surely you're not going to request I come down here every few days, are you?"

"Just clearing up a few details," Sato said, his voice mild. "In fact," he opened a file and placed a single sheet of paper in front of her. "We have a new development."

Columns of numbers filled the printout, blurring together.

"What is this?"

"GRS's bank account. Note the last transaction in this column," Sato said, pointing at the bottom of the page where the balance showed a long string of numbers.

Zoe frowned, picked up the paper, and scanned the entry. "That's a deposit…and the date…twelve million dollars? Yesterday? It was deposited yesterday?" She wasn't making any sense, but she couldn't get the words to come out coherently. "How could that happen? Jack and Connor are both…gone. Where did it come from?"

Sato looked at her a long moment, then said, "Apparently it was a computer error."

"What? What are you talking about?"

"The bank has researched this account and discovered that twelve million dollars was transferred by mistake to Jack's personal account. They have corrected the error and replaced the money."

"But…you said that the money had disappeared from Jack's account, too. Where was it transferred?"

Sato plucked the paper from her hand and shuffled it into the file, a trace of huffiness in his movements. "We are tracing it, but it is back now. Frozen," he added in a stern voice that indicated he expected her to run down to her local bank branch and ask the teller for a withdrawal slip the moment she left, even though she didn't have access to Jack's business account. "Did you have any knowledge of this transfer, either the initial transfer from GRS's account or the subsequent transfer out of Mr. Andrews's account?"

"No," Zoe said, drawing back from him, her forehead wrinkling as her eyebrows crunched together. "I don't know anything about that."

"What about the transfer back into the GRS account yesterday?"

"How could I know about that? You just told me." Sato

stared at her, so she continued, "I don't have access to that account. I don't know what's in there."

Abruptly, Sato stood. "Thank you for your time," he said, every syllable conveying anything but thanks. "We'll be in touch."

"When?" Zoe asked, standing as well. "Should I mark down a certain day on my calendar each week? Mondays are always terrible. Should we just get it over with then?"

The older man pushed away from the wall. "That won't be necessary," he said, opening the door. He exchanged a look with his partner. Sato left the room without looking back. His partner gestured for Zoe to precede him out the door, saying, "I'll walk you out. I don't think we've met, officially." He extended his hand as they walked down the narrow gray hallway. "Special Agent Mort Vazarri."

Zoe took his hand. "You already know my name. And probably more about me than I know about myself," Zoe said, not quite sure why she threw the quip in there. If she'd said those same words to Sato, she was sure there would have been a bite, a bitterness in her tone, but this guy, Vazarri, seemed different. Despite Sato's suave, stylish exterior, his attitude broadcast his bloated opinion of himself. Vazarri didn't have any of that. There was something about his face, a kindness, a reserve, which suggested he hadn't marked her down as "accomplice," as Sato seemed to have done.

"Call me Mort," he said. "Everybody does."

He led her through the corridors of cubicles and offices. As they neared the lobby, Zoe said, "Can I ask you a question, um, Mort?" It felt a little awkward using his first name, but he'd just asked her to use it, so it would have been weird to use his last name.

"Sure," he replied, pausing in the hallway, his tone easy and relaxed.

Zoe wasn't sure if Sato and...Mort...were intentionally

going for the good cop versus bad cop routine, but even if they weren't, she certainly felt more comfortable with Mort. This might be her only chance to get some of her questions answered. Despite her woolly, disengaged state, during the last few days, thoughts had been popping up at random. She'd pushed them away and snuggled back down into her cocoon of detachment, but she knew those questions wouldn't go away. They'd always be there and Sato's insinuations that Jack might be alive had shaken her up and broken through the protective layer of disassociation. "The memory card...were you able to locate it? I told the Polizia that it had to be on the bottom of the canal somewhere near where I went in the water."

Mort raised his eyebrows slightly as if her question surprised him. He probably expected her to ask about Jack. But she wasn't going there right now. She was firmly back in denial land. Thinking about anything related to Jack was an emotional quagmire anyway she looked at it. *Nope, not going there right now.*

Mort seemed to pick his words carefully. "Several items were recovered, including a memory card. Unfortunately, it was too corrupted to extract any data."

"I see," Zoe said, her mind racing faster than it had in days. "What about Eddie? Have you...talked to her? Do you know where she is?" A tremor of fear pulsed through her. The number of people involved in this little drama had plunged. Besides herself, there was only Roy, who was tucked away in some Italian hospital following a lengthy surgery, and Eddie. Zoe had no doubt that Eddie would spin all sorts of stories, implicating anyone but herself in the events of the last few days.

"I, personally, haven't spoken to her. She's in custody in Las Vegas. Interestingly, there were several memory cards at her place of business, all with sensitive information on them. I can't say much more than that." Mort resumed moving down the hallway. "There's an article in today's *Sentinel* by Jenny Singletarry. You might want to check it out."

Ж

HELEN HURRIED ACROSS THE LOBBY, her silk shirt rippling and her high heels clicking. A pair of black Michael Kors jeans—it was casual day—completed her ensemble. "How did it go?"

Zoe shrugged. "The same, I guess. They asked questions, I answered." She didn't mention the bombshell Sato had dropped about the money or his questions about Jack. Helen was still having trouble adjusting her perception of Jack. "You didn't have to come with me," Zoe said as they walked to the car.

"Right. My best friend is being questioned by the FBI for the third time this week, and I'll just hope it goes okay. Right."

"I do appreciate it," Zoe said as they came out of the building and a blast of muggy air buffeted them. "Can I borrow your phone?" Zoe asked. Her cell phone had gone into the canal with her, so she figured it was either still in the canal or, if it had been fished out of the water along with the memory card, it was locked away in some Italian evidence holding area.

Getting a new cell phone had been low on her priority list. An extremely long shower followed by hours of sleep had been her only real desires after leaving Sato and Mort's original interrogation, but it was obvious she needed to return to the real world, and purchasing a cell phone was just one thing she needed to think about. Getting her car back from Vegas was another. She hoped it was still parked in the parking garage at The Venetian.

"Here you go," Helen said, handing her the phone, then digging in her carry-on sized purse for her keys.

By the time Helen pulled out of the parking lot and merged onto the freeway, Zoe had found the article. She scrolled down, squinting in the bright sun to read the text, then she dropped back against the seat. "Eddie and Francesca were involved in identity theft," she said.

Helen blended seamlessly into the fast lane, then cut a glance at Zoe. "Are you sure? Identity theft? I mean, I know it's a problem, but murder?"

"Local Businessman's Death Tied to International Identity Theft Ring," Zoe said, reading the headline aloud. "This is by the same reporter who dug up the truth about GRS. Her track record is pretty good, so I bet she's right on this, too. This wasn't a few names or credit card numbers for quick hits of cash or goods."

Zoe scrolled down the article and read, "The thieves specialized in providing deluxe identity replacement—histories going back five to ten years with job records, medical histories, bank accounts, utility bills, even mortgage records, all for fifteen to twenty thousand dollars a person. 'Clients,'" Zoe smirked as she read the word, "could choose from a variety of locations within the United States for their new identity. There was even a special family package. The innovative ID thieves kept their on-line activities to a minimum, never receiving or sending data digitally, relying instead on couriers to shuttle the information back and forth from Venice, their home base to various distribution points around Europe, the United States, and Canada."

Helen tilted her head in acknowledgement, her gold hoop earrings glittering as they swayed, "Okay, that sounds lucrative. No wonder Francesca picked Venice. It's an international destination—about as far away as she could get from Naples, but still be in Italy, and there would be lots of tourists. Her couriers could slip in and out easily, and someone like Eddie with her Venetian glass business would have a legitimate reason to travel there on business. No wonder they were partners."

"Eddie and Francesca certainly had the same business philosophy," Zoe said dryly. "Eliminate anyone who got in their way. Connor was a threat to Francesca's fake ID business, and Jack was a threat to her very existence. No wonder she went after both of them."

"What I don't understand is why Francesca and Roy let Jack…well, live in the first place, back when they staged her death," Helen murmured, her attention on changing lanes and avoiding the car braking in front of her. Then she seemed to realize what she'd said and looked quickly at Zoe to see how she was handling the topic.

It was that concerned, walking-on-eggshell glance that got to Zoe. She closed her eyes. "It's okay," she said, opening her eyes and squaring her shoulders.

Talking about Jack with Helen was different from talking about him with her new best friends at the FBI. She could do this, at least for a little bit. After all, Helen had stood up for her after Zoe had ditched her and left town. The least Zoe could do was fill in the blanks for her.

"In the beginning, I think it must have been Roy who convinced Francesca that Jack wasn't a risk. Roy didn't want to kill him. Roy placated Francesca by saying that he'd keep an eye on Jack and make sure he didn't find out. If Jack did discover the truth, Roy must have told Francesca that he'd take care of Jack, but I don't think Roy would have. He tried to warn us off in Naples. Roy followed us to Venice and tried to convince Francesca not to kill us. And, in the end, he was the one who prevented her from shooting Jack."

The car was silent as they left the freeway and navigated the streets of Zoe's neighborhood. "Want to get some take out and come over to our house?" Helen asked, as they rolled to a stop in front of Zoe's house.

Zoe climbed out. "No, I need some time alone."

"Okay," Helen said, "I'll let you off this time, but I'm not going to let you become a recluse. You already spend too much time by yourself as it is. It's not good for you to be cooped up in your house all day."

Zoe grinned. "What are you talking about? I just got back from Europe."

Helen rolled her eyes. "Next week. Lunch?"

"Sure." Zoe swung the door shut, grabbed her mail, and turned for a final wave before she rounded the house to enter through the back door to the kitchen. Inside, she dropped the mail on the counter.

Ж

MORT left Zoe in the lobby with her friend and returned to his desk. Sato was shrugging into his suit jacket. "I'm heading out."

"Meeting Chloe?" Mort asked.

"She's out of town. Cousin's wedding," Sato said with distaste, pulling his shirtsleeves and adjusting his tie.

"You didn't want to go with her?"

"You're kidding, right? Never go to a wedding with a chick. It messes with their minds."

"Come by our house tonight then. Pizza and a movie," Mort offered.

"Nah. There's a new tapas bar in Uptown," Sato said as he handed off the Jack Andrews file to Mort.

"You were kind of hard on her," Mort said, lifting the file to Sato's back. He was already moving to the door.

Sato jostled his car keys impatiently as he turned back. "We had to know. We had to ask her, see her reaction."

"So you don't think she was acting? She was genuinely shocked at the thought Andrews might be alive?"

"Yeah," Sato said, his eyebrows coming down in a frown.

"Didn't you?"

"I thought so, too," Mort said.

Sato gave him a nod, a little raise of his chin. "Almost got this one wrapped up. See you Monday."

Mort tapped the file against his palm. Things were coming together. Stefano was responsible for Connor Freeman's death, which had been initiated at the behest of Francesca, who was living under an assumed identity. Her exclusive identity theft ring, which catered to the champagne and caviar set in the criminal world had been exposed, and her accomplice, Eddie, would soon be facing a wide range of charges.

Yep, it was all coming together neatly. Even the missing money was back. Neat and tidy, all loose ends tied up. Too neatly? Sato was good at reading people, and he'd thought Zoe Hunter had been truly shocked at the idea Jack had survived. Mort agreed with that assessment. Her face had that shell-shocked immobility he'd seen before that was difficult to fake. And the paperwork, his specialty, was in order. He'd poured over the bank forms earlier today and couldn't find a decimal point out of place.

He reached to toss the file in the bin at the side of his desk along with their other closed cases. A few more days and their part in this investigation would be mostly over. His hand hovered in mid-air. After a few seconds, he dropped it on his desk instead. He'd just keep an eye on things.

X

ZOE had made herself a huge bowl of mac-and-cheese. Comfort food. After she rinsed the bowl, she wiped the cabinets down. When she got to the little glass jar half-filled with change, she paused. Her travel fund. Well, she was an international traveler now. No passport stamp to show for it, she thought ruefully. How hard was it going to be to get a new passport? Maybe that nice investigator, Mort, would help her out. She crossed her arms and leaned against the counter. The kitchen looked exactly the same. The unfinished ceiling gaped, exposing wood and wiring. The island was covered with a spread of paper and her laptop, which was off. She hadn't touched it since she'd returned.

A gust of wind rattled the window screen, the sink in the hall bathroom dripped with a steady plink in four-four time that she could have set a metronome by. The air conditioner clicked on with a gusty heave. All familiar, comforting sounds, but there were a whole symphony of missing sounds. The creak of the floorboard upstairs under Jack's foot, the low murmur of his voice, which had always carried down stairs when he was on the phone, the thud of his closet door when he closed it.

Zoe shook her head. Work. She'd work. She had plenty to do. She needed to find a new tenant for Kiki's office. As for GRS's office…she didn't know if she could rent it. Would she even have access to it? She'd have to find out. That could wait. Right now, she'd focus on her e-mail. Her next editing job from Smart Travel was probably sitting in her e-mail waiting for her. While she waited for her computer to whir through its start-up routine, she opened the stack of mail. Helen had brought it in for her each day and she had a pile of bills (too many), catalogues (why did they send them to her? She hadn't bought anything from a catalogue in years), and junk mail.

She was several envelopes deep into the stack when she opened a credit card offer, dropped the envelope into the trash, then slapped the preprinted offer into the stack to be shredded. Then she paused, running her fingers over the paper. It was lumpy as if something else had been placed inside the folded paper that offered her free balance transfers and a low APR. She picked it up, unfolding the paper.

A thin woven bracelet fell into her palm. She frowned,

smoothing the creases in the paper as she scanned it. Instead of a chart with dates and interest rates, there was a white lined sheet of paper with a ragged edge, like it had been torn from a notebook. Her heart began to beat faster as she studied a small sketch of water and buildings. Venice. Amazing how a few strokes of black ink could convey the arched bridges, the flash of light on the water, the buildings on either side of the water. The rest of the page was blank, except for the slight imprint where the bracelet had rested.

She twisted the bracelet in her hand, its texture silky and its color dark red shot through with copper and gold strands. Her heart was thudding as she realized it was hair. Her hair.

"Jack," she whispered. "I'm gonna kill you when you show up."

But she was smiling.

## THE END

# NOTE FROM THE AUTHOR

THANKS FOR READING *ELUSIVE*! IF you enjoyed it, I hope you'll consider leaving an on-line review—just a few lines is all that's required. Honest reviews help readers decide if a book is their cup of tea, and reviews are one of the most helpful ways to support authors.

If you'd like me to drop you a line when I have a new book out, sign up for my newsletter at SaraRosett.com/sig-nup. You'll get access to exclusive content and subscriber-only giveaways.

I had a wonderful time writing and researching *Elusive*. While the events involving Zoe and Jack are purely fictional, the mention of the mafia member who was arrested because of his discarded designer socks came straight from the head-lines.

You can view pictures that inspired me as well as some photos from my trip to Naples and Venice at the *Elusive* board on Pinterest.

You can find out more about me and my books at my web-site, www.SaraRosett.com.

*Sara*

# ACKNOWLEDGMENTS

MANY THANKS TO MY FIRST readers Lauren Rosett as well as John and Edwyna Honderich. Mark Honderich provided expertise on Dallas traffic and locales. David P. Vandagriff, AKA The Passive Guy, helped with legal questions. Thanks to TJ, who helped get the manuscript ready for readers. Couldn't have done it without you all. Thanks so much!

# ABOUT THE AUTHOR

Sara Rosett writes cozy mysteries (the Ellie Avery series and the Murder on Location series) and an international heist series (the On the Run series).

Sara is a travel junkie, loves all things bookish, and considers dark chocolate a daily requirement. Her stories and essays have appeared in *Chicken Soup for the Military Wife's Soul*, *Georgia Magazine*, *The Writer*, and *Romantic Times Book Review*. *Publishers Weekly* called Sara's books, "satisfying," "well-executed," and "sparkling."

Connect with Sara at www.SaraRosett.com and join her newsletter at www.sararosett.com/signup.

Facebook: AuthorSaraRosett
Twitter: SaraRosett
Pinterest: SRosett
Instagram: SaraRosett

# OTHER BOOKS BY

# SARA ROSETT

This is Sara Rosett's complete library at the time of publication, but Sara has new books coming out all the time. Sign up for her newsletter to stay up to date on new releases.

*Murder on Location* series
*Death in the English Countryside*
*Death in an English Cottage*
*Death in a Stately Home*
*Death in an Elegant City*
*Menace at the Christmas Market (novella)*
*Death in an English Garden*

*On the Run* series

*Elusive*
*Secretive*
*Deceptive*
*Suspicious*

*Devious*

*Ellie Avery* series

*Moving is Murder*
*Staying Home is a Killer*
*Getting Away is Deadly*
*Magnolias, Moonlight, and Murder*
*Mint Juleps, Mayhem, and Murder*
*Mimosas, Mischief, and Murder*
*Mistletoe, Merriment and Murder*
*Milkshakes, Mermaids, and Murder*
*Marriage, Monsters-in-law, and Murder*
*Mother's Day, Muffins, and Murder*